Mere Reflection

By

Elizabeth Wehman

Summit Street Publishing

MERE REFLECTION
Published by Summit Street Publishing
131 West Grand River
Owosso, Michigan 48867

ISBN 978-0-9905580-9-5
ISBN 978-1-7326522-0-0 (ebook)

Publishing in the United States by Summit Street Publishing, Owosso, Michigan

Library of Congress Cataloging-in-Publication data
Wehman, Elizabeth
Mere Reflection/Elizabeth Wehman-1st ed.   2019903980
Lifetime of Callie; 2
Scripture quotations taken from The Holy Bible, New International Version®NIV® Copyright ©1973, 1978, 1984, 2011 by Biblica, Inc.™

Used by permission. All rights reserved worldwide.

Printed in the United States of America
2019

Cover Photo: Emily E. Lawson Photography
Back Cover Photo: Angela Foltz-Lamphere
Cover Model: Lila Beth Anderson
Cover Art: Kristina Sweers

I would like to dedicate *Mere Reflection* to my three children, Emily Elizabeth Wehman-Lawson, Rebekah Leigh Wehman, and Ethan Paul Wehman. May I always be the reflection you need in life of our ultimate Creator and may you allow God to use you in the same way.

Acknowledgements

The joy of publishing continues in my life and for that, I'm eternally grateful. Grateful to God for His amazing gifts. Grateful for the opportunity to use my creative talents to serve Him. Grateful for the challenge each novel brings to hone my skills. Grateful for all the support and push I've received from all of you, my readers. What a blessing all of this is in my life.

Nothing prepares you for being a published author. You have dreams of it for almost a lifetime, but when it finally happens, the benefits and joy are far beyond anything you could ever imagine. God puts just the right people, experiences, and resources in your life to prepare you for the journey. His timing is always perfect.

This book was difficult to write. Between a seasonal job, daily duties, starting up a local writing group, and life ~ things just kept getting in the way. I grew frustrated as many clamored for the sequel to *Just a Train Ride*. What started as a simple Christmas novella turned into a full-length novel complete with much more than just a simple romance.

To all of my readers. I'm amazed at your tenacity to keep following me and my career. I'm so honored that something I write brings you joy, makes you think, or even takes you away from the stress of the world for just a few pages. You all bring me great joy.

I'm thankful for my editors, Kathryn Frazier, Meline Scheidel, and Emily Lawson who challenge me beyond what I think I could do, yet encouraging me that I'm capable. I will forever be grateful to them for their skill and expertise. Also to Emily at Emily E. Lawson Photography who captures exactly what is in my head...in an amazing cover photo. To Angela Foltz-Lamphere for getting my back cover shot in Chicago. And to my sweet cousin, twice removed, Lila Anderson for her willingness to use her beautiful Atkinson-bred eyes for an amazing front cover. Thank you sweet, adventurous, fun girl.

Thank you to all who make this fourth dream a reality.

Elizabeth Wehman
Psalm 34:8

Chapter 1

It had all happened so fast. Just last week, Blaine Taylor had been working as a waitress in one of the biggest cities in America, and now...her life had changed faster than the weather on a typical Chicago day. And it all began on a train ride.

Today, she sat on the edge of a bed surrounded by white-and - yellow daisy wallpaper in the home of a complete stranger. Yes, she felt somewhat connected to the elderly woman she met on the train just a few short days ago. Callie was kind, but fragile.

Callie's face revealed the marks of a woman who had lived a long life, with wrinkles marking both smiles and tears. Blaine often caught herself staring at the old woman's face. Her face reflected peace, an unexplainable contentment that intrigued Blaine. Often the world claims that faces like Callie's reveal an easy life, void of fear or calamity, but Blaine knew otherwise because Callie told her life story on the train.

Blaine gazed across the room at herself in the reflection of a large mirror over a dresser. Her face was opposite of Callie's face. She could see dark circles under her eyes. A permanent wrinkle in her forehead gave her a perplexed, fearful look. Relaxing her face, didn't help. Her reflection seemed permanent. Callie's facial expressions revealed a look of hope, almost anticipation. It was the complete opposite of Blaine's. Blaine wondered why.

Despite the faint scent of moth balls, the lavender tones of the quilt, curtains, and even a few down-filled pillows screamed princess. The bed was comfortable. For the past two nights, she'd fallen asleep beneath its warm covers. Lately, she felt she couldn't get enough of it. Rubbing her arms to warm herself in the cool room, she knew better than to dwell on the thought of crawling back in right now. Callie would need her soon.

Blaine wondered if it would be advantageous to unpack the duffle bag she'd brought with her on the train. Her gut instincts answered her question. Never have expectations. Callie had convinced her to stay through the Christmas holidays under the pretense that Blaine was to be her caregiver. Blaine allowed herself to believe it was the real reason she now sat in this spare bedroom in the small Michigan community. As nice as Callie seemed, it would be a big job to care for this elderly patient.

A growl down deep in her stomach brought Blaine back to realizing her need to take the offer. She picked up her heavy bag and placed it on the bed to dig for a few mints she had left from the hospital. After removing clothing, two pairs of shoes, and her makeup, Blaine tipped the bag, shaking the items onto the bed. Two twenty-dollar bills, three quarters and a few dimes spilled onto the quilt. One more shake spread crumbs of saltines over the bedspread. Blaine dug into the bottom to find the opened sandwich bag with three crackers left. She placed a stale cracker into her mouth, as she dug into the corners of the bag for the mints.

The stomach growls came with an aggressive intensity. Despite the muffin she'd had for breakfast, she felt like she hadn't eaten in a week. These leftover crackers needed to hold her until she could make lunch for Callie and herself. She wondered if she'd ever feel relaxed enough here to just go find something to eat.

Delicate snowflakes drifted past the paned windowed glass. Perhaps she could find a nice scented candle somewhere and place it on the small table beside her bed. It might kill the subtle scent of an old woman at a doctor's office.

A voice calling from the living room interrupted her thoughts. Blaine cracked the door to the bedroom enough to see Callie trying to maneuver her walker into the kitchen. Blaine returned to her bag and shoved the clothes, shoes, and money back into it so she could go to Callie's aid.

"Why didn't you call me to help you?" Blaine questioned the old woman, more out of annoyance than compassion, when she reached her.

Blaine had been a waitress most of her working life. She knew how to wait on a person's beck and call. But this job would try her patience. How much care would Callie actually need? The thought of bathing her gave Blaine a stomach-ache. She would need to keep perspective. Don't get attached, keep to yourself and do your job.

With her hand wrapped around Callie's waist, Blaine led her to the kitchen. Helping her to a nearby chair, Callie placed her walker beside her.

"I'm here to help you," Blaine scolded the old woman. "Call for me. I don't mind."

Callie rummaged through papers on the table, "We need to make a grocery list or we're going to starve."

Blaine picked up a blank slip of paper, "You name off some things and I'll add them to the list. Callie rattled off some odds and ends.

"The doctor said I shouldn't sit around all day. Do you think that walk from the living room counts as exercise? Do you think you could manage to find the grocer this morning?"

Blaine left the grocery list to fill Callie's tea kettle as she'd done for the past two days. "No worries. I'll get dressed soon. How close is the store?"

"Just up the road. As soon as I get some tea, let's finish the list."

Opening a cupboard door, Blaine grabbed a mug and plopped in a tea bag from Callie's supply. She found plenty in the sealed mason jar. Callie's medicine must be making her extra thirsty. She'd better pay attention to things like this. She could see the police report now, 'Cause of Death - Young Inexperienced Caregiver.'

"We need to decide what exactly you want me to do while I'm here." Blaine didn't bother to remove her exasperated tone. Callie could be a stubborn patient when it came to helping her. This job was going to try her patience.

While Blaine poured the boiling water over Callie's tea bag, the aroma of raspberry drifted from the cup. Returning the mug to the table, she glanced at the old woman now fiddling with her hair.

"I need a haircut. Something."

Callie's hair was a bit unmanageable right now. Not only did it need a good wash, but a curling iron and hair spray might tame the tangled mess sticking out from the hair net.

"I've done hair before. Perhaps I can help."

Callie smiled. "Oh would you? I'm sure I won't be able to get a hair appointment during the holidays."

Blaine placed the steaming mug of tea in front of Callie, "Of course. That's a good start. Have you ever used a curling iron?"

Callie laughed as she held the mug up to blow across it. "Um no. I use wire curlers. The old fashioned way."

"Wire curlers?" Blaine sat down across from her new friend. "Sounds archaic."

Callie smiled, "Perhaps, but we can try your curling iron. It would be nice to look normal again."

Callie glanced at the young woman whose hair was never out of sorts. She knew, without a doubt, she was frustrating Blaine. She sensed it for the past day or two. She wanted this whole arrangement to work, but for how long? She ushered up a silent help prayer. She knew He'd know the details. That one simple plea would result in supernatural assistance and always beyond what she deserved.

Blaine sipped on a tall glass of orange juice left over from their breakfast. Quickly she stood and went to a drawer in the kitchen.

Callie wished she could still move as easily as her caregiver. "Blaine, let's finish the list."

Back at the table Blaine began writing down items Callie recited.

"Milk. Eggs. Toilet paper. But we need the larger pack and not the normal four-roll pack I usually buy. That won't be enough for Mason and us." The thought of having to purchase a larger package made Callie joyous. Company. When was the last time she needed to buy extra supplies for guests? She smiled at the thought.

As the list grew long yet complete, Blaine finished the last gulp of her orange juice. "Callie. We need to talk."

The exasperation in Blaine's voice stopped the mental recitation of the grocery aisles and what they contained. "Of course."

"You gotta get used to the fact that I'm here to help you. I'm not a house guest." Blaine pulled at her pony tail, tightening it to her head. "I'm here to work. Take care of you. Give me a chance to help you. Okay?"

Callie folded her hands in her lap and leaned into the table. "I'm sorry."

Blaine laid her head down on the table, "And stop apologizing."

Callie bit her lip. She'd about said it again. Despite only wanting to be humble, kind...it probably did sound annoying at times. She wanted Blaine to be with her. She needed to show appreciation without being sappy sweet or overly polite. "Okay." She sighed. "I'll try."

"Now let's go over what you expect from me?"

"What?" Callie was confused.

Blaine smirked at her across the table. "Let's pretend I'm a caregiver. You're interviewing me for the job. Tell me some of the things you'd have me do as your employee?"

Callie sat up straighter, feeling empowered. She took a deep breath. "Good idea. Okay, well...let's see." Blaine raised eyebrows caused Callie's recent confidence to wane like a quick release of air from a balloon.

"Well I need help getting out of chairs." It was bad. Callie knew it. But it made Blaine chuckle.

"That's a given, Callie."

Callie knew she could think of things. There had to be legitimate needs. Ways for Blaine to help her. She remembered the start of her grocery list. Taking it away from Blaine she held it up. "I need you to run errands."

Blaine nodded. "Good. What else?"

"Perhaps some light housekeeping. I can't make beds very well. I need someone to sweep, perhaps dust."

Blaine motioned for Callie to give her more. "Good. Keep going."

"Cook."

"Well, you're gonna have to help me a little there. I'm not a very good cook."

Callie felt her insides relax a bit. "I'll help you. We'll do it together."

Blaine acknowledged with a nod.

"Laundry. The stairs give me trouble."

"Good. Right."

Callie tapped the table. "And one more important thing." She knew the moment needed something light. Something for Blaine to know that she wasn't becoming a slave in Callie's home.

"What?"

"I need someone to make us popcorn and watch those sappy, horrible Christmas romances on cable television with me."

Blaine grimaced. "No. I can't."

Callie leaned back in her chair and crossed her arms. "Then you can't work for me."

"You're impossible!"

"I hope not."

"So you need help with care? Laundry? Housekeeping? Cooking? Errands? Anything else?"

Callie was determined, "The movies?"

The young woman's exasperated face spread into a casual grin. "Okay, the movies."

"And...in the next few days, we need a few Christmas decorations put up. Like the tree?"

"Decorating?" Blaine's eyes opened wider.

"It'll be fun. This old house needs some Christmas spirit."

Blaine rubbed the back of her neck. Callie needed to rally something more. She'd never had a caregiver before. If she needed anything, she called her neighbor Miriam. This arrangement had been a last minute attempt to get this young woman into her home. It had worked, but she had to keep up the charade. It wasn't she who needed Blaine as much as she knew Blaine needed her, but she couldn't let Blaine know that or the unraveling of her scheme would happen like a dropped stitch on a knitted blanket.

Blaine leaned forward, "What about my pay?"

This would solidify it. What would Callie pay someone to care for her daily needs? They discussed a number and Blaine agreed. The number brought a little trepidation to Callie's normal budget, but if God was in this, He would supply. And what did she really know about caregiving costs these days? "Now there are sheets in the dryer. Why don't you bring those up and put them on your bed?"

Blaine picked up the empty clothes basket by the door leading down to the basement. "We're gonna make quite the team, you and I."

Callie watched the young woman disappear down her stairs. 'You have no idea, sweet girl.'

Blaine pulled warm sheets out of the dryer. Piling them in her basket, she realized that this was it. Her life now. She liked Callie. She really did. But how long could she do this?

Here Blaine was, caring for a complete stranger who didn't quite fit that description. Blaine might have met Callie just days before, but at this moment, the title of stranger seemed cold and foreign. As odd as it seemed.

She was looking for a new life. Her life with her boyfriend Kyle, back in Chicago, was relentless frustration. Her head knew it, but her heart had only known his presence. He did seem to care whether she came home from work each night. His friends were her friends. There were good times, but lately, the frustrations overpowered the good.

She recently came to realize one thing: Kyle's life was all about him. He controlled her actions, food, existence, but also her will, choices, and even her body. His last request or demand of her was something she just couldn't shrug off. Surely, all men weren't like Kyle. In the short time she'd known Mason, she felt this wasn't true. And after hearing Miles and Callie's love story on the train, she knew things could be different.

Blaine hefted the basket to her hip and started up the stairs. When she reached the top of the stairs, Callie was still at the kitchen table jotting notes down on their grocery list.

"Blaine, check and see how many orange juice cans are in the freezer, would you?"

Blaine placed the basket at her feet and pulled open the freezer door. As she gazed around to find cans of frozen juice concentrate a smell assaulted her senses. Blaine swallowed hard. It didn't seem to help. The familiar surge made her cover her mouth. She glanced over at Callie, who was still concentrating on her list.

Blaine nearly tripped over the basket as she made a dash to the bathroom.

"Blaine, be careful honey."

Blaine didn't have time to respond, nor could she speak, so she nodded.

Racing into the room, she slammed the door behind her and almost didn't make it in time. Blaine's belly released the cracker as well as the juice she'd consumed at the table. After a few deep breaths, Blaine sat back wiping her mouth with the back of her hand. She'd forgotten to switch on the ceiling fan this time to cover her retching sounds. Leaning toward the switch, she felt her stomach grumble.

How long would she be able to keep her secret from Callie? Everything she read had said to keep eating small amounts to diminish her queasy stomach. How was she supposed to keep eating when all it did was make her feel more miserable? And she still didn't feel comfortable rummaging through Callie's cupboards or refrigerator for food.

She'd only been sick a few times since her arrival at Callie's house. Callie had been asleep both of the other times, but today, she'd watched her run to the bathroom.

Blaine flushed down her breakfast. Standing up she washed her face with cold water and looked in the mirror. She saw the look of fear she'd often had when trying to hide facts from those around her. Wiping her face with a nearby towel, she waited a few moments for the wave of nausea to pass.

Coming back into the kitchen, Blaine glanced at Callie who still seemed intent on finishing up the grocery list. Blaine sighed in relief. Perhaps keeping her secret from Callie wasn't going to be as hard as she thought.

Sitting down across from Callie, Blaine studied her face for any recognition of what had happened in the bathroom. Callie appeared indifferent and seemed intent on putting the last item on her list. "I think I have it ready for you." She laid her pen down and looked up at Blaine. "Are you okay, dear? You look a little pale."

As in true form, Blaine lied. "No make-up yet, Callie."

Callie patted her hand, "Do you remember where the store is? Remember I pointed it out to you when we came into town the other day."

Blaine picked up her phone from off the table. "Tell me the name of the store again?"

Callie recited the name and Blaine plugged it into her phone. "Butlers at 602 Sycamore Street."

"Must be it. I don't know any other store on Sycamore but Butlers."

"I'll get a shower in," Blaine picked up the list, folded it and stood to shove it into her pocket. "And put on some make-up."

Blaine went down the hall to her room. Shutting the door behind her she again placed her hand over her mouth until the next wave of nausea went away. Grabbing a few clean clothes, she went to the bathroom to get ready for the day. She'd stay in the room for a while just in case she felt sick again.

As she entered the bathroom this time, she remembered to flip on the overhead fan as well as the light. A hum followed that would surely mask the sound of a pregnant woman losing more of her breakfast from the old woman just outside the door.

Chapter 2

"What would you like for Christmas? Callie asked. "Is there something special you'd like?"

Blaine stopped peeling the potato. What? No one had ever asked her that. Her own mother had never bothered to ask even when she was a little girl. This woman was indeed a strange one. "What do you mean?"

"It's Christmas, isn't it?"

Blaine again stripped the peeling off a potato. "I guess."

"Well then?"

"How would you get out to buy me this so-called-thing for Christmas? You can't drive anywhere. Right?"

Callie shook her index finger at her, "I have my ways, young lady."

What would she say? What would be reasonable? Blaine struggled to think of something. "I don't need anything from you. Christmas is just a stupid holiday filled with everything commercial and frivolous. Isn't it? I'm a stranger. I don't think it's necessary for you to get me anything. We'll just pretend it's like any other day," Blaine thought, as she'd done her entire life.

"I'm not taking 'nothing' for an answer." Callie grabbed a box of chicken broth from the pantry beside the stove. "It's Christmas. Everyone spending Christmas with me gets a gift. Even you."

More conflicting thoughts stole away Blaine's joy. Not even Kyle had gotten her something for Christmas, especially something she'd asked for. She decided to put the woman to a test. A small one, but a test nonetheless. Blaine's feet had been cold ever since she'd arrived at Callie's house. "Um, how 'bout slippers?"

"Slippers? Yes." Callie grinned at her as if she'd found out the most secret part of Blaine's heart. "Good idea. Anything else? What's your favorite color?"

Blaine's face grew warm. She wasn't used to this. She scrambled to come up with a color. "Lavender, maybe..."

"Are those potatoes peeled yet?"

Blaine rinsed off the five peeled potatoes and handed them to Callie who took a large carving knife and diced them into pieces.

"After dinner, I think we better get some cookies made. Mason can't come home for Christmas to find his grandmother doesn't have any homemade cookies baked for him. Will you be too tired?"

Blaine scolded. "Of course not, but you're gonna have to help me if you want something homemade. It's hard for me to make anything not from a tube or a box."

"I may have to do it from a chair at the kitchen table, but I'll help you. Standing here is wearing me out. Get the milk out of the fridge, honey."

Blaine returned with the milk jug.

"Pour in about two cups, love."

Blaine's eyes misted over when Callie called her 'love.' What would it have been like to have a grandmother like Callie. The difference between Callie and her own grandmother was like comparing a thunderstorm to a rainbow. Blaine's grandmother was tall, skinny, her face revealed the kind of life she'd endured. Relatives from Blaine's past were a part of her life due to obligation. It didn't feel the same with Callie.

Everyone had told Blaine how important she was in their lives, yet no one bothered to show her. She realized they all made promises they never kept. Disappointments led to frustration, frustration led to denial until Blaine just stopped trying to trust.

She always felt the blame for all the things that went wrong. Blaine crossed her arms, she'd long closed the compartment door to love. Real love.

Callie interrupted her thoughts. "Just keep pouring and I'll tell you when to stop."

Helping Callie cook wasn't all that bad. She was learning something new. She found she almost enjoyed it.

"Mason will be home soon. If those crazy business people in Chicago let him off early. I can't wait to see him."

Blaine loved how much Callie adored her grandson, Mason. Even she was anxious to have someone young around for a change.

"Another good thing to come out of having a heart attack and open heart surgery."

"What's that, Callie?"

"My grandson coming home for Christmas. We'll have to get to the store and get him a few things, too."

"So now Christmas shopping is on my list of requirements?"

Callie touched her arm. "Is that okay?"

She loved shopping. Perhaps that's how Callie would get her something. She'd bought her own presents before, she could do it again. "Okay."

"Christmas is going to be so wonderful this year. Perhaps Mason can get his folks on the computer and we can have a conversation with them." Callie added.

"His parents?"

"Yes, my daughter and her husband. Mason's parents?" Callie seemed to be trying her best to remind her, but in a kind way. "The ones in Africa. Remember?"

"I remember."

"If Mason brings his computer, we can talk to them like he and I did this past summer."

Blaine wondered about Mason's parents. What were they thinking of Callie asking a perfect stranger to help her? She'd overheard a few of the phone conversations to Africa during the past two days. Callie had called them to keep them updated on her health. Surely, Callie had told them about her.

"Doesn't this smell good?"

Blaine had to agree. The chicken and potatoes smelled delicious. Her nauseous morning was now replaced with a desire to eat everything in sight.

"Blaine honey, are you sure there isn't anyone else you'd rather spend Christmas with than me?"

Callie had asked her this before. Blaine always shook her head. She wondered if it was a lure to get her to leave for Christmas, but then Callie always seemed to be including her on all the upcoming celebrations.

"No, Callie...unless perhaps you'd like me to leave?"

Callie stopped stirring. "What? Don't be silly. You're my caregiver. I need you here. Through the holidays. I just don't want to keep you from being elsewhere."

Blaine assured her she'd be staying to do her job. Blaine hoped Callie accepted the reasoning because if she didn't...there would be no place for Blaine to go.

Overwhelmed was an understatement. The stack of work on Mason McAnder's desk threatened to topple each time his supervisor stomped to the coffee machine. Mason had never been this far behind in his account estimates. His trip to see Nana in the hospital, just two short weeks ago, had proven his inability to take even two or three days off without dire consequences.

Mason grabbed his coffee cup for another swig only to find the liquid stone cold. He grimaced. He needed a break to not only get a fresh cup, but to stretch. He'd been working without interruptions for the past four hours. Lunch was out of the question today.

"How you comin' on the Carhouse file, Mason?" His boss stood behind him and Mason was certain he was reviewing the opened Santer files visible on his desktop.

Mason swiveled around on his chair. He wasn't sure how to tell the boss he hadn't even started that file yet. Lying wasn't an option. "Um, not there yet? As soon as I'm done with the Santer's file, I'll start..."

"No...that Santer file needs to be done before Carhouse. Finish that first," his boss exhaled, sounding as exasperated as if he had just heard how much his wife had spent on Christmas, and stomped back into his office.

Mason turned back to his desk and shook his head. He felt guilty wanting a fresh cup of coffee. He knew what needed to be done. He'd been adding figures on this same statement for hours. He knew all of his accounts needed estimated sale figures this time of year. They needed to know totals for tax abatements and if they should be lowered. Why did his boss assume he didn't know...all of that?

Mason was planted on the bottom rung of the company ladder. For now, all he had to show were splinters. Nothing could prevent this other than to do his best, even when he accomplished his goals, it seemed to go unnoticed. He wondered how long it would take before someone realized the hours he put in. What if he wasn't cutting it in the workplace?

His thoughts were interrupted.

"Mason," his boss called from inside his office door.

Mason tried hard not to feel irritated. How could he finish up the account if he had to stop to hear another lecture?

Standing, Mason brushed imaginary crumbs from the front of his sweater. How embarrassing it would be to have bagel flakes speckled down his black sweater? A co-worker in the next cubicle whispered, "Good luck," accompanied with a look of annoyance. She seemed to realize the exasperation of being held to the fire to work harder, yet being interrupted.

Mason did the mandatory knock on the side of the door jam. His boss had returned to his desk. "Come in, Mason."

"Close the door behind you."

Mason rubbed his hands down his pant legs.

"Having to go home to be with your sick mother has put you way behind."

Mason shook his head, "It's my nana. I'm sorry, my grandmother. She just had a massive heart attack. Open heart surgery. I'd apologize, but it was a family emergency."

"Life happens. I understand that. Do you plan to take more days off?"

Mason knew his voice would soon be shaking. Not from fear, but frustration. He hated it when work priorities came before something as important as a sick family member. "I think she'll be fine. There's someone there taking care of her now."

"Good. Good. How much longer on the Santer's file?"

"I think I can finish it before lunch, although..."

"Well, get to it. If you don't finish both of those and the ten other files on your desk, I'm afraid you'll have to work a few days next week. Got it?"

Mason wanted to defend himself but it wouldn't change his boss's mind. Nana was more important than this job, but it probably wasn't a good idea to tell his boss that. And next week was Christmas. He'd bought his ticket at the station yesterday. He'd be at Nana's house all next week. Was the boss serious about working through holidays?

"I have phone calls to make." His boss picked up his phone and dismissed him with a wave of his hand.

Before Mason could say another word, his boss was talking to his secretary on the other line. He struggled with understanding his manager's motives. He'd just told him his progress, and now he threatened him. Who makes someone work through a scheduled Christmas vacation?

Returning to his desk, Mason studied his screen to figure out where he'd left off. The whole interruption put him behind even more. Picking up his cup he decided that another interruption wouldn't change a thing. He needed caffeine.

One of Mason's co-workers stood over the coffee machine and poured himself a large portion. "That guy puts me into the stratosphere. He's so rude," he said, placing the now empty pot back on the sizzling burner.

Mason didn't want to chat, he wasn't in the mood, but was it too much to ask for a fresh cup of coffee? He sighed. He hated listening to co-workers talking smack about the boss. And he still didn't have any coffee.

He turned to leave. The guy didn't seem upset that he hadn't responded, nor did Mason have time to explain. He struggled to focus back on his screen. Where was he again? Someone came up close behind him and took his cup.

"I'll get you a fresh cup, Mason." Megan was the floor secretary. He often smelled her sweet scent–a subtle scent of honeysuckle and vanilla-before she ever reached his desk. But today, he was too busy to notice. She must have seen Mason getting back to his desk without a refill.

"Thanks Megan. I appreciate it."

"Want any cream? Sugar?"

Mason shook his head. "Black is fine."

Megan flashed him a pretty smile, "No worries. Give me a sec, I'll make another pot."

Mason turned back to his screen and began to decipher another line of numbers. Megan was an amazing secretary. She was always alert. Ready to help and above all, she was gorgeous. Not only did the office run smoothly during her shift, Mason had been trying to get up enough nerve to ask her out again.

Most everyone in the office got along well. For this, Mason was thankful. Each took time out of their own busy schedules to teach him, offering suggestions and give advice whether he needed it or not. He had grown to appreciate each one in some small way after being at the corporation for just over a year.

Soon Megan was back with not only one of her gorgeous smiles but also with a cup of steaming hot coffee. She placed it right beside Mason and touched his shoulder. "Get my attention if you need more." Mason wanted to thank her, but she only left her scent lingering in the air.

Many people, in the office, told Mason how much Megan liked him. He doubted it. Megan did give him much more attention than anyone else, but she was the secretary. Mason would probably never attract someone so hot, her presence often made him unable to speak well even when the opportunity arose for just small talk. At this moment, he was thankful for her.

Soon everyone headed out for lunch. Miguel, one of Mason's favorite co-workers, approached his desk. "Hey guy. Want me to bring you back something? You look swamped."

Mason stood up to pull out his wallet, "Where you headed?"

"Marcos. Want tacos?"

Mason smiled. Tacos would work well. He could easily eat them at his desk. "Yes, please. Here," he handed Miguel a twenty-dollar bill. "Get me three."

"Everything on them?"

"Loaded. Yup. Thanks Miguel." Mason knew Miguel wouldn't end at tacos. He'd get a Mountain Dew and probably some kind of homemade cookies out of the deal, too.

"Get back to work," Miguel teased as he stuffed the bill into his coat pocket.

As Mason finished up the Santer's account he glanced at the pile of accounts still waiting his perusal. Some would take him an hour or two to finish, others up to four or more hours. Today was Thursday. He had only Friday left to finish most of them before heading back to Michigan to see Nana for the upcoming holidays.

After talking to his boss, he now wasn't even sure he could go home for Christmas. The office was closed all next week. Friday afternoon was even blocked off for a party at work, but Mason knew he'd not be able to attend very long. That thought almost brought a smile to his face. He hated the office parties anyway. He wasn't a drinker and that seemed to be the only reason to have a party at FP Franklin.

Plunging into the Carhouse account, he knew it would probably take him the rest of the afternoon to finish. That would mean leaving the smaller accounts for this evening and into tomorrow.

As he figured the beginning balances for the accounts, he thought of Nana. She was his world here in the states. Being an only child, and with his parents in Africa, she was the only family he knew stateside. And with her being ill, that meant he was the only one here to care for her. She'd had such an ordeal on the train. He hated even coming back to Chicago after her surgery.

Mason stopped for a moment and thought of Blaine. He glanced out the window. He could see snow beginning to fall outside. He prayed often that he'd made the right decision to allow Blaine to care for Nana. She was a stranger.

He'd seen the connection Nana had begun to form with Blaine at the hospital. Nana wasn't one to meet a stranger and decide so quickly to invite that person to go home with her. Yet Nana had seemed determined to keep Blaine with her. Close. Mason felt a pull to get to know the woman as well.

He'd not had a serious relationship with a woman other than a girl he liked in high school. Yes, he was attracted to Megan, but that was about all. She'd always been kind to him and they'd been on a few dates. Yet since meeting Blaine, he couldn't help but wonder about her, too.

Despite his work schedule, Mason had been looking for possible young women to date. He hated being alone all the time. Returning home to an empty house. Spending his weekends alone or at work. He wondered when and if one of these young women could be someone he could fall in love with.

But what if he had given Blaine too much responsibility? He was just too busy to worry about it. Whether she was good for Nana or not, worrying would get him nowhere. He'd find out soon enough.

Running his hand through his thick dark hair, he pushed it off his forehead. Rows and rows of figures on his Excel worksheet were causing his eyesight to blur. With the Carhouse file complete, he proceeded to dig into a new account.

He couldn't wait to finish his work, but the nagging feeling of having to tell Nana he wouldn't be home for Christmas made him work harder. Even if he pulled an all-nighter he didn't know if he could finish all the requested files in time. A pit formed in his stomach thinking about not spending Christmas with them. He had to do that last year and it'd been a miserable holiday.

Chapter 3

Callie watched as Blaine scooped shortening out of a baking cup and put it into the mixer on the kitchen counter. She was such a beautiful young woman yet so haunted by something. What would make someone like her stop her life to come to Callie's aid?

"What now, Callie?"

Stirred from her thoughts, Callie had barely heard her question.

"I put in a cup of shortening or what did you call it?"

"Lard. Just manufactured different now. Now put in one cup of brown sugar and a cup of white."

"Who knew there were so many different kinds of sugar."

Callie laughed. This girl really didn't know how to bake. If she got anything from being with Callie, she'd at least learn to bake.

Perhaps she could stretch out her illness longer. Although that would be a lie, because she was feeling better now than she had in years. That heart cleaning procedure made her feel like she was seventy-five again, instead of her years into ninety.

The tug on her heart was the same as when God told her to take in Joey, their foster child, those long years ago. Before her daughter

Amy had been born. But as with Joey, Callie felt that this young woman needed her. She sensed it. She knew it. But would it end as it had with Joey? She prayed not.

"Okay, now what?"

"Two eggs. Oh no."

Blaine glanced at her. "What?"

"Eggs. I hope we have at least two left. I remember scrambling the last few before heading off to see Mason in Chicago." She'd so enjoyed her trip to see her grandson. She knew it was probably the worst idea she'd ever had to visit him in November, but she wouldn't have traded the visit for anything. He had been so hospitable and thankful she'd come to visit. A young person's life is often marked by loneliness, especially in a place as large as Chicago.

"You have some," Blaine pulled out a carton from the refrigerator. "I bought them at the store yesterday."

"Did I put eggs on the list?" Callie might feel like a seventy-year-old, but her memory was clearly still at age ninety. "It's hard to believe Sunday is Christmas Eve. Let's plan to have Mason's favorite dinner that night. How does that sound, Blaine?"

"I'm sure he'll like that. What is it?"

"Pizza."

Blaine laughed as if she were remembering a favorite memory. "That's hilarious. Homemade pizza?"

Callie laughed. "Heavens, no. Homemade, as Mason puts it, is 'lame'. We'll order out."

"Are you sure there is a pizza place open on Christmas Eve, Callie?"

Callie sat up straighter, "You're right, Blaine. I didn't think of that. That child just loves pizza. I only have it when he comes to visit. He only likes one kind, from the small place downtown."

"One of the first meals we had together was pizza."

"Mason loves his pizza."

"Who doesn't? In fact, it was my idea to have it, not Mason." Blaine made a face of what appeared to Callie to be odd. It was as if she didn't like the sound of eating pizza. What young person didn't like a good pizza? "Now what do we need?"

"Now add a teaspoon of vanilla and of salt."

"I hope these turn out okay," Blaine put in the last two ingredients and flipped on the noisy mixer. The hum made Callie realize how much she'd missed baking. She rarely did it anymore.

"They'll be delicious. Did you turn on the oven?"

"Yes, remember." Blaine got out the baking sheets she'd asked Callie about just a few minutes before. "Three hundred and fifty degrees."

Callie was growing tired. "Do you think you can finish up the rest? Add those dry ingredients on the recipe there and plop them on a baking sheet. Bake for twelve minutes, each pan."

"I guess." Blaine glanced her way, "You okay?"

"Of course. Getting weary. Thanks Blaine for all your help today."

Blaine gave her a thumbs up. "It's my job, remember?"

Callie sighed, "For which, I'm extremely thankful."

Callie stretched as she stood up and inched her walker and her tired body to the living room couch. She used to run circles around other women in preparing for the holidays. Not now. She couldn't wait for Mason to get home and get the tree down from the upstairs attic. He could help Blaine decorate. It would be fun watching the kids decorate the artificial tree on Christmas Eve. She normally didn't wait so long to put it up, but this year was different.

Kids. She knew Mason and Blaine weren't youngsters, but having them home for Christmas would be wonderful. She wondered if Mason was as eager to be home.

"Putting cookies in the oven now," Blaine called from the kitchen. "How long do they have to bake again?"

Callie called out the twelve minute cooking time again to Blaine. Mumbling to herself she said, *'Who says it's only old women who are forgetful?'*

"What did you say?" Blaine again yelled from the kitchen.

Callie hollered louder. "I'd love a warm cookie out of the oven." The smell of the baking drifted out and into the living room. What was better than the aromas of holiday baking?

Before long, Blaine brought Callie a sample of her hard work. Callie pointed to a napkin holder on the table, can you grab me one of those, too, dear?" Picking up a cookie with overly brown edges, Callie waved her hand toward her feet. "This looks good. Can you grab me that afghan over there too, Blaine?"

Callie was sure, by Blaine's slow actions that soon the girl would be throwing things at her. She knew she was demanding, but she wanted to be sure Blaine knew she was needed.

Blaine picked up an afghan from off the side of Callie's couch and placed it over her. With a bit of an annoyed tone she asked, "Anything else?"

"No. Thank you. Just finish up baking those cookies."

Blaine sighed. "Okay."

"As soon as you're finished, we'll watch a Christmas movie."

Blaine flashed her an irritated look.

It made Callie laugh.

Blaine couldn't wait. A Christmas movie. She'd just as soon sit down and have two minutes to tweet someone. But who? If she had a friend left in the world, she'd snapchat them a photo of her slaving in Callie's kitchen. But who would care.

Life wasn't all that bad. She munched on a warm cookie. She agreed, they weren't all that horrible. She went for a glass of milk. Hollering into the other room, she asked Callie if she wanted one, too. Of course she did. Blaine went for two cups instead of one.

She'd leave all the dishes in the sink for tomorrow morning, convincing herself wasn't hard. She'd done plenty of work. She was legitimately earning her wages. Yet it was better than waiting tables during the busy holidays.

Kyle would laugh his head off to see Blaine spending time watching sappy Christmas movies with an elderly person. His idea of a great holiday event was to hit the local bar until he couldn't stand up anymore. Blaine had drug him back to their apartment so many times like that, especially during the holidays.

Blaine thought of Mason joining them. They'd only spent two nights together while Callie was in the hospital, but Blaine had enjoyed getting to know him. She wondered about his love life? Did he have a girlfriend? She hadn't thought to ask him? He was unlike any guy Blaine had ever known. She was pretty sure he would never be interested in someone like her.

Mason glanced over his computer screen. Snow speckled the air outside the office window. The occasional creak of the glass made Mason believe that the wind was picking up, too. Everyone had left the office. Yawning, he felt the pressure in his head building into what would prove to be a headache the size of the stacks of paperwork on his desk. His phone rang.

"Hello, Mason McAnder, how can I help you?

It was his supervisor. He began in on a particular item of paperwork that hadn't been entered into the computer yet. Mason tried to suppress his frustrated tone, "I'll find it and finish it before I leave."

Mason knew it would take him probably longer to enter the information for that account than any other one on the desk. He hit the "X" on the top right side of the document he'd just started and began searching for that file. Before finishing up the phone call, Mason imagined the man at least acknowledging that he was still at work. But nothing came. Not even a greeting for a good evening. He probably shouldn't expect anything.

Hanging up the phone he rubbed his temples. He could literally work through Christmas and never finish these accounts. He hoped management could see how overworked and understaffed they were in this department. The workload was killing him.

Before he could enter the first name of the company on the new document now up on his screen, his phone rang again. He wondered if he should just send it to voice mail instead of answering it, but then he thought of Nana. What if it were another emergency?

Mason cradled the phone on his right shoulder to not hinder his progress, "Hello, this is Mason McAnder." A cheerful greeting at the other end made him sit up straighter and smile, "Mom."

"Mason, are you busy?"

"Of course. How're you doin?" A call in the middle of the day was unusual from his mother.

"Wonderful, son. Dad's right here, too." A brief moment lapsed, "Hey son."

"Is everything okay?"

"We just wanted to let you know, we're in the states. Just landed at LaGuardia. We should be at Nana's tomorrow."

"What? Really?" Mason closed his eyes. "You're home?"

"Yup. We thought it best to get back here for Mom. We want to surprise her. You know how she can be when she knows we're traveling. She'd worry herself sick if she knew we had jumped on a plane to spend the holidays with her."

"How did you manage it?"

"The agency gave us permission and also paid for it out of the 'emergency fund' account."

"Nana is gonna be so stoked." Mason took in a deep breath and exhaled from relief.

His mother's voice added, "Don't tell her. When will you arrive?"

Mason glanced at the stack of papers on his desk. He'd finish up the last of the documents his boss needed, the rest were in his briefcase. He'd have to do a few while home. "I can't leave Chicago until Sunday, but I should be home by five or so. It'll be so awesome to spend Christmas with you."

"Have you talked to her? How is she feeling?"

"Blaine said her color is good, but says she tires easily."

"Blaine?"

"The caregiver I told you about. She's awesome. Nana loves her."

Her mother's voice sounded skeptical, "Caregiver? Which service did you hire her from?"

"No. Nana met her-" Mason stopped himself. It was going to sound like he pulled Blaine from strangers on a sidewalk. Who was he kidding? He wasn't even sure he'd done the right thing by not finding a reputable care giving agency to hire someone. Saying it out loud to his mother would sound even worse. "I'll explain the whole story when you arrive. You can meet her yourself."

"Well, okay then." His mother sounded less than thrilled about the idea. She still treated him like he wasn't old enough to find an appropriate night's meal, let alone a caregiver for her mother.

"Nana is gonna be so happy. This will be a great surprise for her. Are you renting a car?"

His father must have taken the phone from his mother and now answered him, "Yes. We're headed your way as soon as we get our luggage. We're pretty sure you wouldn't be available to come and get us anyway." Mason was thrilled that another thing hadn't gone to the top of his to-do list. He hadn't even done any Christmas shopping yet and Nana had texted him two more ideas for Blaine. He'd planned on spending time before he left to finish that up for her.

"Well, have a good flight the rest of the way. See you soon."

"We love you, son. You travel safe, too." His mother now returned to the phone and sounded reassuring and kind. It made him miss her more. The surprise would make Nana's Christmas even better to have her daughter and son-in-law home.

He hung up the phone and then hit the 'block calls' button on his phone. He had to work like crazy to finish these last few contracts.

Soon a janitor came into the office, plugged in a sweeper and swept the floor around Mason. He needed to quit for the day. There had to be a better way to climb the corporate ladder.

Chapter 4

Bright December morning light penetrated the thin blanket over Blaine's head. Blaine blinked awake hearing a noise from the hallway. She'd left her door open a bit each night to listen for any movement from Callie. She realized the sound came from Callie pushing her walker down the hall. Pulling the heavy comforter and blankets off her legs, Blaine scooted out of bed.

Opening the door she found Callie bent over her walker, shuffling toward the bathroom, her flowered robe sliding off one shoulder.

"Callie."

Callie jumped, tugging the bathrobe up, "Blaine. Are you trying to give me another heart attack?"

Blaine drew closer, "Why didn't you wake me?"

"I bother you enough. I wanted you to sleep. I'm wearing you out with all these trips to the potty."

Blaine grimaced, she'd also been using the bathroom much more these days. Blaine got a kick out of Callie calling the bathroom a *potty*. "Is this the first time you've been up tonight?"

Callie glanced up at her. "If I say yes, will you let me go?"

Folding her arms, Blaine responded, "It isn't, is it?" Blaine hoped there wouldn't soon be a competition for the bathroom. What if she needed it in a hurry again?

Callie seemed determined to maneuver her laborious trek down the hallway, her hair stuck up in odd places beneath a pink hair net. Blaine imagined these net things were to keep your hair looking nice for another day but Callie was losing the battle.

"I wish you'd let me do my job."

Callie continued her walk to the bathroom, "I'm feeling better. I can get to the potty alone. I've been doing it for ninety plus years now."

"I know, but that doesn't mean you should continue to do it alone."

Callie pushed her walker around the nearest corner as she disappeared into the bathroom. Waving Blaine off, over her shoulder she mumbled, "Go back to bed and get warm. I'll be fine. Give this old woman some privacy."

Blaine had been standing guard since they got home from the hospital every time Callie used the "potty" as she called it. She didn't want her falling while in there and Blaine not hearing it.

Callie shut the door, but called through it, "You're gonna get sick by running around here in your skivvies."

Blaine felt warm enough in her yoga pants, although it would be nice if she had a robe. For some reason, it was one thing she hadn't packed from Kyle's apartment.

Callie called out through the closed door, "Get back in bed, I'll be out in a jiffy."

Blaine's feet were cold now, despite the green shag carpeting. Folding and rubbing her arms, Blaine went back into the guest bedroom. Blaine enjoyed being lazy these days as her body seemed to be craving sleep. It was quite the difference after her days living with Kyle. He always insisted they jog before heading to work, despite the fact that Blaine had spent a full shift waiting on tables the night before and hadn't hit the pillow until midnight. Exercising was important to Kyle, he expected no less from her.

Blaine thought of Mason as she snuggled down deep into the warmth of her bed. How would Mason treat her when he arrived home? What if he totally realized how he'd actually left his Nana to a complete stranger? He had to have felt guilt in doing that. What if he had simply been nice to her in order to find someone to care for his grandmother? She scowled. Trust had long been cheated from her.

If she laid there another minute, she'd be second-guessing everything that had happened in the past few days. Instead, she got up, found a heavy sweatshirt on a chair beside her bed and pulled it over her head. She adjusted it and flipped the hoody part off her head. It kept off the cold of the morning until the furnace kicked on higher to warm Callie's house.

Heading into the kitchen, Blaine flipped on a light switch and clicked on a stove burner. The blue flame came to life as Blaine filled the tea kettle with water. She wished she could afford a coffee maker, yet she was determined to save as much of her earnings as possible.

She'd contrived an alternative plan in case this job didn't last long. She wanted to do everything in her power to get on her own. It was a safety net. Nothing was ever sure or secure. She always needed to remember that.

Setting the filled pot on the burner, she pulled two coffee mugs out of the cupboard, and placed them on the counter. The warmth of the small burner cut through the damp, cool air of the kitchen. Blaine rubbed her arms, thankful that most of her queasy stomach came after she ate.

What she wouldn't give for a cappuccino or a latte right now. The coffee maker was probably the only thing she missed of Kyle or her old life. How odd that she didn't miss anything else.

Blaine grabbed the jar of instant coffee and shrugged. Perhaps she could persuade Mason to go with her to find a Starbucks. She knew it wasn't Chicago, but what city in America didn't have a Starbucks?

Callie scooted her way into the kitchen just as Blaine stirred the coffee in mugs steaming with hot water. "I'm gonna get you to like instant coffee yet, my dear." Callie laughed.

Blaine gave her an "are you kidding me" look which made her giggle. "What's wrong, Blaine?"

Blaine alternated between one foot and another, "Don't tease me Callie. There has to be a Starbucks here somewhere."

"A what?"

"Starbucks?"

"Never heard of it?" The look Blaine gave Callie made her laugh.

"In the whole town?"

"I don't think so. Although I've never needed one. What do they sell?"

Blaine frowned at Callie like she'd revealed to her there wasn't a Santa. "Coffee!"

"No worries. We have a perfectly good tea kettle." Callie had been teasing Blaine ever since they'd arrived home that instant coffee was the way to go. Yet the frustration and shock on Blaine's face that first morning was unforgettable. At first she'd tried to hide it and now, they'd grown so accustomed to each other, she didn't hide the fact that she hated the stuff. In Callie's mind, coffee was coffee. Surely there couldn't be that much of a difference.

Blaine finished stirring the cups and carried them into the living room where Callie sat in her favorite chair. The old woman never missed a morning to sit and read what appeared to be a very, worn book with a leather cover. Blaine placed Callie's cup on the table beside her.

Callie beamed, "Thank you."

Blaine sat on the couch, pulling her legs underneath her for warmth and placed a blanket over her. It always took a few minutes for the house to warm.

Callie took her book off the table and opened it on her lap. "Think I'll read about Elisabeth and Mary."

Blaine looked out the front window at a fresh layer of snow that had come in the night. Cars passed the house. Blaine loved not having to worry about a commute in the morning. Getting out into the frigid temperatures, finding just the right outfit that agreed with Kyle's standards, and hoping the line at Starbucks wasn't too long.

Glancing at Callie she noticed the intent stare she had while reading

"Callie, what are you reading?"

"My Bible."

Blaine took another long swig of coffee and grimaced. A Bible. She didn't know much about what a Bible had to say but she imagined it to be old, ancient words, written long ago by some theologian. How could an old book like that hold a person's attention? She hated to interrupt her, but she was curious. "Callie? Do you read the same thing in the Bible every day?"

Callie looked up, keeping her finger on what appeared to be the section she was reading from. "No. I read something new each day."

"How long have you been reading a Bible?"

"My whole life." Callie's finger moved again.

Blaine didn't get it. "Why?"

"I never see it in the same way twice. One day it is gentle reminders of something I've read over and over again. It helps me to remember God's promises or His words of how to live my life. Other days," Callie sat back, "I'm amazed that after so many years, I read something new or with different thoughts. Like I've never seen it before." Callie removed her finger from the page, her attention now interrupted by Blaine's questions, "Blaine. I've read the Bible through many times. I can't even count how many and each time I find something new. Every time."

Blaine tilted her head. "How can that be?"

"God tells us that His words are living and active. It is evident to me when each day reveals something different."

"That's impossible. I've never read a book that read differently each time I read it."

"The words all stay the same, yet somehow they speak differently or have new meaning each time. It's hard to explain, but it never makes me doubt God's words."

Blaine wanted to ask more, but now the woman's finger continued to move down a page. She'd read for a while then either close her eyes or act as if she was thinking about what she was reading or maybe she was taking small naps. It was odd, yet Blaine could clearly see that the religious book was important to Callie. Who was she to doubt it?

Her reading today had given Callie lots to be thankful for. She glanced in Blaine's direction as the young woman stared out onto the lawn. Each morning brought a new scene and Callie often daydreamed as Blaine seemed to be doing. Today's daybreak brought a bit of fresh snow, almost covering, but leaving patches of yellowed grass here and there. Branches were barren of leaves and the lack of green looked stark against the fresh, white powder.

Watching her cemented the realization that she was growing fond of this young woman. God had delivered her again from having to be a burden to her family, yet another reason for thankfulness.

Blaine's eyes found her gazing at her, "Are we supposed to get more snow today?"

Callie leaned back in her rocking recliner, sipping her now lukewarm coffee. "The weatherman said last night we might get two or three inches today."

As they sipped their coffee, Callie took the opportunity to finish the story that she'd started during their conversation they'd had on the train two weeks before she became abruptly ill. She wasn't sure exactly where she'd left off, but as always, God prompted her to finish it. "Blaine. Do you remember where I left off in telling you about my husband?" Miles had left for war only to return a different person.

Blaine took another sip of coffee. Despite the grimace and her wrinkled forehead, she nodded. "Um, I think something happened to Miles or something he did."

Callie asked, "Would you like me to continue?"

"Sure."

"Was it when he tried to take his life?"

Callie saw recognition reflect on Blaine's face.

"I think so. You found him in the garage doing something. I imagined he'd tried to commit suicide." Blaine set down her mug on a side table. "But why would he do that? Why would he try and take his life after all you and he had been through? Like he didn't appreciate your efforts in helping him after the war."

Callie recalled now, "It wasn't that he wanted to hurt me. He just wanted the bad thoughts to stop. War had changed Miles. He didn't realize how much until he came home."

Blaine shrugged, "I don't understand."

Callie started, "I think many people believe committing suicide is selfish. It leaves so many questions and great hurt to those left behind."

"You're telling me."

Callie realized she'd said something that brought a knowing look to Blaine's face. What if telling Blaine her story was actually helping Blaine through something that had been troubling her. Callie continued, "Sometimes when a person is suicidal, they not only want to stop their own hurt, but they might also believe that their loved one would be better off without them. I truly believe Miles never wanted to hurt me or our daughter."

"I'm sure that's part of it." Blaine clutched her blanket tighter. "But I still believe it is an easy way to quit. A sure way to fix your grief but puts horrible scars in the hearts of those around you."

"You're right, honey, it does. But back in 1945 and in the years to follow, we didn't talk about such things. There wasn't a family in the United States that hadn't been affected by the war." Callie twisted the tissue in her lap. "But we didn't acknowledge the way the war had changed us. The horrors of war were kept quiet in an attempt to protect those that hadn't experienced it. Men didn't want to recount their ordeals. Miles was one of them. He kept things to himself. I can only imagine the insecurities and fear he experienced during the war, and during those first few years following his return to normal life."

"So what happened? That day?"

Callie had never fully told the story to anyone. Not even Amy knew the depth of that afternoon in the garage. She'd hid it from her. Miles had enough issues. He didn't want his daughter to know he'd made the attempt.

"I found him. In the garage." Callie sighed. "He had shut all the doors. Closed all the windows on a hot, July day. That's what tipped me off because I could hear the engine gunning on our old Dodge truck."

Callie rushed to the garage to see if Miles was testing out something he'd just fixed on the car. But if he were doing that, he wouldn't have closed the garage doors. The windows to the building were always at least cracked as he worked on the cars or cleaned the blades of the lawnmower. Suspicion grew when she found all the windows closed tight.

Callie didn't want to know whether her premonition of what he was doing was indeed what she imagined. Why would he think of doing something so harsh? So permanent to her. And what about Amy? It was her birthday.

Her hand went to open the garage door which fortunately was not locked. Callie could smell the fumes of exhaust seeping out from beneath the door. Anger grew in her heart as she looked through the window of the door and saw Miles sitting quietly in the driver's seat of the pickup truck. His head bowed. He didn't see her.

Flipping the garage door open, she stared into the garage to see if the slamming of it against the back wall startled Miles. His head didn't move. What if she were too late? What if enough fumes had entered the car and it was all over.

Before she could get the courage to find out, Callie held her breath, ran to the overhead door, and pulled it up. Soon the stuffy, fumed garage became clear again. She turned back to the car to see Miles looking at her from inside the car. Relief flooded her heart, but it was immediately replaced by anger and resentment. *How dare he?*

As she crossed the garage and opened a window, Miles began to lower the driver's side window slowly. His face revealed sorrow and tears slipped down his rough cheeks. Callie stared into his eyes.

Maybe he was a stranger after all. He put his face into his hands, his shoulders shook, and he started to sob.

"I knew at that moment," Callie recalled with tears now filling her eyes, turning her coffee cup in her hands. "My husband needed more help than even I could give him. He needed a supernatural awakening. Something to jar him to his senses."

"Supernatural?" Blaine pursed her lips.

"Sometimes God needs to wake us up. Open our eyes. He did it for me that day, but I could only pray that somehow He would grasp her husband's heart and change it for the better."

"So then what did you do?"

"I committed a cowardly act." Callie fiddled with her wedding ring still on her finger and twisted it to clearly see the diamond. "I reached into the car, turned off the motor, and took the keys. Without saying a word to Miles, I left him sitting in the car. I couldn't comfort him. Nor could I do much of anything else.

"As he continued to sob, I turned and left. Leaving him all alone. I was livid." Callie shivered, despite the blanket covering her legs. "It wasn't the proudest moment of my life, but that's what I did. I couldn't face him. How could he think that his death wouldn't affect others? Me, Amy, his mother, and even other family members? Leaving him there was the easiest thing I could do, because if I had really told him how I felt at that moment, I was afraid of what he'd do. Would he try it again. I didn't want to take that chance."

Blaine clutched her forearms.

"Are you cold honey? Turn the heat up more."

"It's fine."

Callie was unsure about whether to continue or not. Blaine wouldn't look at her. Was she really that affected by Miles' story?

"I remember one thing you said in the hospital, Callie. You said that Miles was never the same." Blaine lifted a stray blonde tendril off her forehead, pushing it behind an ear.

"He wasn't." Telling the story brought up so many emotions for Callie. Her next words always brought her relief. "What appeared to be one of the worst things in his life, in our lives, turned out to be the turning point in Miles' life."

"That afternoon, I feared what he would do. Should I have comforted him? I'd just left him sitting there. All alone. In that blue pickup in the garage. He must have had the keys to the other car in his pocket, because it wasn't much more than fifteen minutes or so and I heard him pull out of the garage and head toward town. I was still so angry that I didn't care. If he didn't think enough of Amy or me to not attempt anything so ludicrous, why did I really care what he tried to do next? If he really wanted to take his life, I would never be able to stop him. I wasn't strong enough to help him. So I just let him go. Let God deal with him."

A catch in Blaine's voice made Callie look over at her, "That must have been hard for you to do." Blaine's eyes grew moist, her nose pink.

"I had no other choice. I had done the best I could to heal his wounds. I'd held him at night during his nightmares. I'd been patient with his outbursts. I loved him, but I couldn't heal his mind, even though..." Callie took a deep breath, "I always wished I could.

"I was afraid. More than any time in my life, I never felt so afraid. Help wasn't available like it is today. All I could think about was how I would support Amy and myself. We would be left alone and penniless. I would have had to go back and live with my parents until I could find a job to support us both. The only thing I could do that afternoon was to get on my knees and plead to God to spare his life. I prayed like I'd never prayed before."

Callie leaned her head back on her lounge chair. She seemed exhausted from recalling her story. She looked wounded. Sad. Blaine knew the feeling well. She'd felt it for years.

A wound, stifled for years, began to bleed in Blaine's heart, upon hearing Callie's story. It felt as if Callie's story had taken a knife and reopened a messy infection that oozed not blood but emotions, forcing Blaine to go into a part of her life that she'd kept hidden for years.

Blaine took her cup off the nearby table, took Callie's now empty mug and put them into the kitchen. Coming back into the living room she blurted out, "I think I'll get in the shower now." She needed to avoid Callie's gaze.

Blaine felt a tug to tell Callie how she really felt about suicide. She'd seen enough of it in her lifetime and hated it. How could someone as loved and cared for as Miles want to do something so selfish? Her mother didn't have anyone to really love her, but Blaine. Despite her being a child, it still wasn't enough to stop her.

Callie watched the young woman rush down the hallway to her room. Something troubled her. What was it?

Callie did the one thing that always brought her comfort. She reached for her Bible. When it was in her hands, she felt comfort, as unreal as that seemed. She bowed her head and prayed. The urge for Blaine was just as strong as her urge to pray for Miles so long ago.

She murmured, "Please keep this child here long enough for me to help her." And she added, "Show me how."

Chapter 5

Blaine flipped on the faucet in the shower. The room was cold and it took a while for the water to turn hot. The heat from the shower moistened the glass door as the tears flowed down Blaine's cheeks. Her stomach was reeling. She wasn't in any mood to eat.

Miles' story shone a bright warning light on her life. It felt real and harsh. Memories made long before Kyle. Her mother had died in a car accident, but she had never told anyone about another night a few weeks before the accident. Years dissipated sending Blaine back as she recalled that horrible night. Stepping into the shower, fear, anxiety and doubt crept into her thoughts as the water now penetrated her hair. She could hear her grandmother's voice.

"Blaine. Turn the oven on for me."

Blaine couldn't reach all the handles of the stove, but she did know how to turn the oven on. She scooted a chair over to the large appliance and reached over the burners to the temperature knob. "What number, Grammy?"

Her Grammy removed a box of chicken nuggets from a plastic shopping bag, turning the box over. "Three. Five. Zero." This wasn't their first cooking experience. Shuffling through the bags she pulled out a carton of milk and a bag of chips. "Where's your Mommy?"

"Sleeping," Blaine turned the knob on the stove and found the three-hundred-fifty mark. She pushed the button and waited to hear the oven blaze on. Gazing down at her thumb, she remembered the day she'd burned herself on an oven rack, she knew to be careful.

Grammy hollered her mother's name toward the bedroom. Blaine got down from her chair, pushing it back to the table. "Can I have some chips, Grammy?"

"Where's your brother?" Blaine shrugged. He'd left her yesterday. Probably spending the night at a friend's house. "No chips. Wait until your nuggets are done." Her grammy screamed her mother's name again toward the bedroom. "The only thing that girl can do well is sleep. Wait here. I'll go wake your-" Her words stopped short as fear filled her eyes. Turning, she rushed into Blaine's mother's room.

Blaine rubbed her belly as it grumbled. She'd found a half eaten pop tart that morning in the pantry, but that's all she'd eaten all day. The peanut butter jar was scrapped clean and the empty bread bag was halfway hanging off the edge of the table. She couldn't wait much longer. She took the bag of chips from the table and quietly pulled the edges apart to open the bag. Without hesitation, she devoured a handful of chips. Surely, Grammy wouldn't care. Blaine only wanted the grumbling in her belly to stop. A few chips fell into her lap. Blaine gobbled them up, too.

Suddenly, Grammy rushed back into the room. Blaine hid the bag of chips by sliding them to the floor at her feet. Grammy grabbed the wall phone, dialed a number quickly, and began shouting into it. "Come quick. It's an emergency. I think my daughter has...," Grammy glanced at Blaine, seated at the table, turned her back and whispered into the phone. As she hung up, her tone changed from soft to harsh. "Where's your mother's bucket?"

Blaine wiped off her mouth with her sleeve. Grammy didn't seem mad at her for eating some chips. She went to the closet beside the empty pantry to find her mother's wash bucket. Her Grammy grabbed the bucket from her and a bottle of Mommy's favorite drink from the refrigerator. All Blaine could think about was to get back to the opened bag of chips under the kitchen table. Her Grammy left the kitchen and ran back into her mother's bedroom.

She hollered back over her shoulder, "Blaine. Go unlock the front door."

Blaine grabbed the bag of chips and took them to the door with her. She unlocked the deadbolt and even remembered to turn the little button inside the doorknob and then went to find the remote control for the television. She placed the bag of chips on the couch.

Blaine crawled up on the couch and devoured more chips from the bag. She could hear Grammy hollering to her mother to swallow her special drink. She overheard her say, "Whiskey always makes me throw up. It's gotta work on you, too."

Blaine wondered if her mother was going to be sick. Putting both hands over her ears, she waited a moment or two before snatching another chip from the bag. Shoving more into her mouth she heard the oven beep. She hollered in the direction of her mother's bedroom, "Grammy, you can put in the nuggets now." She'd do it herself, but she'd always been scolded to never open the oven door by herself. Her Grammy said she'd burn herself and she'd done it before. The scarred welt still evident on her thumb.

The only thing Blaine could hear from the bedroom was her Grammy pleading with her mother. Blaine had a mouthful of chips, so she put her hands back over her ears for a few moments. She always hated to hear someone else throw up.

Blaine slid off the couch, tucking the bag of chips under her arm. While heading into the kitchen, she found the remote control on the floor by the door. Pointing it at the television she soon found one of her favorite cartoons and climbed back up on the couch. Without realizing it, she finished off the entire bag of chips. Fear crept into her heart for fear she'd get into trouble, but her tummy felt a bit better.

A loud bang startled Blaine as someone pounded on the front door, screaming from the other side. "Paramedics!" Blaine tucked the empty bag under a couch pillow.

What was a paramedic? Before Blaine could yell to her Grammy, they knocked again. She screamed into the other room, "Grammy!"

Her Grammy yelled back. "Answer the door, Blaine. Let them in."

Blaine hated opening the door. She got scared, reached for a blanket at the other end of the couch and pulled it close. Her mother had told her time after time to never open the door for anyone. Only Grammy.

Grammy came into the room wringing her hands on a towel. She opened the door. The men had on uniforms and eyed Blaine. They were carrying black bags. Her mother would be mad that Grammy had let strangers into the house. Two other men pushed a bed on wheels into the room. Following them through the front door was a policeman. Blaine covered her head with the blanket. Perhaps they wouldn't see her.

Blaine could hear heavy footsteps coming nearer, she shivered. What if someone found out she'd eaten nearly the whole bag of chips? A man spoke softly to her.

"Hey honey. What's your name?"

Blaine knew to never open the door to strangers, but having a man talk to her made her almost wet her pants.

"Sweetie?"

The police officer touched her leg. Blaine pulled it back under her blanket. "I have something for you."

Blaine wondered if it was more food. She was still hungry, despite the chips. She felt something soft touch her leg. She pulled the blanket slowly down from one eye to look.

The man's eyes sparkled, "It's a teddy bear. Do you like teddy bears?"

Blaine wasn't sure what to do. Speak to him or pull the blanket back up over her head. Admiring the plush bear she saw friendly, brown eyes and felt the soft fur against her leg. Blaine reached out and took the bear, hugging it to her chest.

The man, with a tight blue shirt with shiny buttons asked again, "What's your name, sweetie?"

Blaine wasn't sure how, but she finally became brave enough to pull the blanket down and gaze at the man. Soon a woman with identical gold buttons and a tie on came through the door. The two people whispered to each other, glancing back at Blaine from time to time.

Blaine was sure they were police. She'd seen them outside her house many times often pulling the neighbor man from the house across the street and putting him into a police car. The woman now sat down by Blaine and stroked her hair. "What's your name, honey?" Blaine wasn't as afraid of the woman. She only hated men. She was nice and Blaine wondered if she could ask her to put the chicken nuggets in the oven.

Blaine crawled off the couch and took the police woman by the hand and led her into the kitchen. Blaine pointed to the box of chicken nuggets on the table and then to the oven.

"Are you hungry, sweetie?"

Blaine grinned big. Maybe the woman would put the nuggets into the oven.

She not only did that, but she also poured Blaine a glass of milk. Soon hot nuggets were on a plate on the table. The police lady, who called herself Suzy, told her the nuggets were hot and to blow on them before putting them in her mouth. Blaine had burned her mouth on one before so she tried hard to wait until she could nibble on an edge. While she ate the men wheeled her mother out on the bed with wheels.

Suzy sat down across from her while she ate and laughed, "Sweetie, I've never seen such a little girl eat so many nuggets all by herself before."

Blaine smiled. The warm chicken nuggets filled her empty tummy.

Her grammy had done nothing but shake her head when she saw Blaine eating at the table.

"She's always hungry." Grammy told Suzy, with tears in her eyes. "She doesn't even realize what her mother just tried to do. I guess that's probably a good thing. How could my daughter want to leave her all alone?"

The nice Suzy now stood up and hugged Grammy. Tears streamed down Grammy's cheeks. Her eyes red and watery. Grammy wiped her nose with her sleeve.

Blaine continued to let the hot water flow over her body doing its best to erase and wash away the memories of that horrible night.

Callie wasn't the only one to ignore a loved one attempting to take their life. Blaine was a child, but why hadn't she asked questions. At least been more concerned about Grammy's tears.

There was so much in Blaine's life that she wanted to forget. That night was one of them. What cold, heartless child would care more about chicken nuggets than about her sick mother carried out on a gurney?

Thinking about that night brought a sob so strong that Blaine covered her mouth. She'd tucked the memory away so long she thought it would never return, yet it came back with a vengeance. Despite being a child, and a hungry one at that, she'd ignored all the sadness around her. Why hadn't she noticed her mother's suicide attempt? What if Blaine would have stopped her mother from trying again? She was heartless, unsympathetic when her mother needed her. Blaine tried to prevent her shaking despite the spray of hot water covering her body. She pressed the heels of her hands into her eyes to stop her tears.

Everything that had happened to her was God's punishment for wanting to eat instead of seeing her mother's pain. Blaine deserved Kyle and his demanding ways. To this day, she'd never been able to stomach chicken nuggets. The thought of smelling them now, repulsed her and Blaine rushed to the toilet bowl.

Drying off, Blaine swallowed the lump in her throat and the heartache that had haunted her for years. She needed to hide the memory once again, wipe her tears away and forget them.

Would she ever feel free to tell someone the truth about her life? She'd wanted to many times, but guilt would hide it again.

When her mother took her life successfully a few weeks later, Blaine knew she deserved to be left alone. Her lies began then. Sometimes she could pretend that it hadn't happened. She was so young, perhaps she remembered the details wrong. But she knew better.

She didn't want anyone to know the truth about her life. They'd feel sorry or worse yet, they find out how uncaring she was to her mother.

One lie would lead to another. She'd tell friends about wonderful birthday and Christmas presents she'd receive. She'd write essays about her amazing summer vacations. On spring breaks, she'd hide at home and then assure everyone that she'd been to Disney World or even on a Hawaiian vacation. Thankfully, she changed schools each year, which protected her from others finding out the truth. Unfamiliar friends would make her stories new again.

The only thing she could do was remain strong. Perhaps that's why she let Kyle have his way. At least he cared whether she existed or not, to use her. She pretended that he made her feel needed, wanted. Maybe she shouldn't have left him.

Picking up her phone after putting on her clothes, she wondered if she should call him. Then she remembered why she'd left him. His last ultimatum had made her feel unloved again.

Lies protected her. Lies satisfied her longing to fit in. Be just like everyone else. But in every case, her lies only alienated her from others. And soon, people would find out the truth and cast her off as a liar. Who wanted a friend they couldn't believe?

Did she want to put Callie's friendship in jeopardy? Did she want to lose a chance to possibly date Mason over more lies? Of course not. How stupid of her to harm their trust? She knew she had a problem, but truth eluded her. Often she'd hidden the truth so long she'd forgotten it.

As she applied her makeup, she thought about how lying had caused more drama in her life. She needed to change. Could she do it? Could she open herself up and be vulnerable? Callie had been nothing but honest with her, even strong enough to tell her the truth. Somehow admitting it brought her strength to try.

She toweled off her hair. There was only one way to find out. She wanted a chance to see if she could keep Callie's trust. A stranger, yet not a stranger. She only needed to keep one thing hidden, but that seemed like her biggest lie of all.

Chapter 6

Blaine spent the afternoon cleaning the house. She'd never worked so hard, but the activity kept her thoughts at bay.

That afternoon, Callie's phone rang. Her face brightened as she responded, "Mason honey, are you coming soon?"

Just as quickly, Callie's face darkened, "Okay. Then when will you arrive?"

Would Mason disappoint Callie too? Blaine hoped all men weren't alike. Perhaps Blaine's perceptions of the guy were wrong.

"Uh huh, I understand."

She didn't. Blaine understood one thing: disappointment and the hurt never went away.

Callie finished her conversation. Swiping the phone off, Callie placed it on the table. "He's been held up. He won't be arriving until late Christmas Eve."

Blaine wanted to console Callie, but she knew nothing could at that moment.

"He has too much work. It's probably because of my emergency surgery."

Blaine knew exactly what to do. Her grammy had done it for her numerous times. Distraction. "I'm sure he's as upset as you, Callie." Even as the words came, Blaine knew better. "Why don't we wrap gifts tonight?"

Callie looked up with a little more hope in her eyes. "Perhaps we should."

They'd finished up the last of the gift wrapping. Callie had grown weary from the busy day. Now in her lounge chair, she drifted off to sleep.

Blaine was tired too, but still wanted to keep busy until time for bed. Callie had told her where she stored her Christmas tree and decorations, and Blaine grew anxious to retrieve it and begin decorating. If she got it down tonight, they could begin putting it up the next morning.

Blaine found a ladder in the garage while Callie snored softly in the next room. She hoped the box was marked as she shuffled around the cold, dark attic. She found a few totes that held Christmas bulbs and lights and brought those into the kitchen. She tried carefully to get it done without waking Callie.

She found a long box that looked as if it could hold an artificial tree. Finding pine branches just under one of the box flaps, she got it down the ladder and placed it on the kitchen floor. It was a process getting all the items out of the attic and down a ladder, and Blaine was shocked she'd done it all without waking Callie.

Her grandmother had once gone out and purchased a real spruce for them. She'd had it delivered to their house right before Christmas. She'd also shown up the same afternoon with bags of bulbs, lights, and even tinsel. Together, she and her brother, as well as Grammy, had decorated the tree while their mother was at work.

They were supposed to be in bed when their mother returned from work, but Grammy had allowed them to stay up past their bedtime to see her reaction.

It would have been better if they had gone to bed.

Blaine remembered that night and tears filled her eyes. She'd refused to even decorate a tree for years. She could still remember the ache in her heart as her mother stripped the tree of the pretty bulbs smashing each one as she yelled at Blaine's grammy for allowing her and her brother to stay up way past their bedtime. A bedtime she never adhered to herself.

She didn't understand at that time why her mother had gotten so angry, but years later she realized it was a symptom of her mother's addiction. Couldn't she see how it left only heartache for them? To this day, it had kept Blaine from any addiction.

Blaine was happy to please Callie for all she was doing to comfort Blaine these past few days. If putting up a tree would help her not feel so lonesome for Mason, Blaine made it her goal to fulfill it. Helping Callie eased the guilt in her own heart.

Mason checked the clock on his computer. He'd gotten to work at seven. Now it was only him and the janitor, and he'd gotten so much work finished without the distractions of co-workers and his supervisor. Now past six he realized that if he didn't get Nana's shopping done, she'd never forgive him. He knew the traffic and crowds would be insane just days before Christmas, but he had no choice.

His grandmother wanted nothing more than to surprise Blaine with gifts. That was typical of Nana. He flipped through the dwindling stack of accounts still on the edge of the desk. The stack was smaller, but it still haunted him. Then he remembered the words his grandfather used to tell him when he'd come over to help him with yard work or to help in his garden, "Just do your best, son. That's the only thing that will matter in the end."

He wanted to take the train home Sunday afternoon. He'd planned on working on a few accounts during the four hour commute. He could then email the files to his boss to look over while he was in Michigan for the holiday. Perhaps if he sent some today the boss might realize he was still working to get everything accomplished.

He attached a few to an email and hit the send button. He'd finish the rest tonight at home after shopping. As he slipped his arms into his coat, someone said, "Hey" behind him. He swung around.

Megan stood in the doorway. "Mason, I'm sorry. I didn't mean to scare you."

After the initial shock, Mason laughed. "Megan. You can't creep up on an overworked employee like that."

Megan smirked.

"Are you about done?"

Mason turned back to his desk to retrieve his computer. He got out his satchel and zipped it inside. "Mostly."

Megan approached him. As usual, her perfume preceded her. Mason slipped the satchel over a shoulder, he couldn't help but notice how amazing she looked with her jet-black hair pulled up at the back of her head, her cheeks bright pink, and her lips covered in Christmas red lipstick.

"Are you going to a party? You look fabulous."

She nodded. "Well, in a way. But first I'm headed out to do some *necessary* shopping."

"Hey, me too." Mason wasn't sure she could help, but he needed some advice to cut this errand short. "What kind of slippers do you wear?"

Megan's dark eyes twinkled, her eyelashes black and long. "What?"

"Slippers," Mason pointed to his feet. "You know?" He was trying to be serious, but the look she gave made him feel odd.

"I know what slippers are, Mason. But why do you ask?"

Mason fumbled his words. "Um." Telling Megan they were for his grandmother's caregiver sounded odd. "She's young. Like you."

"Oh," Megan squinted at him as if to question who exactly he was thinking of buying a gift for. "So you need a bit of advice on what to buy?"

Mason had to think quickly. He'd been attracted to Megan. They'd gone on a few dates. She was beautiful, and in fact they'd had long discussions about their relationship, but Mason had struggled to commit to her. "My Nana has a young woman looking after her and she always has to buy something for everyone or it 'isn't Christmas'. You know." Then shrugged. "I have no clue. Literally."

Megan pulled her phone out of her purse. "Well, let's see. I can show you what I would like and maybe that would help?" Megan twirled, "Let's go."

Mason breathed out a sigh of relief. If Megan helped him his errand for Nana wouldn't be so overwhelming. Megan's thumbs typed in a message on her phone.

She slipped the phone into her black pea coat's pocket. "I'll just shop with you. How does that sound?"

"Do you have other plans? I don't want to put you out."

"Nonsense," Megan waved her hand in response. "I was going shopping, but now I won't have to do it alone."

"Um, I guess." Mason buttoned his coat. "If you wouldn't mind? That'd be great."

Megan flashed him a mysterious smile. Like she knew a secret.

"Could we get a housecoat, too?"

A quizzical look replaced the confident one. "Housecoat?"

Mason shrugged, "Robe?"

She tapped his arm. "Right. Yes, we can get both. Do you know her size?

Mason took a deep breath. Panic must have shown on his face, because Megan patted his arm. "No worries. We'll figure it out. C'mon."

Mason wondered if this evening was an official date. Perhaps he could buy Megan dinner, as thanks for helping him. He didn't really care, he was just relieved to have help.

Blaine had gotten the last of the lights checked from the box now sitting on the floor of the kitchen. She'd found three working strands and hoped that was enough to decorate the tree in the box at her feet. She could hear Callie stirring in the other room. Dropping the strand, she went to check on her.

"How was your nap?" Blaine went into the living room. She'd forgotten she'd put a strand of silver garland around her neck until she adjusted her sweater. As slipped the decoration off, she glanced at Callie to see if she'd noticed.

"What was that?"

She couldn't keep anything from this woman. "What?"

Callie clucked her tongue and pointed her finger at her. "Blaine, where did you get that garland?"

"From...the...kitchen." Blaine pointed behind her.

"The kitchen? I don't keep garland in the kitchen."

Blaine dropped into a chair. "The attic." She paused, cringed for her reaction.

"Blaine. You didn't?"

Blaine said, "Maybe."

Callie shook her head. "Help me up. I need to use the potty."

Blaine held Callie's arm as she rose to head to the bathroom. "I'm sorry, Callie. I just thought if I got the tree down we could decorate it. Surprise Mason."

Callie was still shaking her head as she held tight to the hand bars of her walker. "You did, did you?"

"Please don't be mad." Blaine knew the feeling of trying to do something good and having it backfire. She felt the years dissipate and saw her mother's face.

"Mad?" Callie stopped and looked into Blaine's face. "Honey, it takes more than that to rile me."

Blaine sighed. She hoped she hadn't hurt Callie's feelings.

Callie and Blaine decided putting up the tree would be the first thing on their agenda the next morning. Soon after breakfast, Callie went to take a shower as Blaine sorted through the boxes in the kitchen.

Callie asked if she had washed the front window before putting up the tree. Blaine went for a bucket and rag. While filling the bucket she heard the back door open. Callie was still finishing up in the bathroom so she wondered who could be coming in the that way without knocking. Shutting off the water, she looked up to see a strange couple in the kitchen.

"Hello?" The woman stared at her like she was probably doing right back.

"Hi."

The man held out his hand to Blaine, "I'm Chuck. And you are?"

Blaine pushed a strand of hair off her face with her sleeve. "Um, Blaine."

The woman now offered her hand. Before she could tell Blaine who she was, Callie came shuffling into the kitchen. Paying attention to her steps, Callie muttered something to Blaine. "I cannot believe you got up into the attic alone, Blaine. You could have fallen..."

"Mom!" The woman went to Callie who had a dumbfounded expression.

Chuck smiled behind them and then looked to Blaine. "We're here to surprise mother."

Callie hugged the woman. "Amy! What are you doing here?"

After Amy hugged her mother, she turned to Blaine. *Who was this girl? And what had she done to her mother's tidy home?*

"Mother." Chuck gave his mother-in-law a hug and then hugged his wife. "I think we surprised her, dear."

They all laughed.

"What? How?" Amy's mother stammered.

"We came as soon as we could."

"But, why? I'm fine."

Amy helped her mother to a chair. "Fine? Didn't you just have a major heart attack and surgery?"

"Well, there was that."

Chuck folded his arms, "Yeah, just that."

Amy's mother bubbled, "How long have you been here? How long will you stay? Why didn't you tell me you were coming?"

Tears filled Amy's eyes. She couldn't believe how fragile her mother looked. Taking an emergency furlough now, instead of the planned June furlough had been a good idea. Knowing she could care for her comforted Amy's heart.

"And who is...?" Amy pointed to Blaine who had a blank and guilty expression on her face.

"This is Blaine. She's my caregiver."

Blaine seemed to force a smile while wringing the rag out on a box placed at her feet.

"Um honey." Amy's mother pointed to the rag as water droplets covered the box at Blaine's feet.

"Oh!" Blaine squeezed the rag over the sink and shook her head, "I'm sorry. Give me a second and I'll get out of here."

"Blaine. Stop. You don't have to go anywhere. This is my daughter, Amy and her husband, Chuck. They're the missionaries. From Africa."

Blaine nodded. "Hello. I'm sorry for this mess. Callie and I were just going to..."

"Yes Mother. What is up with this?" Amy waved her hands around the cluttered, box-stacked kitchen.

"Blaine wanted to surprise me. I think. And she got the Christmas tree down from the attic. We had been waiting for Mason to get home, but I guess she decided to do it on her own."

Amy eyed the girl who stood in the middle of the room, wringing the rag in her hands.

"I did want it as a surprise. I didn't know you were coming home. I wanted to surprise Callie." She cringed. "And Mason."

Amy glanced at her mother, then back to Blaine. "You know Mason?"

Her mother patted the chair beside her. "Sit down, Amy. We have lots to catch you up on. How about some tea?"

"Got any Vernors, Mom?" Chuck smiled.

Blaine went to the fridge and got a can for Chuck.

He popped the tab and took a long swig. "This is divine."

"Blaine and I met on the train home from Chicago. She's a godsend to me."

Amy couldn't believe her ears. "You met on the train? What train?"

"The one from Chicago."

"Two weeks ago?"

"Yes. Isn't that wonderful?"

At that moment, Amy knew she'd returned where she was needed the most. Just wait until she saw Mason! She would ask why a stranger was caring for her mother.

Chapter 7

Chicago bustled with the shoppers that haunt stores just hours before Christmas, anxious and aggressive. Packed store escalators, long check-out lines, and limited sizes added to the frustration. Mason hated shopping, but even more so in an atmosphere like this.

Megan seemed oblivious. For some reason she continued to hang on Mason like they were an item. Mason wondered when the time would come for him to make a decision about Megan. They enjoyed their times together.

As they entered the lingerie department, Mason's collar grew moist. He hated to think of having to carry his coat, but if he didn't take it off soon, he'd melt on the spot. Perhaps it hadn't been such a magnificent idea to request Megan's help. As he passed skimpy panties and colorful bras, it seemed the department oozed seduction and lace. Why did they have to place the bathrobes in this department?

"You're as red as a Santa's suit." Megan whispered, "Uncomfortable?"

Mason couldn't lie. "Maybe." Stepping away from her he added, "Yes."

Despite Megan smelling like a million bucks, he hurried to the robe section for protection. The bulky, pink fluffy robes reminded him of his mother and Nana.

Megan continued her litany of questions. "What does this young lady like? Classy or comfortable? What's her favorite color?"

Mason couldn't remember what Callie had told him. Of all things for his grandmother to ask him to purchase. Unzipping his coat, he slipped it off. He could feel sweat trickle down his back. He grimaced, remembering he also had to find slippers.

Megan seemed to grow frustrated. "Mason, don't make this difficult," tilting her head to one side waiting for him to answer. "You're so cute when you're nervous."

Did he have to explain Blaine to Megan? He was purchasing some pretty intimate things for a woman he hardly knew. He didn't know her favorite color. What did he know about her? He blurted it out before he even thought it through, "She likes pizza."

Megan smirked. "What?" Her raised eyebrow made it worse.

Mason shook his head. "I mean. She seems like someone who likes comfort. And," he knew he'd have to admit it. "And to be honest, I don't know her very well."

"Mason McAnder, have you gone on a date with this girl?"

Mason answered meekly, "Date?" Mason needed to be careful here. If he said the wrong thing, he'd give Megan the impression that he'd found someone else. Before he could answer he asked himself, *had I?* "I met her when I was at the hospital with Nana."

"And your grandmother, I mean Nana, is buying her gifts? Does she know her?"

"Not exactly." Mason felt his collar grow damp. "She met her on the train." He knew it would better in the long run to just come clean. "We did have dinner together." The look he received made him consider his reaction if the tables were turned. He didn't blame her for the questions. "She was on the train with my Nana when she had her heart attack. She was kind enough to stay with her in the hospital until I arrived." Mason took hold of a nearby clothes rack for support.

"That was nice of her." Megan turned quickly, perusing through some more clothes.

"Now she's staying with my Nana. Taking care of her until I get home."

"So," Megan seemed to want to ask a million questions. "Not for long?"

Mason sighed. "I don't know. We'll see how she works out."

"Okay. How old is she?"

"I mean," Mason felt trapped. He was steaming even without his coat. "She's your age. That's why I need your help."

Megan scooted closer as a woman pushed past them. "Okay." Megan took a deep breath, pointing to another rack a few feet away. "Follow me."

Mason followed like a puppy. If he didn't need a woman's suggestion, he wouldn't be feeling so trapped. He'd never shopped for a woman before, other than his mom or nana. He struggled with trying to figure out what color Blaine had worn at the hospital. Nothing came other than the pretty sweater she'd worn when they went to get pizza. He remembered how the color had looked so nice on her. Then it came to him.

"Purple."

Megan interjected, "Purple?" like it was some kind of foul color.

"A light purple." Mason shrugged. "Is it lavender?" He suddenly remembered.

"Okay," Megan nodded, turning back to a rack of robes, pulling one out, gazing at it and then putting it back. One after another.

Weren't all robes alike? Mason wanted to ask. As he perused the room he realized, he was the only male in the whole department. Mason's head throbbed.

"How about this one?"

Mason reviewed Megan's choice. It was nice, yet it made him blush. It was a silky, deep purple. He looked away. "Yeah, no."

"Why?"

He looked back at Megan and she looked at him with exasperation in her eyes. "I think it's too..."

"Yes?"

"Silky."

Megan rolled her eyes. "Provocative. Something you wouldn't buy for just a caregiver." She put the robe back on the rack. "So you think you need something a bit more conservative?"

Mason nodded, "Exactly." He turned and found a lavender plush robe beside him. He pulled it out. "Like this one." It looked warm and comfortable. He pictured Megan with completely different tastes than Blaine. It surprised him that he even surmised this.

"That's pretty." Megan came closer to him and then asked another impossible question. "What size?"

Mason wondered if he could just disappear into the coat department across the aisle. "Size?"

Megan seemed to grow impatient. "Let's do it this way. Is she taller or shorter than me?"

Mason quickly glanced at Megan. "About the same."

"Okay," Megan twirled in front of him, "Is she skinny or large?"

Mason smiled, "You both are just right." He mentally complimented himself for such a great answer, but Megan's look revealed otherwise.

"Well, I wear a small."

"Perfect. That's probably what she wears, too."

Megan sighed. "What else did you need?"

"Slippers?"

"That should be easy. If she's about my size, she probably wears my size as well."

"She could take them back if they don't fit, right?"

Megan walked away, but called back to him, "Yes, keep the receipts."

It didn't seem a legitimate way to go find slippers, but Megan led him right through the bra and panty department again. For once in his life, he considered ditching a pretty girl and running for the nearest escalator, but that wouldn't solve his dilemma.

Mason soon went to find a check-out to purchase the gifts as Megan wandered back into the bra section. Of course the line stretched out into the main aisle. He couldn't wait to chide Nana for sending him on this mission.

As he purchased the items, even the cashier complimented him on his choices. She was about Blaine's age, which made Mason proud. He could never be certain women were serious, friendly, or just flirting with him.

Megan grabbed his arm when he finished, "Anything else, Mason?"

He hated to ask Megan to stay with him any longer. He did want one more thing, but he thought perhaps he could find the other item by himself. "I don't want to keep you any longer. I'm sure you have other shopping to do yourself."

"I do, but I don't mind. What is it?"

"That's the problem." Mason put his wallet back in his back pocket. "I'm not sure yet. Maybe jewelry?" He shrugged.

"You're in luck. That's my specialty."

Why did Mason have a feeling that's what Megan would say? *Who was this girl Mason now seemed intent on buying gifts for? Were the gifts he bought really for his nana to give this new girl or was it a ruse Mason was using to cover that he had to purchase gifts for another girl? Surely, Mason wouldn't have asked her to help if they were for someone he really had a crush on. Would he?*

"Mason?" She had to ask. If she didn't her Christmas would be ruined. She didn't want to think that he was going home to see his nana when really he was heading home to get acquainted with another girl.

Mason fumbled with his packages, tightening the straps of his computer case as he walked. "Hmmm?"

"Is she pretty?"

Mason looked around, as if he'd missed seeing someone. "Who?"

"The girl staying with your nana?"

"Yes." Mason's eyes revealed the truth. She was.

"Are you interested in her?"

Mason stopped, as if gathering his thoughts. "I'm not gonna lie to you Megan."

Megan held her breath. She didn't want to hear. Mason was a catch. She knew it. Everyone around her knew it. She'd been lucky enough to catch his attention herself. He was husband material, someone she'd been imagining herself growing old with. She'd been happy to have him finally giving her the attention she'd desired for months. His answer might seal her fate.

"She is pretty. But Megan, I really don't know her. Like I said, we just met two weeks ago. I'm sure she's a very nice girl, but that's about all I know about her."

"You had pizza together." Megan felt her temperature rise.

"Yes." Mason raised his hands in the air. Packages and all. "That's not a crime."

"No. It's not." Megan pulled her phone out of her coat pocket. She needed a distraction. A reason to leave him before she got really mad. "Hey, I do have to meet someone else." She turned and kissed him on the cheek. "I hoped I helped you."

Mason grinned. "Yes you did. Thanks. I really appreciate it."

Megan couldn't do anything but leave him standing alone in the middle of the store. She needed some air. Even though they'd had a couple of dates, Megan thought for sure Mason would be shopping for her. He hadn't made another date with her tonight, so she expected she wouldn't be getting anything from him for Christmas. She thought of the nice tie she'd bought him a few weeks earlier. Maybe her father would like it instead.

Mason left the large department store and headed further into town. He knew his last stop would be an easy purchase. Nana had picked out a pretty ornament when she was visiting around Thanksgiving at the German Marketplace. He hoped it was still available and he wouldn't have to shop for a substitute. He always made an effort to watch her enthusiasm when she shopped, and to try and remember the things she'd put back on the shelf without purchasing. Just like his father had taught him.

His shopping would be finally finished. He felt bad that the gifts he'd sent his parents were now on route to Africa. Perhaps he could pick up some of their favorite candy so at least they'd have something to unwrap on Christmas morning from him. Just as he wondered what to get them, Mason passed a famous popcorn shop and knew exactly what would please his father.

Arriving at his apartment almost three hours later, he was exhausted. He wanted to look over a few more figures before going to bed, but he was starving. There wasn't much to eat in his apartment so he'd stopped by a local deli for his favorite soup and a sandwich.

As he sat down to eat, for some reason he couldn't get Megan off his mind. He was pretty sure he'd offended her tonight. Even though they'd never officially called themselves a couple, he had been pursuing her a bit in the last few months. And why not, she was a nice girl. He liked spending time with her. But what now? And why hadn't he ever made it official? Maybe he should try and talk to her about it before he left for Nana's house. His thoughts kept returning to Blaine, even though he really knew nothing about her. Would Christmas at Nana's house change that?

Chapter 8

Blaine felt awkward after Mason's parents arrived. As she busied herself by washing the window in the living room, she could hear snippets of the conversation from the kitchen. She felt intrusive, but what could she do? She also wanted to clean up the mess she'd made in the kitchen. The only way to do that was to begin moving it into the living room.

Blaine returned to the kitchen and motioned toward one of the boxes, "I think I'll take this tree into the other room."

Chuck moved toward the box, "Let me help you." Before picking up the box, he turned to Blaine. "Blaine, right?"

Blaine nodded. "Yes."

"She's a God-send, Chuck. This girl has been an angel ever since I met her on the train."

Blaine felt her face flush. "Your mother has been very good to me."

"I needed to be." Callie leaned toward Amy and winked. "She knows everything about me."

Amy seemed to eye Blaine suspiciously. "How did you two meet, exactly?"

As Callie chattered on about the waiting room in Chicago and how Blaine helped her get to the train and then even sat with her, it sounded preposterous. While following Chuck into the living room with another box, she shook her head. What was she doing here? If Callie were her mother, she'd be skeptical, too.

Chuck set the box in front of the large picture window. "Mom always likes the tree here. She wants the neighbors to see it at night." Chuck pointed to the houses across the street. "Where are you from, Blaine?"

"Chicago."

"Do you know Mason in Chicago?"

"Chicago's a very big place."

Blaine couldn't get over how much Mason looked like his Dad, except not as tall.

"I didn't know him before meeting Callie, if that's what you mean?"

"So...you met Mother on the train and now you're taking care of her?"

Blaine sighed, then nodded. Her thoughts were blocked by wondering whether she needed to find another place where she could spend Christmas.

"Do you want all the Christmas boxes in here?" Chuck motioned for Blaine to go before him into the kitchen. Callie had lots of questions for Amy. "Your furlough wasn't until June. How did you manage to get that moved to now?" Many more ranged from why they didn't call to how long they could stay. Blaine listened intently-just waiting to hear her name as she and Chuck moved the remaining boxes into the living room.

Hearing only whispers, Blaine decided maybe the family needed some space. Perhaps she could go take a nap. Lord knew she needed one. She'd been fighting exhaustion for days now. But then she knew she needed to think, too. Having no clue as to where she'd go, Blaine snuck off to her room to get her coat.

Returning to the kitchen, Callie saw her, "Blaine, where are you going, sweetie?"

"Callie, why don't I mail those Christmas cards you addressed this morning?"

"But Blaine, I haven't gotten stamps yet."

"No problem. I'll stop at the post office."

"The car keys are by the door."

Seeing concern on Amy's face, Blaine held up her hand to Callie, "No Callie. It's fine. I'd rather walk. It's just a block or two, right?"

"Yes. Do you remember?"

"I think so."

"It's awfully cold out there, Blaine. Are you sure you want to walk?"

Blaine patted Callie on the back and did her best to console her with a genuine-like smile, "I'm from Chicago, remember. I love walking in the cold." Pulling on her mittens, she wrapped a scarf around her neck, "Where are those cards?"

Relief flooded Blaine's soul as she escaped out the kitchen door and into the garage. She stuffed the envelopes into her oversized purse and left through the garage door at the back of the house. Walking around the side of the house, a blast of Michigan cold slapped her cheeks. She reached for her hood and slipped it over her head. The arctic blast didn't compare to the emotional chill inside Callie's house and now filling her heart.

She headed down the sidewalk, not looking outside for the past hour, she hadn't realized how the weather had turned into blizzard-like conditions. The snow stung her cheeks as she realized, she had no clue where the post office was. Her lies were only continuing.

As Amy heard the door shut from the garage, she gazed back at her mother. "Are you crazy?" As soon as the words left her mouth, she knew she should have spoken differently.

"Amy!"

"Mother, you don't know this girl at all. You met her last week and now she's living in the same house with you?"

"Amy, calm down and it was two weeks ago." Her mother pulled her sweater tighter around her bulging middle. "We need to talk about this."

Chuck pulled out a chair and gave her a look of 'be careful.' She knew what it meant; she usually got it when her mouth worked faster than her brain.

"I'm sorry, Mother. I don't mean to sound harsh. This is just odd. Why wouldn't you hire a professional with reliable credentials to come and help you? Why would Mason allow a stranger to help you?"

Callie stood. "Amy, you have no idea what you are talking about. I appreciate your concern, but I'm not stupid. I did think this through. In fact, believe it or not, God still uses old women like me to fulfill his purposes in life. Do you believe that?"

Amy saw the look in her mother's eyes that almost matched her husband who now sat back in his chair and folded his arms. He'd given her the lecture on the way to Callie's house. How not to jump to conclusions. How to diplomatically figure out who this girl really was. All of it. They'd gone over it, but Amy had once again jumped to what she believed to be only logical conclusions.

Her mother still stood, despite her shaky limbs. "This girl is not a stranger to me. She's had and is living a hard life. She has issues I'm not even sure I'll understand or pry from her, but she's giving and kind. Look at what she did while I was sleeping." Callie motioned around the kitchen and into the living room. "She managed to get into the attic and pull down my Christmas tree. Who would do that for a stranger? She's not living here because she wants anything from me. She's living here because I asked her. I'm paying her, just as I would any another caregiver. Why is it so hard for you to understand? You and Chuck just walk in here and assume things that aren't true. I'm not so elderly that I can't make rational decisions. No matter what you believe."

Amy now stood, "I'm sorry, Mother. You're right. I don't know all the details. Now please, sit down. Tell me about her."

She wasn't sure her mother would calm down. She was defending this girl like she would her own grandchild. There had to be more to the story and Amy now understood she needed to listen carefully. If she didn't, it appeared she'd be kicked out of the house while a stranger took over her mother's care.

Blaine's hands were frozen, but she'd managed to find the post office thanks to her phone. Now she wasn't sure what to do after getting stamps on Callie's cards and mailing them. Should she return to the house? Adjusting her mittens she spotted what appeared to be a coffee shop across the road. Blaine wondered if she was more excited about the coffee she'd finally be able to buy or the fact that she didn't need to return back to Callie's house right away.

A small bell rang as she entered the store. Two smiling teens behind a counter asked her if they could help her. She scanned the blackboard against the wall behind the counter. "I'd like a mint mocha please."

"Comin' right up." A young man smiled at her. A shock of dark brown hair fell over his eyes.

Blaine slapped her mittened hands together and stomped her feet to bring feeling back into them. Growing warm again, she shivered. She needed to stay for a while and get warm. Waiting for her drink, she spotted an empty table up against the windows at the front of the little shop.

Service was fast. She paid for her drink and sat down. An older man leaned against one of the windows, and smiled at her as she sat down. Chicago coffee patrons rarely stopped long enough to sit down, or even offer a smile. *Must be the small town charm.*

Her hands were still cold, but she pulled them from her mittens and slid them around the warm, fresh cup of mocha. The smell brought a sense of heaven into her life.

Pulling out her phone, she wondered if Mason was available to talk. It was close to lunch. She hated to bother him.

He'd told her to call if there was another emergency. If his grandmother needed him. Did that apply to her as well?

She looked up Mason's number on her cell phone. What would he do if she did call? Would he hang up on her? He'd probably not answer if he was busy. Or would he, perhaps he'd assume something was wrong with Callie.

Blaine hated her indecisiveness. She'd had it her entire life. Issues like...if she should call the police when a man came home with her mother and made her feel afraid, if she should call Grammy when her mother was incoherent and couldn't get the box of cereal down from the cupboard, or if she should call an almost stranger to ask him if his parents would kick her out of his Nana's house. Blaine was always afraid of the consequences.

She'd done it once. Just once. When she was a little girl, she'd called her grammy because she was hungry.

If there was one thing Blaine could do well, it was to obey. Usually, without question. She'd not listened to a man her mother had brought home one night. He'd told her to turn down the volume of the television. She'd paid dearly with a bruise across her cheek which remained black and blue for weeks.

Blaine tiptoed into her mother's bedroom. She hated waking her up. She turned a bit and whispered into the phone, "Grammy, she's sleeping. I'll get in trouble for waking her up."

Grammy told her to do it anyway.

Her mother's bedroom smelled of a pungent sweetness combined with the familiar cigarette smoke. Her mother wasn't in any kind of pajamas, but she lay on her stomach, a bare shoulder exposed. Blaine nudged the shoulder and mumbled, "Mommmy?"

Grammy yelled at Mommy through the phone, hurting Blaine's ear. Lowering the phone she placed it on her mother's ear. But nothing happened.

She raised the receiver to her ear, "Grammy she won't wake up."

Her Grammy now yelled at her, "Yell at her Blaine. Make her hear you."

Blaine shook her head. She hated yelling at her mother. There had always been lots of hollering in the house. She nudged her again and spoke louder, "Momma?"

Her mother opened one eye and shut it again.

Blaine again raised the receiver to her ear. "She isn't gonna wake up." Blaine turned and tiptoed out of the room. "I'm hungry, Grammy."

She could hear her Grammy sigh, "Blaine I'm at the store. Give me an hour or so. Find yourself some bread."

There wasn't anything in the house to eat. She'd looked all afternoon. She could open the only can in the pantry, but she couldn't read the label yet to know what it was. What if she opened a can of green peas? She hated peas. They were green and squishy.

Whenever she called someone for help, it often just made matters worse.

Blaine glanced at the cell phone in her lap. Would Mason get angry if she called to tell him that she was worried about his parents and what they thought of her? Of course he would. Why would anyone want to hear a stranger nark on their parents?

Tears sprung to her eyes. She blew on her coffee trying to suppress them. If there was a happy note to the day, she loved the coffee. It'd been so long since she'd had something so tasty. The smell of mint tickled her nose, warming it.

Across the room she spotted another young woman seated by herself drinking coffee. She watched her as she pulled out a notebook and began to write things down. She was poised and pretty.

Unwrapping a scarf from around her neck, Blaine watched as she picked up her phone and dialed someone.

Soon the young woman was chatting away to possibly a friend. Perhaps it was her mother. Blaine felt the jealousy she'd always had when she envisioned someone having a personal friend or even an affectionate mother to talk to. She'd never had that. Life had always seemed unfair to her.

What would she tell Mason about his parents? They seemed aloof. Untrusting? Skeptical? How many more fears could she add or imagine?

Blaine sipped more of her coffee. This time a warm sensation filled her mouth and throat. The mint in the drink cleared her sinuses. Tears filled her eyes, she used her napkin to wipe them. She tried to focus on something else rather than her emotions.

Would she ever have someone she could call? Worst of all, would there ever be anyone she could call who would care if there was ever a real emergency? Blaine felt more alone than ever.

Chapter 9

Blaine trudged back to Callie's house as snow continued to layer the sidewalk making it slippery in places. A pelting sound on her hood from the snow mixed with the crunching under her feet.

Rounding the corner, she was on the last stretch to Callie's street. Her face felt numb as sharp pellets stung her face. The mint from the coffee now making her stomach queasy. A strong wind awakened dead leaves that skittered across the snow like tumbleweeds. Tree branches twisted in the wind, a few snapped over her head. The weather had gone from bad to worse while she'd been trying to stay hidden. Almost like her life.

Zipping her coat, she pulled her scarf higher to cover her mouth and cheeks, to shield her eyes from the stinging pellets. It felt like Chicago, but the small sidewalk and rustic houses didn't provide any comfort from the bitter wind. Doubt crept in even more. Why was she here? She even had begun to miss her co-workers at the diner. She'd never called to officially quit. Why should she? With the doubt came guilt. Guilt for leaving Kyle without an explanation, despite the fact he didn't really even deserve one.

Did anyone miss her? She did have a friend at the diner where she worked. Another waitress. They always had fun when they shared shifts together. Had she noticed Blaine was gone? Or would she be mad at her that the diner had been left short-handed during one of the busiest times in the city? The thought made her heart ache and soon she realized she wasn't going to make it home without leaving her mark on the fresh snow at the base of a tree. She removed her scarf just in time. That seven dollar coffee had been a waste.

The snow began to fall harder. The wind was making a legitimate effort to steer her off the sidewalk. She put her head down and trudged a bit faster, even though she didn't want to fall. What would she find back at Callie's house? What if her luggage was packed and waiting on the front porch? Callie wouldn't let them do that to her? Would she?

The cold not only brought numbness to her fingers and toes, but on this day it brought another horrible childhood memory. Blaine dreaded each time a cold walk reminded her. She was so young, yet her memory so vivid. The tightness of her mother's hand covering her own as they walked and walked. Despite how she felt now, she'd never felt so tired, afraid, or cold as that day.

"Blaine, you need to walk faster."

"But Momma, my legs ache and I can't feel my toes."

Blaine's Momma knelt down beside her and tightened the string of her hat, tying it tighter, "I know baby. I'm sorry. But if we don't keep moving..." Tears filled her Momma's eyes. "I have an idea. It's our only solution.

Standing, she picked up Blaine's hand and gripped it tight, pulling her forward. "C'mon. We have to keep moving."

Blaine stumbled. As her Momma glared down at her, she wasn't sure if she saw anger or pity in her eyes. She was too cold to care whether she was making her mad or not.

She grew tired. The only thing she wanted was to crawl up on Grammy's lap and fall asleep. Her stomach had long ago stopped grumbling. She was too cold to even be hungry anymore.

"We're almost there baby. C'mon."

Blaine and her momma passed all the stores on Canal Street. Festive decorations adorned each window, toys of all kinds were surrounded by stuffed animals. It was Christmas time. She tried to distract herself with the pretty lights. Her feet were beginning to hurt with each step. "Momma, where are we gonna stop? I'm so tired."

Blaine's Momma didn't respond. She wore no mittens, her hands turning white in the cold, she stared off down the street as if looking for something. "We're nearly there, baby. Hang on."

Soon they approached a building with a large sign out front that looked like a cross. It glowed red against the dark, brick building.

"Where are we going, Momma?"

Again, her Momma ignored her question. Blaine was used to it. They walked through the door below the sign and warmth hit Blaine's cheeks.

Her Momma talked to a man at a desk and he nodded.

Blaine stomped her feet. She couldn't feel her toes anymore. She shivered despite her winter coat and mittens. Her fingers and toes burned and ached. All she wanted to do was sit down and cry, but if she did, Momma would scold her. Instead, she slumped beside her on the floor. She wasn't sure if her Momma would make her, but she couldn't walk another step. The floor smelled of cleaner used in some of the gas station bathrooms they'd used that week.

Soon a large black woman approached her mother and asked her a few questions. Her mother mumbled, "She's so little and so cold. Can't we stay. Just tonight?"

She stooped, speaking softly. Blaine was afraid to look at her, so the woman took her chin and turned it toward her face, "Hey little one. What's your name?"

Blaine tried to answer, but her lips felt like they were swollen.

The woman picked her up. Blaine could feel the warmth from her body envelope her and she put her head on her shoulder. That's when she heard the woman holler, "John, come get this baby. She's nearly froze."

Blaine remembered the pain that night. Despite being warm and covered in heavy blankets, her feet hurt so bad she cried. Her Momma had disappeared into the night, leaving her by herself. But Blaine hadn't cared. The black woman had stripped off her old clothes and replaced them with warm, soft clothes. She sat in a rocking chair across from Blaine's cot. Rocking. Back and forth. Back and forth. Blaine couldn't keep her eyes open any longer. For the first time in a long time, Blaine felt safe. Secure. Warm. Her last thought before sleep came was, maybe she could stay here with this lady forever.

That's how she felt now. Alone, cold and lately she'd been so tired. Could she handle all of this? Did she even want to try?

Thinking back to that moment with her mother, she remembered one thing: Her mother had done everything in her power to keep her safe that night. Whenever they'd get kicked out of an apartment, her mother always did her best to find her shelter.

Blaine thought back to the time she'd been left alone with the lady from the shelter. She'd overheard the conversation just before she'd fallen asleep. The lady had told her mother there wasn't room for her. They'd keep Blaine and do their best to protect her through the night, but Blaine's mother needed to find another place to stay. Her mother made the lady promise that she'd protect her through the night. The woman agreed, but said, "If you don't return in the morning, we'll call protective services."

The next morning, after sleeping better than she'd done for days, her mother was at the bottom of the stairs when she descended them to get some breakfast. She'd come back for Blaine...she always did. Until she was gone.

Blaine reached down and patted her stomach. Despite anything, Blaine would protect her child, too. At least her mother had taught her something.

Mason packed up the last of his clothes and stuffed them into a suitcase. He wanted to get all packed tonight because he had one more account to finish up.

He stuffed the shopping bags into a backpack. Nana would have to wrap them. He was sure she wouldn't care. She could wrap presents better anyway.

As he sat on his sofa, he thought about calling home. Perhaps if Blaine knew his parents would arrive soon, it might be better. His mother could be a bit dramatic at times and he still wasn't sure how she was going to feel about having Blaine as Nana's caregiver.

What if Blaine had grown tired of taking care of Nana by now? What would he do? Would his parents also feel sorry for Blaine and see how much she needed a family? Blaine had dropped everything to be with Nana. Surely they'd care for her just as Nana and he had done.

Food was scarce in his apartment. Grabbing a bottled water from the fridge, he returned to the couch as his phone rang. It was Megan.

Should he answer it? He cringed and swiped the bar, "Hey Megan."

"Mason. Are you still home?"

"Yeah. Leaving tomorrow. Why?"

"Nice. I was wondering." Loud music blared in the background, and Megan spoke louder. "Can we have dinner again before you leave?"

Mason hadn't had dinner. Perhaps it was time to discuss their relationship in depth before he did head to Nana's house. But what would he tell her? He didn't know Blaine enough to say that he didn't want to ever date Megan again. He was still up in the air about them both.

"Let me know what you want and I'll have it ready for you when you get here."

Perhaps talking it all out would do them both good. "Um, sure. Order me a southwest burger."

"Fries?"

"Yeah, sounds great. See you in a bit."

He went for his coat.

Megan scooted her chair closer to the table against the large window. She caught a glimpse of Mason coming down the sidewalk and waved to him. Adjusting her skirt just a little higher, she could see her reflection in the window, smiling at what she saw.

Who was this girl he'd been buying presents for? He'd never mentioned meeting anyone lately. If there was someone new, she needed to get to the next step with Mason before he could fall for someone other than her.

Her stomach churned from hunger, she hadn't wanted to eat all day. Mason was the first guy who hadn't come on to her first, by asking him out she was venturing into new territory.

The restaurant was cool, but she wasn't about to cover up what she'd put out on display for Mason. She had guys all over the restaurant eyeing her, so she knew she'd worn exactly what she needed to. All she had to do was reel him in.

Mason was different, that was for sure. She'd never met anyone like him before. As other restaurant patrons passed, she drummed her fingers on the table. Where was he?

From the first day she'd met him, she knew he'd be the one for her. He was kind, gentle, and his reputation was impeccable. They'd chatted about his family and how he'd been raised in Africa as a missionary kid. Her parents would be thrilled with him. If she could only get him home to introduce him to them. He'd look great on her arm...from this day forward. She knew it and if she didn't take a chance on him, she'd regret it for the rest of her life. This was her time to shine. She murmured, "Merry Christmas, Megan."

Mason came through the front doors of the large restaurant in search of the table by the window where he'd seen Megan.

"I'm with that girl," Mason pointed in Megan's direction, "over there."

The guy nodded, "Very good. This way please." The guy escorted him to Megan's table.

Megan stood when he got closer, "I'm so glad you came, Mason."

Megan never looked *this* good. She wore a bright red dress, and Mason could feel his face grow warm at the length. Her black spike heels and low neckline didn't help his comfort levels. Heat spread to his entire body, she was drop-dead gorgeous.

What was he going to do? What could he do at this point? Walk out?

As he approached her, Megan came to him and pecked him on the cheek. "Hey. I'm so glad you got out on a cold night to come and eat with me."

If Megan was making him feel uncomfortable, he was sure she was getting attention from every other male in the room.

"You look beautiful tonight." He slid out of his coat, his heat intensifying even more.

Megan twirled in front of him before sitting back down. He wanted to crawl under the table.

"It's just us. I thought it would be nice to have a pre-Christmas celebration."

Before he could answer, the waiter arrived with their food. Mason's burger looked hot and juicy. Megan had ordered a salad.

"Can I get you anything else?"

Megan flipped a cloth napkin to her lap and smiled, "We're good thanks." Looking at Mason she added, "Just what you ordered."

Mason nodded. His burger looked delicious. "Thanks for ordering for me."

"No problem. Would you pray for us?"

Mason nodded. As he bowed his head he felt her hand grab hold of his. He peeked at Megan who had her head bowed.

He needed to carefully craft his words for this prayer. "Dear Lord. Thank you for this food. Thanks for good friends." He hesitated, *Oh God, help me.* The nervousness he'd felt in the panty department coming back with a vengeance. "Thanks for someone to share it with. Please be with us through the next few days as I travel and also as we celebrate your birth. Help us always to remember the true meaning of the holiday. In Jesus' name, Amen." He hoped God heard the plea from his heart in the middle.

"Amen," Megan added.

She pulled her hand away. "Your prayers always seem so sincere."

He grabbed a bottle of ketchup on the table and squirted it on his fries. "I hope so. That is always my intention."

Megan sliced a grape tomato in half and popped it into her mouth. "How's that Santer account coming?"

"Finished it this morning. I'm so glad. That thing has been haunting me for weeks."

"I know." Megan chewed some more of her salad. If he had known she was eating healthy he would have asked for something a little more appropriate, but his stomach growled. "Wanna fry?"

Megan shook her head. "I've had enough carbs this week to last me for a while. My roommate is obsessed with Christmas food. She bakes all kinds of cookies, candies…I can't handle all that for very long." She giggled.

Mason took a large bite of his burger, always annoyed at how girls had such food fetishes. "So," he chewed a bit more to be able to talk, "what're your plans for tomorrow and Monday?" Anything to get off the subject of food.

"I'm going to my parent's house," Megan picked up her water glass and took a long drink.

"What about your siblings?"

She nodded. "My sister and brother. I haven't seen them since I believe," Megan tapped her forefinger to her lips as if she had to think about her answer, "Fourth of July?"

"That's a long time to not be with your family."

"It's hard to get together."

Mason ate a few more of his fries, "I got a call the other day from my parents. They've come home to see Nana for Christmas."

"That's cool. I'm sure she'll be surprised."

They chatted through their meals about their Christmas plans. What they enjoyed about Christmas as children and what they didn't. Mason related his African Christmas experiences to her. Megan always seemed attentive to how he had been raised in a foreign country.

They finished their meals and Megan asked if he wanted to head across the street to a local book store. "They have this magnificent fireplace there. Almost like what you find in Colorado ski lodges. It's in the center of the store, with lounge chairs surrounding it. Have you seen it?"

Mason had heard about it, and he had wanted to see it. It also might be a better place for them to talk. It was hard to hear each other in the noisy restaurant. "I haven't. Sounds like a nice place to spend an evening."

Megan squealed, "I've been so wanting to take you there. I know how much you like books."

"Books are my favorite." Before he could react, Megan reached around for her coat.

Mason stood to help her. He hoped the cover-up would stop the gawkers as they headed for the restaurant's door.

They headed across the street. The Chicago wind was gusty, even among the tall buildings. Megan kept inching closer to him until she hooked her arm through his. She looked up at him and smiled.

They found the fireplace at the center of the new store, along with other couples snuggled up close on the surrounding sofas. She shed her coat, sat on the sofa, and patted the seat next to her. He took off his own jacket, but somehow it didn't give him any relief from his body temperature now rising to an all-time high. The radiating heat from the open flamed fire wasn't helping him.

As Megan snuggled close, he realized this conversation was going to be harder than he thought. Yet at this moment, he still had no clue about what he was going to say to her. He chided himself for thinking that he wasn't interested in Megan anymore, just because he'd met another girl just two short weeks ago. He'd be a fool to let her go completely. Just yet.

Chapter 10

Blaine came into the garage. Stomping her feet, she did her best to alert the family inside that she'd returned. No surprises. She was grateful to not find her things in a heap at the back door.

Tapping lightly on the door before she entered assured her that they knew she was now back.

Callie waved from her chair at the kitchen table. "Blaine. Honey. You must be frozen." She began to rise from her chair but Chuck waved her to sit back down. He made his way to Blaine.

She was cold, to be sure. As Chuck approached her, she grew colder in a different way. What was he going to say to her?

"Can I help you with your coat?" He smiled and held out his arms.

Blaine peeled off her mittens and scarf. Still shivering, she unzipped her coat and placed the bundle in Chuck's arms.

Callie called from her chair, "Honey, where have you been? I've been worried about you."

"I'm sorry. I stopped for coffee." Her stomach churned some more at the thought.

Callie chided, "Honey, it's turned so cold and snowy out there. Come sit down here and get warm."

Callie's table appeared to have become a meeting-place of sorts. Papers were sprawled over it. A computer was open, as if everyone had been looking at something, their chairs scooted close.

"We've been showing Mom some photos from our mission field," Amy said while pushing her hair back behind an ear.

Callie glowed, "You should see some of these Blaine. They've been watching a family of giraffes near their property."

"Giraffes?" *Who had an opportunity to see wild animals in their back yard?*

Chuck came from hanging up her coat and motioned to her. "Come sit down Blaine." Now she knew where Mason got his manners.

Amy was smiling. "Has mother been making you drink that instant coffee of hers?"

Blaine shivered, "It wasn't all that bad." She hated to lie, but didn't want Amy to think her ungrateful.

"Oh honey, I can only take it a day or two and I'm headed out for a good dose of real caffeine. Is the coffee shop downtown a nice one?"

Blaine nodded again as she bent down to remove her boots. "Not like Chicago, but not bad."

"Mason has taken us to some pretty amazing coffee places in Chicago. You must miss those." Amy's expression seemed concerned. Almost, sympathetic.

"Hard to beat a good Starbucks."

Amy nodded. "You're right about that."

Everyone seemed much more relaxed. Blaine sighed. She wished Mason was here to see them all together.

"Sit down with us." Callie patted the chair beside her. "You can see the rest of their photos with us."

"I could start supper." Blaine lingered in the kitchen for a bit more. "We'll need to make a little more chili." She hoped her stomach could handle frying up some hamburger. At the moment, she wasn't so sure.

Callie patted the chair next to her. "We'll get it going soon enough. It's only four or so." She patted the chair again, "C'mon Blaine. Sit here with me."

The next few minutes were filled with some amazing photos from Africa. Amy narrated all of them for the group. Chuck added his perspective as well. The family of giraffes they had been watching was mesmerizing. Blaine couldn't imagine seeing wildlife in such a natural environment.

The photos seemed to be taken by a professional photographer. She soon got caught up in the wonder of being in a far-away country via computer.

Soon Callie asked Blaine to head to the basement for a pound of hamburger from the freezer. Fear filled her heart. Could she do it without feeling sick? What if she had to run to the bathroom with them all in the room? If any of them found out her condition, it would definitely land her out in the cold again. This time, permanently.

When she returned to the kitchen, Chuck offered to help her. Blaine handed him the burger and a frying pan. She thought it might be better for her to chop an onion instead of having to smell raw meat.

Amy and Callie chatted on about people in the community. Families they'd both received Christmas greetings from. How were Miriam and Ethel doing? Callie grew animated as she responded. She seemed so enamored to have Amy and Chuck home.

Blaine dumped chopped onions in the meat while Chuck used a spatula to separate clumps of ground beef into diced pieces. "Thanks," Blaine needed fresh air. "I think I left my boots outside. I'll be right back." She rushed to the back door and just opened it to the fresh air outside. Breathing deep, the fresh air helped settle her stomach.

When she returned to the kitchen, Chuck was finishing up browning the meat, "I like to cook. We have to make so many things from scratch in Africa, I almost forget how easy it is to whip up a small meal here in the states."

Blaine rinsed off the cutting board in the sink and then turned back to Chuck.

"Hey Callie, where's the fixings for chili?"

Callie pointed to the canned goods section of her kitchen. "That front cupboard right by the stove, Chuck. You'll find a can of tomato sauce, chili beans, and diced tomatoes there."

The mention of all those food items did it. Blaine couldn't stop herself. She ran for the bathroom. She wanted to utter something over her shoulder like, 'I'll be right back' or 'Excuse me' but she didn't have time.

"What's wrong with Blaine?" Amy looked at her mother with concern in her eyes. "Do you think she's feeling all right?"

Her mother sighed. "She does that sometimes. She seems to be fighting a bug."

"That's all we need. We'll all be sick through Christmas."

Her mother motioned to Chuck, "Why don't you two set the table for us? We can eat soon, I'm sure."

Amy wasn't sure but it seemed like her mother wasn't telling her everything.

After spending the evening with Megan at the book store, Mason learned more things about Blaine he didn't know. Some good, other traits caused him concern. They'd found some picture books of the places in Africa he'd been able to visit while living there and he loved showing Megan photos of what he considered his homeland.

Megan seemed intrigued by his life as a missionary kid. He loved talking about his adventures there, growing up in a foreign country.

Yet he knew he needed to be up front and open with her. If not now, when?

"Hey Megan, I think we need to talk about a few things. I hate to do this right before Christmas, but I don't want you to get the wrong impression of me."

Megan fidgeted, pulling her skirt down in the process. "What about Mason? She seemed oblivious to what he might want to tell her.

"I like you."

"I like you, too Mason." She looked right at him, "Please don't add a *but* to that statement." She closed her eyes.

Mason sighed. She seemed to know. Without him even having to mention it. But he proceeded anyway. "I'm torn." Megan's eyes flashed open. Her dark eyelashes wide, her eyes grew moist. "I have met another girl. Her name is Blaine." Mason shifted to looking at his hands which now twisted around the other. "My Nana met her when she left me a couple of weeks back. Do you remember that?" Mason looked back up.

"When she had the heart attack?"

"Yes." Mason took in a deep breath, "We became acquainted in the hospital. During surgery and while Nana was in the hospital. She asked Blaine to go home with her to help take care of her. Be her caregiver."

"The caregiver. Okay." Megan bit her bottom lip.

Mason didn't know how to make this sound any better, so he just blurted out, "I'm attracted to her." He paused a moment to watch Megan's shoulders droop. "But, I just don't know her very well."

All at once, Megan seemed to grow a backbone and she sat up straight, "Are you telling me that you're not sure about her yet, so you want to leave me hanging while you go home to investigate whether she's a better catch than me?"

"I mean," Mason wanted to be honest, but this sounded about as ridiculous as him letting a stranger care for his grandmother. "Maybe."

Megan stood, picked up her coat and slid into it. "Mason McAnder, that is the most...ridiculous," Megan's voice grew louder, "cold-hearted. Insidious comment, I've ever heard."

She was right. It was. "I don't want to pretend with you. You're a nice girl. I want us to be honest with each other."

"Honest." Megan buttoned her coat and flipped her scarf around her neck. "Well let me be honest. No one does that to me. There isn't a single guy around here that would ever do that to a girl like me. Would you guys?"

Ten or so men around them shook their heads.

Mason rubbed the top of his forehead with the tips of his fingers. She was right. No one would. Only him. Why was being honest with a girl one of the hardest things he'd ever done?

Mason had followed her outside. He was probably just a few steps behind her, so she turned, stopping in front of him. "Can't we just keep seeing each other? See where this whole thing will go?" She hated to plead, but she didn't feel like she had a choice.

"Megan," he moved closer to her and took her hand. "Listen. Let's get through the holidays. Then we'll talk again."

"I don't like being second best. I never have."

Mason dropped her hand, "Our relationship hasn't even been officially established yet, has it?"

Megan shook her head.

"I know we enjoy each other's company, but that's all it has been up to now. Right?"

Megan knew if she didn't agree, she'd never get another chance. So she nodded her head, reluctantly. But instead of letting it go all his way, she kissed him. "I'll be waiting to find out what you decide, but in the meantime...," she turned and called back over her shoulder as she headed for her apartment, "I might find someone different myself."

She left him standing there on the sidewalk. Alone. For the first time, Megan felt she didn't have a chance with the one guy she wanted to spend the rest of her life with.

Chapter 11

Mason woke the next morning with a massive headache. He hadn't slept well. As he looked out his apartment window at the traffic below, he sipped on coffee. All he wanted to do was get on a train and leave Chicago. Back to Nana's house and his family. He rubbed his throbbing temples trying to figure out how things had spiraled out of control the night before.

It wasn't like he was cheating on someone. He was single. Yet he hated giving girls wrong messages. He always had. At one time he'd thought he really liked Megan. He'd even pursued her.

His exasperation with Megan kept getting interrupted by thoughts of Blaine. Remembering her in Nana's room, curled up in a hospital chair and looking so uncomfortable, yet so relaxed at the same time. He loved the way she'd looked at him across a room, as if he were someone she'd known all along. He didn't realize it at the time, but he was attracted to her almost immediately.

As he thought about her at Nana's and having the ability to get to know her better, he realized how eager he was to leave today. There were many things to consider with Blaine. According to Nana, she had a boyfriend. Someone she'd left in Chicago. What had happened with that? Was she still in love with him? More importantly, did she have a relationship with God? He'd never had the chance to ask her. Was she even attracted to him?

Perhaps he shouldn't have mentioned anything to Megan. What if Blaine did have a boyfriend and wanted nothing to do with God in her life? If that was the case, there wouldn't be any reason for Mason to consider her. He wished he'd had more time to get to know her at the hospital.

It would be good to see his parents again. He missed them and his Dad and he had always had a great relationship. They talked about everything. He was thankful they'd returned home for Nana's sake, but he needed his Dad's advice right now, too.

Seeing his computer on the kitchen table, he knew he needed an hour or two to finish the last account he had been working on, even though all he wanted to do was pack up and head to the train station, but his train didn't leave until late that afternoon. Sitting here, dissolved in his thoughts, was only going to frustrate him more. If he finished this account, he would only have one left to do the days after Christmas at Nana's house.

Women weren't the only thing he wanted to talk over with his Dad. He'd been so agitated lately about his job. Should he keep it or not? Maybe getting away from it for a while would help him refocus. Did he want a career which kept him working non-stop even during a holiday? He got paid well, but living in Chicago hadn't allowed him to save much money. Perhaps he needed to explore other paths in his life.

Flipping the page on a sheet beside his computer, he couldn't wait to finish the account. Then maybe he could get in a short nap while on the train to Nana's house, instead of working. To clear his head.

Blaine opened her eyes to a quiet house. Yesterday had been a nightmare, but it had ended better. She'd told the family she wasn't feeling well and they seemed to believe that excuse, but how long could she keep up the charades. Thankfully, there was another bedroom in the house for Chuck and Amy. She wasn't obligated to give up her room for them. Her now familiar room gave her a comfortable, warm feeling. For some reason, it felt safe. A haven of sorts, yet so unexplainable. She'd been wandering for years, and she never felt so safe. Why here?

She listened for Callie's bedroom door to creak open. She'd grown accustomed to listening, so she could get up to help her. Then she remembered, Mason would be home today. The thought brought her relief. They'd just gotten acquainted in the hospital, but he didn't really know her, nor did she know him. It would be nice to spend a few days together again.

Would he treat her the same way he did at the hospital? So many questions filled her heart. Could she keep her secret hidden from him as well as the whole family? What if they found out? They were a good Christian family. An unwed mother wasn't always welcome in a place like that.

Hearing the creak of Callie's door, Blaine pushed back the down comforter and slipped out of bed. The morning chill caused her to shiver. If only she had a robe. Upon opening the door she found Amy at Callie's side, helping her down the hallway. They both chimed, "Good morning Blaine."

"Crawl back into bed, honey. Amy's helping me." Callie called over her shoulder. "We weren't sure if you were feeling better this morning?"

"I'm feeling a bit better."

"Go back to bed. Amy will help me this morning."

Blaine slowly closed her bedroom door. She climbed back into her bed. What if this was the beginning of the end? Perhaps they were becoming aware of her secret after all.

Mason left for the train before lunch. After securing his apartment, he adjusted his backpack firmly onto his shoulder and pulled up the handle of his luggage. He smiled in relief, he was finally headed to Michigan for Christmas.

The snow hadn't let up. Mason allowed the heavy snowflakes to speckle his face, blinking back the wetness from his eyes. He felt free from a heavy burden, *the stress of work finally over.* It would be good to leave the busy city. Residents scurried around preparing for the next day. Without a doubt, it was Christmas Eve. The entire city's population seemed crazy over the approaching holidays.

The walk to the train station seemed to put him in a Christmas mood. The stores bulged with customers, residents packed up cars outside their apartments, the wind swirled the snow in multiple directions around the skyscrapers. Many people destined for other places, like Mason, dragged luggage behind them, making their way to waiting cabs or the closest transportation available.

A vendor on a street corner was selling candied nuts. The aroma of cinnamon and sugar filled the air. Mason stopped to buy a bag to enjoy on the train.

"Mason, what's up?" Someone patted him on the shoulder. Mason turned to see the man whose desk sat directly behind his at work.

"Miguel." Mason took the man's hand and gave him a solid handshake.

"Headed home?" Miguel pointed to his luggage.

"Yeah. Finally."

"You've been kicking butt trying to get things done at work. I've been watching you. You are valuable, my friend."

Mason shook his head. "Just doing my job."

Miguel put his hand on his shoulder, "No man, I'm serious. You're dedicated, man. I actually don't want to work that hard. For anyone."

They both laughed. "You work hard too, man."

"Glad I can fool you so well." Miguel ordered his own bag of flavored nuts from the vendor. "Where's home, Mason?"

"Michigan. Well, that's where my Nana lives."

"Where in Michigan?"

"A small town outside of Flint." Mason wasn't sure if anyone had ever heard of the small town before so he'd rarely mentioned it.

"Near Flint. Isn't that where they're having a water crisis?"

Mason nodded. "Yup. The one and only."

"Crazy how I know that."

"It's been a hot topic in the news."

"Right." Miguel nodded. "I have a friend near there. He lives in Lansing. He works for a financial advisor there. They're always looking for people to hire. If you're ever interested in living closer to your Nana, I can hook you up."

Mason nearly choked on a nut he'd popped in his mouth. "What?"

"Yeah." Miguel smiled. "If I didn't love Chicago so much, I wouldn't be working at FP Franklin myself. There are better places to rise in the industry. Not just there."

"Well thanks, Miguel." Mason turned to leave. He waved over his shoulder, "Have a great Christmas."

Mason thought about the job comment all the way to Union Station.

Chapter 12

The day before Christmas was a disaster for Blaine. Everything she tried to do for Callie ended up in failure. Amy kept stepping in. She'd get her tea, fix her breakfast, wash some of her laundry, and even wrap the last of her presents.

Blaine felt lost. What could she do? She finally got enough courage to ask Callie about the tree. "Can I put up the tree this afternoon?"

Callie eyes twinkled, "Oh Blaine, yes. Let's do it. Amy and Chuck are here to help."

Blaine sighed. Would she have to leave Callie on Christmas Eve? She really didn't want to. Admitting that this job was her only lifeline would be embarrassing, but that's exactly what it was for Blaine. The thoughts of leaving meant spending the holidays by herself. In a hotel or worse yet, a homeless shelter. The thought made her heart ache. She'd been gullible enough to believe it might be different with Callie.

With Amy here, Blaine felt useless.

Callie watched as Blaine pried open the box which held her Christmas tree. The young girl seemed sullen and extra quiet today. Amy had been helping more because they both thought Blaine hadn't been feeling well. Something was wrong now though. Callie could sense it. Amy came into the room and took over inserting the branches into the tree stand as Blaine folded her arms and stepped back.

Callie reached for a small box setting by itself among all the Christmas décor totes scattered about the floor. Something inside made her suddenly realize what might be happening. "Blaine, can you come here?"

Blaine made her way through the maze of totes in the room. "Look in here." Callie pried opened the lid. The container held a favorite ornament of Callie's. She lifted the glass ornament out of a red box and held up the glass Santa. The red and white painted jolly ole' man twirled, light reflecting off his gold beard. She held it out to Blaine. "My father gave me this ornament when I was a little girl."

Blaine touched it, "He's cool."

Callie laughed, "And old." She held it out to Blaine, "Will you put it on the tree first? It's my favorite."

Blaine nodded. "Of course."

Amy turned to them now, "Where are the ornament hooks, Mother?"

"Here they are," Blaine added, "in this tote." She held up another small box filled with tiny wire hooks.

"Good job, Blaine. I always end up searching for that box every year." Callie clapped her hands. "I'm so happy to have you all here helping me this year. This will be such a special Christmas." Callie took out a tissue from under her sleeve and wiped her eyes.

Amy was so into decorating the tree she must not have heard Callie ask Blaine to hang the Santa ornament. She held out her hand to Blaine for the Santa ornament she was carefully holding.

Callie saw her. "No Amy. I want Blaine to put that one on the tree."

Blaine held out the ornament to Amy. "It's okay. She can do it."

Callie spoke up quickly, "No Blaine. I asked you."

Amy stepped back and smiled.

Blaine glanced back at her for approval. Callie pointed to the tree. "Go ahead. In front there."

Blaine slipped the hook through the ornament loop and put the Santa directly on a branch at the front. She stepped back and glanced at Callie as if to seek her approval.

"Perfect. Thank you. We always make it a special event to place the first ornament on the tree. I'm happy you're here to do it this year, Blaine."

Callie watched as Blaine kept her eyes on Amy, as if to gage her reaction. Amy seemed oblivious.

Chuck had been reading the newspaper in a nearby chair. Setting his paper down on the floor, he asked, "Mother, where are those green ones you have? They're my favorite."

Callie knew exactly which ones he was asking for. She rummaged through a few ornament containers in one of the totes. "Blaine, can you check that tote?"

"In this one?" Blaine pulled off the lid. "What do they look like?"

"They're green." Chuck began rummaging through the tote at Callie's feet.

"They're not just green, Chuck." Callie snickered, giving him the look of knowing what he was up to.

Chuck glanced her way and laughed. "They have a large *S* on each one."

"These?" Blaine held out the green and white ornament box to Chuck.

"That a girl, Blaine. That's them." Chuck grinned. "These are my favorite."

Amy laughed. "Just because they have Michigan State emblems on them." She looked at Blaine, "That's his favorite football team."

"It's the *only* team," Chuck opened the box, carefully putting each one in a prominent place on the tree.

Blaine's phone chirped from the table.

Callie watched Blaine weave her way through the maze of boxes to answer it.

"Hello." She ducked into the kitchen.

Amy leaned close to Callie. "Does she have somewhere to go today?"

What kind of question was that? Amy knew Blaine was spending the holidays with them. Callie shook her head, "No. She's here for the holidays." She was growing frustrated with her questions. "With us."

She overheard Blaine's conversation from the kitchen.

"Mason. Where are you?"

"Are you on the train?" Blaine asked Mason. She was shocked he'd called her and not his parents.

"Yes. Finally. I'll be there in a few hours."

Blaine sagged against the wall.

"Have my parents arrived yet?"

"Yes, they're here."

"And?" Mason hesitated a moment.

"Um, not sure they like me being here all that much." What else could she say? She felt it was true.

"Give 'em a chance. They don't know you well yet."

"Neither do you?"

"That's true."

Blaine didn't want to appear too excited or forward. "I'm glad you're coming."

Mason's voice seemed light and excited as well. "I can't wait to see my folks. I miss them."

It was understandable he wanted to see his parents. Blaine knew she needed to subdue her excitement about having Mason around again. He was returning home to see his family, not necessarily her.

"And you and Nana, of course." Mason added.

Blaine chided herself. She had to remember, she was only a caregiver.

"What are you doing?"

"Putting up the tree." Blaine could overhear the communication in the living room about whether Chuck's prestigious ornaments had to take up the entire front of Callie's tree.

"Cool. I'm sure Mom and Dad are enjoying helping Nana with that."

"We all are."

"Who got to put the Santa ornament on the tree?"

Blaine couldn't believe he knew about that. "Um...the Santa ornament?"

"That's Nana's favorite. She says it has to be the first one on the tree. Usually I get the job, but I'm sure Mom did it. Am I right?"

Amy? Was she the one to always do it? Guilt now filled Blaine's heart. What if she'd overstepped her bounds? But Callie had purposely told her it would be her job this year. Blaine's shoulders relaxed. "Callie asked me to do it."

Mason sounded surprised. "That's awesome."

What did that mean? As she said goodbye and pushed *end*, she began to wonder about the coming week. Perhaps she was simply an intruder and Callie was feeling sorry for her.

"Is she talking to Mason?" Amy whispered to Chuck as she placed the last of the Michigan State ornaments on the tree.

Chuck stopped hanging ornaments on the tree and listened. He hadn't been eavesdropping like his wife seemed to be doing. After a few moments of listening, he shrugged his shoulders. "Maybe."

"I think so," Amy's mother gasped. "Why would he call her and not us?"

Amy glanced at her mother. She seemed oblivious, separating pearl garland. Chuck had seen that look on his wife's face many times, suspicion was her specialty.

Her mother leaned forward in her chair, "They became friends while visiting me in the hospital. It's fine." The look on her face said it all. She approved of their friendship.

"Chuck!" Amy looked at him for answers. She always expected him to fix the problems. "Did you hear what Mother just said?"

Chuck was humming a Christmas carol. "Mother, where's the tinsel?"

Amy put her hands on her hips. "You're no help."

"I put six bulbs on the tree."

Amy shook her head, "Never mind."

Chuck opened his palms to the ceiling and shrugged, "What?"

Blaine returned to the front room, slipping her phone into her pocket.

"When does he arrive?" Callie asked.

Blaine nodded. "He's on the train now. Said he'd be here in a few hours."

Callie clapped her hands. "I'm so happy. I can't wait for us to all be together. What a wonderful Christmas we'll have."

Blaine smiled at her friend. Being with her whole family would be good medicine for the frail woman who now looked far from the patient in the hospital only a two short weeks before. She seemed so excited; glowing in anticipation. Like a child on Christmas Eve.

"Did he mention what time his train arrives?" Chuck looked to Blaine for an answer.

"Five fifteen." Blaine wanted nothing more than to be the one to go pick up Mason, but she hesitated to offer. Mason wanted to see his parents more than her. As she weighed whether she should speak up or just let them all figure it out, Callie spoke.

"Blaine? Why don't you go and pick up Mason? If you're feeling up to it."

Amy's mouth fell open, watching Callie for a response. Callie seemed not to notice.

Blaine pointed to Amy and Chuck, "Maybe they would like to go, Callie. They haven't seen him in a while."

Callie added quickly, "They've been complaining about how cold it is today. You're used to the cold, Blaine. Living in Chicago and all."

Callie winked at her. She was pretty sure Amy and Chuck didn't notice.

Chuck leaned down, kissing his wife's cheek, "Callie's right. We have all week to be with him." Chuck smiled back at Callie.

"You don't mind, do you dear?" Callie asked her.

Blaine subdued her excitement as best she could. "No, I can go."

"Then it's all settled." Callie sat up straighter in her chair. "I can't wait to see my boy."

The train sprayed snow along the tracks like a snowplow after a blizzard. Mason felt as if he was on the #1225 Polar Express. Based in Michigan, he wondered if his family would have the opportunity to go see it while he was home. He'd always loved trains.

Mason's thoughts drifted to Blaine. She seemed shy on the phone. He'd wondered how his parents had reacted to her being with Nana, since she was a stranger and all.

The four-hour trip dragged as Mason flipped through magazines he'd never had the chance to read, but mostly he watched out the window as the landscape changed like the towns along the way. As the train traveled north the snow piles grew deeper revealing only a few leftover shocks and stubs of corn stalks left in the fields.

The vibe on the train car was merry. Babies were being snuggled by mothers or jostled on a Daddy's bouncing leg to disrupt their cries. Passengers peered out windows, murmuring to each other. It felt like an eternity before he finally heard the whistle blow and the conductor announce the next stop at a depot close to Nana's hometown.

Mason gathered his luggage and backpack and ducked to look out the window at the approaching depot, lights from the windows blazed into the darkness, illuminating the snow-covered sidewalks. A multi-lighted Christmas tree sat outside a door, a glow of lights strung along the eave line.

Following others off the train, Mason couldn't wait to see who had come to the station to pick him up. He hoped Nana hadn't gotten out in the cold. It would probably be his dad. It would be like him to leave the women at home in the warmth. The departure was slow and tedious as other passengers gathered their belongings stored around the seats. Parents stuffed miscellaneous toys and electronic iPads into duffle bags.

As he descended the stairs onto the depot's platform he looked up to see if anyone familiar stood outside to greet him. The platform, to the right, was empty. The cold wind of the late afternoon stung his eyes, making them water and causing him to squint. He didn't blame anyone for not standing outside to greet him or the other passengers. But as he hit the last step, glancing to the left to avoid the sting of the western wind, he saw Blaine standing alone by the decorated tree.

What a sight! He'd almost forgotten how pretty she was. He made his way to her. Her face lit up, her cheeks red from the cold, she shivered.

He grew solemn and made his way to her, "Blaine, why didn't you wait inside? It's freezing out here."

She smiled. Her hair wispy under her coat's fur-lined hood. Her mystic blue eyes now caused him to shiver. "It's fine. I wanted to be sure you saw me here. Can I help," she held out her hand, "with your backpack?"

Mason giggled. "Of course. Thank you. It's kinda heavy. I had to bring my laptop and other things."

"I'm not a weakling," she took hold of a strap and slung it over her shoulder. "Other things?"

"That isn't any of your business." Mason was only kidding, but it sounded a bit harsh, so he added, "It *is* Christmas."

Blaine nodded, "Oh." She motioned to where the car was sitting in the parking lot.

Even though they didn't know each other all that well yet, Mason gave her a sideways hug. "I'm happy to see you."

"It's nice to see a familiar face."

Her statement made them both laughed. Mason was pretty sure Blaine felt the same way he did. Still basically strangers.

"Where is everyone?"

Blaine nodded, "They're fixing dinner and decorating the tree."

"Sounds Christmasy!" Mason picked up the handle of his luggage again. "Let's go home. For Christmas."

Home for Christmas. It was something Blaine had only ever dreamed of and never experienced first-hand. Her dreams rarely came true. She wondered, as they made their way back to Callie's car, if this year would be any different. Christmas was the very next day.

Chapter 13

Callie felt her heart swell. Everyone was home. Feeling blessed, she couldn't help but think about how a heart attack might have kept her from experiencing this moment. *All things work together for good.*

Sensing her own mortality, she couldn't thank God enough for allowing her the opportunity to enjoy another Christmas. Everyone she loved, most on earth was now seated around the dinner table. And she was there, in the midst of it all.

Blaine was seated next to her, sitting quietly with her hands in her lap. She looked as if she felt out of place. Callie reached over and squeezed the young girl's hand. Blaine was proof that God could still use her, frail as she was, to help others. She still had a purpose and for that, she couldn't help but give thanks.

It was Christmas Eve. She'd spent the last few holidays alone. Last year, she'd only been able to talk to Mason and Amy on the phone. This year, he was sitting at her table. Her heart attack and surgery had brought her a bit of normalcy as far as her health was concerned. She felt better than she had in years. God was faithful.

Even to an old woman who had been stupid enough to travel to Chicago by herself.

Soon the dishes were done as everyone sat in the living room chatting about life. Snowflakes floated through the air out the patio window. Snow was beginning to pile high. The glow of the tree's Christmas bulbs cast reflections against the walls. Amy turned off the overhead lights and lit a few candles around the room.

Conversation merged from one subject to the next after Mason joined them. They talked about Chuck and Amy's projects in Africa. How they'd had a few political uprisings in the past six months and the safety of their village. They talked about the stresses regarding Mason's job.

Blaine sat and listened. They laughed about Callie's blunders around surgery time and how chatty she was right after it. Mason loved teasing his nana, but it wasn't wasted as Nana could taunt right back.

As their family subjects seemed to be all talked out, Amy turned to Blaine. Innocent questions soon felt like an interrogation.

Did she have family? Where were her parents? Blaine squirmed. How much should she tell them? She hated to think her only option was to lie. Would Amy like her better if she thought she grew up in a regular home?

"My grandmother took me in when I needed someone."

"Your grandmother raised you?"

Blaine knew this wasn't all true. Her grandmother felt sorry for her. "Yes, partially. I lived with my aunt and cousins when I was younger."

"That must have been hard on your grandmother."

Blaine took this to mean that she'd been difficult to raise. "I learned to do things for myself."

"Oh dear."

"I mean, whenever I called my grandmother, she'd help me."

Callie chimed in, "I'm sure she was good to you, right dear?"

Blaine nodded. What could she say? Her grandmother only helped when she grew desperate and called her. Even after her mother committed suicide, her grandmother stopped by to see her from time to time, but as a teenager living with her, she let her do most anything she wanted. Blaine grew more nervous that she'd say something to make her seem less of a normal person. She couldn't compare any of her life to this typical family.

Soon she stood up and excused herself. She didn't have to use the restroom, but she went there for solitude and quietness for a moment. She wanted the questions to stop. While in the bathroom she thought about the moment she'd had to move in with her grandmother. Most of the time, all it did was haunt her.

Blaine hated to admit how much of the personal conversation she was hearing through her bedroom door. The social worker sitting at the kitchen table was loud, despite her Grandmother's quiet voice.

She'd been directed to go to her room, just after they'd arrived to talk to Grandmother, as if she were some kind of child. She knew what it all meant. It wasn't working out at her Aunt's house and they'd placed Blaine back into foster care. Blaine was too young to live alone, despite being almost sixteen. If they were deciding her fate, she wanted to hear the outcome.

"You are all she has," the social worker's tone sounded demanding and overbearing.

"You don't think I know that," answered Blaine's Grandmother in a hushed tone. "But I'm an old woman."

"You don't expect us to put her in the foster system, do you?"

Silence penetrated the door between Blaine and her grandmother. She heard the strike of a match and knew her grandmother was lighting up a cigarette. A distinct sound of the first drag and then the exhale.

"Do you?" The harsh woman asked again.

Blaine could hear a kitchen chair scrap across the linoleum, her Grandmother's steps crossed the room and the refrigerator opened. She heard a bottle placed on the counter as she popped the cap. She'd grabbed a beer. This had to be her sixth one that morning. "I do know what I want to happen. I want my daughter back. I want her to raise this child that she seemed desperate to protect. Even from the beginning." Grandmother sat back down in the chair with another scrap.

"We hate putting girls, like Blaine, into the foster care system. No one wants a teenager. They're usually frustrated, sassy, and unmanageable."

"Blaine's is that, and more. I can't seem to make her realize she's gotta stop lying. We've all done everything we know to stop her nasty habit." Blaine heard the bottle hit the table again.

"See," the social worker voiced her frustration, "you're the only one able to understand her. Deal with her."

"But I can't, that's the problem." The words were drawn out as Grandmother's voice grew more irritated and angry.

Blaine couldn't help it, she opened the bedroom door a crack and peeked around the corner. The social worker faced her at the table. Her Grandmother had her back to her. The social worker was writing some things down on the papers now scattered across the table.

"I've been around for as long as I can handle." Another drag. "I've been the one to be sure that child," Grandmother pointed back at her bedroom door, "had food. Had a bit of comfort when her," Blaine winced at the swear words "...mother couldn't even get out of bed to check on her. The television watched her more than her mother. I've given up the last eighteen years of my own life to watch over these kids. Thankfully, her brother is now old enough to be on his own, but Blaine..."

Blaine shut the door and stood against the back of it. She didn't want to hear what her grandmother was going to say. Shutting her eyes, she held her breath and knew the mere paneled door wouldn't keep the words out.

"She'll have to be on her own, too."

Blaine cringed. Alone. On her own. Could she even survive something like that? Where would she go?

"I can't allow that."

More silence. She knew that by the time this government lady would leave, her Grandmother would have finally had too much to drink and would head to bed to sleep off the afternoon.

"I'm on a fixed income. Would her benefits now be transferred to me?"

"I can arrange that. All you need to do is sign here and she's yours until she turns eighteen. Although she can chose for herself at the age of seventeen, according to the courts. That's just shy of two years. I'm sure you can manage that. She'll be around to help you. I'm sure you'd appreciate someone to help with a few things around the house."

Blaine knew what that statement would lead to and she knew, without a doubt, she'd refuse to help. Grandmother would not use her as a slave as her aunt had done. She wanted to have fun like every other teenager she knew. No one was going to demand work from her. It wasn't her fault that her mother died. She'd killed herself.

More swear words penetrated the air.

Blaine couldn't help herself. She had to look again.

Grandmother was signing a paper. "How long before I get my first check?"

"No longer than sixty days."

"Sixty days," Grandmother mumbled more swear words. "And what am I supposed to use to feed her until then?"

"I'll do my best to get your money to you quicker." The social worker scooped up all the papers on the table and shoved them into a manila folder. "Thank you. I think this is the best option for Blaine. Perhaps, in time, you'll know that, too."

Grandmother took another long drag on her cigarette. "Or perhaps she'll get knocked up by a boy and he'll take over. Just like her mother did. Like mother, like daughter...right?"

The social worker slipped the folder into a briefcase on the table and snapped it shut. "Well, for Blaine's sake, let's hope not."

Mason watched as Blaine left the room. Glancing at his mother, he whispered. "Mom, take it easy."

His mother eyed him. "I'm just trying to get to know her better."

"Maybe, but I think you're scaring her," he spoke softly. "Give her a break. I don't think she's had a life she's proud of."

Mason's mother looked down at her feet. "I don't mean to pry. I am just curious."

Nana whispered. "From all I know, she's had a rough life. Not an easy start. Right now, I feel strongly that she needs us."

Chuck nodded. "Let's just enjoy being together. As we chat and spend more time together, we'll learn more, I'm sure."

Callie voiced her concern. "I love Blaine. She's been so helpful the last two weeks. She's a hard worker and helped me get well. I love her company." She straightened taller in her chair, "I think it's important she's here with me. With us." She smiled, "Let's make an extra effort to help her feel welcome. And more than anything, I think she needs us right now, too."

Amy nodded. "I'm sorry. I'll try not to be so nosey."

Blaine returned and conversation went to the state of the government, the weather, and about various friends in the community. She tried to blend into the scene, not saying much.

Chuck stood up and stretched. "I think we need a family activity. How about a puzzle?"

Everyone cheered. Their enthusiasm over a puzzle surprised Blaine.

Mason held out his cup of coffee, "I'm actually digging sitting here. Doing nothing. It's been super crazy at work. I'm whipped."

"Well, not me." Chuck nodded, "Mother, where are those puzzles?"

Callie motioned to Chuck where he could find a puzzle and told Amy where the card table and chairs were stored.

"Do you like puzzles?" Mason asked Blaine.

She shrugged. "Um. I don't know." *What would it sound like to admit she'd only done one or two at school?*

"Well then," Mason patted her knee, "this should be a treat for you. It's our family tradition. I know it probably seems a bit lame. Christmas, just wouldn't be Christmas without the family puzzle. If that makes any sense."

Chuck snapped the legs of the card table in place, opened a puzzle box, and dumped the pieces on the table. "It's a mountain scene. Should be a challenge."

Mason and Blaine sat on the couch while his parents began to sort through the pile of pieces before them.

Callie sat forward in her chair. "Amy. I need your help."

Amy glanced at Callie.

Blaine stood quickly. "I'll help you Callie."

Callie shooed her off. "You can't help me this time. I need help wrapping presents."

Blaine couldn't help but scowl. "I thought we had all your presents wrapped?"

Callie shook her head and pushed herself to stand. "Not all of them."

Mason must have noticed Callie's questioning look. He snapped his fingers and said, "Oh shoot, let me get my backpack."

Blaine crouched in the corner of the couch, not knowing quite how to react.

Mason interjected. "I have a few to wrap myself." He winked at Blaine, "I'll be right back."

As the three family members left the room, Chuck motioned to Blaine. "Come help me, Blaine. We need to find the edges."

Blaine sat in the chair across the table from Chuck.

"See these." He held up a piece that had a flat edge. "We need to get the edges together first. There's always a process."

Blaine nodded and began sorting through the pieces.

"You seemed suspicious when Callie announced she had presents to wrap."

Blaine shook her head. "I thought we'd gotten them all wrapped yesterday."

Chuck smiled, "I think they are some Mason brought with him from Chicago." He leaned over the table and whispered to Blaine. "I hope it's Chicago caramel corn. I love that stuff."

Blaine agreed with a nod. "It is the best."

"Hey, I have a few questions to ask you."

Blaine cringed. The interrogation would continue. "What's your favorite color?"

Blaine relaxed a bit, "Lavender."

"Ah," Chuck smiled. "No wonder you like Mother's guest room."

"I love that room."

Chuck handed her two more straight edged pieces. "Here, put these over there with those. There about the same color."

Blaine obeyed. "What's yours?" Trying to divert the interrogation off of her.

Chuck's eyes sparkled as he answered, "Orange." He nodded. "You should see some orange colors in African fabric. It's amazing. Kinda like a burning sun on the horizon."

"You must live an amazing life there."

"I feel blessed to have the opportunity to be there. Even in saying that, I realize that sometimes we complain and mutter about their customs, and the food...well, it isn't always something to brag about, but yes, there are moments like a morning sunrise or the way music flows from the voices of the believers that you can't explain in words. I love the people. I'm thankful that is where God decided we should be."

Mason approached the puzzle table with a grin on his face.

Blaine smiled. He seemed happy to be home with his family. He sat down beside Blaine.

"Is Dad cheating, Blaine?"

Chuck laughed, "Mason, it's a puzzle, not Monopoly."

Mason leaned into Blaine. "Word of advice. Never play Monopoly with my Dad. He comes across as this too-good-to-be-true, missionary type, guy until you give him property and a little money. Then..." Mason sat back and put his hands in the air as if a policeman had told him to.

Chuck looked shocked at his son's comments. "What?"

Mason leaned toward Blaine again, "Let's just say, he shows his sinful nature."

Blaine felt stunned. "Is that a good or a bad thing?"

Chuck waved Mason off. "Don't listen to him."

"Oh Blaine, you need to listen. Be thankful this is just a puzzle."

Both men laughed.

Blaine was caught off guard. It became clear that these two were the fun part of the McAnder family. She smiled.

Chuck tossed a piece to Mason. "Put that in its place and stop spreading rumors."

Mason shook his head. "They're not rumors."

Mason placed the piece where his father had pointed and told them both. "I think the presents are almost all wrapped."

"Good," Chuck added. "That will get your mother to stop fussing for at least..." He looked down at his watch. "At least through the next hour or so."

"It's surprising there isn't a Christmas Eve service tonight at church?" Mason placed a piece between two others to see if it fit.

"I went to church on Christmas Eve one time. It was when I was little. I don't remember all that happened, but I do remember watching a small, real baby they put in a cradle at the front of the stage. His little feet and hands were about all you could see of him as the music played." Blaine stopped thinking about it and then realized it was the only time she'd ever set foot in a church. "The church bus picked me up. My mother wanted to attend a party and I guess she thought it was a good thing for me to do instead of having to pay a babysitter." Panic grew in Blaine's heart to see the men staring back at her. "What?"

"Nothing. I need that piece right there." Chuck pointed to a piece she held in her hand. Blaine handed it to him.

"Did you go there often?" Mason asked.

"Only that one night."

Mason concentrated on the puzzle piece he held.

"It wasn't a big deal. I think of that baby sometimes. He seemed to be the center of attention that night. Babies usually are, but that night, he seemed to be the focus. I often wondered why."

Mason selected another piece, testing it in various places around the puzzle's edge.

Chuck's determination showed as he tried his own place for the piece in his hand. "We used Mason as the baby Jesus one year. He was about nine months old. His mother had dressed him in red shorts and a white dress shirt. He hated it."

Mason stopped his search, "You'd of hated it, too. Did you see the stuff she used to dress me in?" Leaning back in his chair, "Remember those suspenders she'd make me wear. A personal wedgy for an entire evening."

Both men laughed.

Blaine watched the determination of both men as they took piece after piece, trying to fit them into the edges of the puzzle.

"That baby is pretty important at Christmas. He symbolizes a wonderful thing in our Christian faith." Despite the religious fervor in his comment, Chuck never raised his head.

Blaine handed two blue puzzle pieces to Mason who seemed intent on creating the sky scene, yet listened to Chuck.

He continued, "Jesus was born to change the world, which thirty-three years later, he did. Do you have a relationship with God, Blaine?"

Blaine stopped rummaging through the green pieces and stared back at Chuck. "A relationship?" That sounded personal and a bit strange.

"We do." Chuck pointed to Mason and then himself.

Blaine felt her palms moisten. "What does that mean?"

"We depend on Him for everything. Our well-being, our daily food, clothing..." Chuck pulled his shirt away from his chest. "Our hope."

Blaine sat back in her chair and folded her arms. She wasn't sure what to say. "I believe in God."

"Good," Chuck smiled at her while fingering a puzzle piece and then studying it. "But even Satan believes in God."

Blaine leaned forward. "He does?"

Chuck and Mason both nodded.

"He tried his best to stop Jesus' ministry at every turn while he was on earth. When Jesus was born, a foreign king tried to kill him. Do you remember wisemen coming to that church service you attended with the little baby?"

Blaine remembered them well. They wore men's bathrobes and crowns on their heads. "Did they look like kings?" They brought gifts to the baby during the program.

"Most Christmas programs make them appear to be kings. They had been told by the king to find where Jesus had been born and then return to tell him so he could worship the baby. But that wasn't his intent. He wanted Jesus dead. So when the kings didn't return to tell them where they'd found Jesus, he issued a law that any male, younger than two years of age, would be killed throughout the land in order to find baby Jesus and destroy him."

"I don't remember that part in the program back then."

Chuck laughed, "Probably not. It isn't the most popular, warm-feeling moment regarding the birth of Jesus, but it did happen. Many boys died due to this law. Many were ripped out of their mother's arms and killed."

"That's horrible."

"It is."

Amy came back from the bedroom and asked Blaine if she knew where to find scotch tape. They must not have all their presents wrapped yet. Blaine left the room to find more.

When Blaine returned to the table, Mason and Chuck were laughing about someone from back home who recently had contacted Mason about visiting him in Chicago. The family encountered him from time to time knowing well that all he wanted from them was to sell them some products from a pyramid scheme. "I was scared to tell him to come and find me, for fear, he'd never leave." Chuck was laughing so hard he couldn't seem to catch his breath.

Callie came back into the room, with Amy following behind her, carrying presents. "We're all done."

The men cheered, through snickers, still trying to recuperate from their giggles.

Turning to Chuck she asked, "What's so funny, you guys?"

Chuck was determined to find a place for the piece he was holding in his hand and seemed to completely not hear his wife's question.

"Chuck!"

Mason elbowed his dad and pointed to his mom.

"Yes Amy, did you say something?"

Amy folded her arms and shook her head. "I'll never get his attention again now that Mason is home."

Callie was now settled back on the couch. Amy tugged a blanket off the end of the couch to cover Callie's legs. "Chuck. Come into the kitchen to help me make some hot cocoa for everyone." She left for the kitchen.

Chuck handed his piece to Mason and stretched as he stood, "On my way." He leaned toward Mason. "Don't get this all done before I return."

Mason crossed his heart. He picked up the box, "It has a thousand pieces, I'm pretty sure Blaine and I will not get it done in the next ten minutes."

Blaine tucked Callie's blanket around her feet and leaned toward her, "Want a cup, Callie?"

Callie smiled and patted Blaine's cheek, "I would love one."

Blaine went to Callie's refrigerator freezer to pull out the plastic container of cookies she'd put in there earlier. Chuck and Amy stopped whispering when she entered the room. They seemed to be searching for something as Chuck lined up mugs on the counter.

"I think I'll get some cookies out, too. Would that be okay?"

Amy turned and smiled, "Of course, Blaine. Mom's cookies are always the best."

"We made them this week." She hoped Mason liked them. Callie hadn't made them, but Blaine had used her recipe.

Chuck added, "I'll get a plate for them, Blaine."

"Thanks." Blaine was growing fond of Chuck. Mason resembled him in many ways.

Blaine pried open the box of cookies, and placed a few on the plate Chuck had handed her.

As Chuck reached over her and snatched one from the plate, Blaine laughed.

"Just testing one."

She returned the container to the freezer. Blaine held her breath as she did it. The smells assaulted her nonetheless, sending her stomach into bouts of swallowing hard.

Chuck mumbled while crunching into a cookie. "Blaine these are good."

Blaine gulped, "Thanks." Returning to the living room, she placed the plate on the edge of the puzzle table.

Mason picked up a cookie, shoved half into his mouth and mumbled identically to his Dad, "Mmm, these are good," then went for another puzzle piece. "Did you make them?"

Blaine sat down, "Do you like them?"

"Almost as good as Nana's." Mason winked at his Nana.

Blaine watched Callie smile and said, "Blaine's baking is getting better and better."

Chuck and Amy soon joined them at the puzzle table and the room grew quiet as everyone sipped their cocoa and munched on homemade cookies.

Despite the fact that it was hard for Blaine to feel at home and comfortable with people she'd only met a few weeks before, she had to admit her comfort levels were improving.

She thought about what Chuck had tried to explain to her about Jesus and His birth. Having a personal relationship with God? The only personal relationship she'd ever searched for in her life was that of a man. Was that the same as with God?

The puzzle began to take shape on the table. The scene of mountains rose over what appeared to be some kind of water. Separated colors now began to form parts of the winter scene.

Amy nudged Chuck. "I'm exhausted. Can you pull yourself away from this puzzle and go to bed with me?"

Chuck had been yawning quite a bit and smiled at his wife. "Yeah. I think I need to turn in, too. The time change is beginning to set in."

"Let's go big guy!" Amy held out her hand to Chuck and he took it. The room grew quiet.

"I'm so happy to be home, Nana."

Callie smiled back at Mason. "I'm so happy to have you here."

Blaine smiled at Mason and Callie. They did appreciate and love each other. Her own life was often marked by wondering whether anyone ever cared about her. A wave of jealousy filled her heart.

"What do you have planned for tomorrow?" Mason picked up his mug of hot chocolate.

"Blaine and I have a nice breakfast planned and then we'll open presents."

"That's your favorite thing to do." Mason laughed at Callie as her eyes gleamed that it was true.

"I've always loved to give things." Callie leaned back in her rocker. "I used to have a hard time keeping secrets, especially from my father. He'd always find a way to finagle them out of me." Callie laughed right out loud. "My mother would get so furious with me.

Soon she refused to tell me what she'd purchased for the other family members, knowing full well that I couldn't keep it from them."

Callie leaned forward, "What is one of your favorite memories about Christmas, Blaine?"

Caught off guard, Blaine tried to think of something. "I did remember going to church that one time."

Mason acknowledged with a nod. "That's a pretty cool memory."

"Anything else, sweetheart?" Callie looked to her as though she had a store of wonderful memories to share with her. Should she make something up? It was sad to think that her memories only included sadness, disappointment, and regret.

"I wish I had some great memory to share with you both, but to be honest, I really don't." Blaine pulled her legs closer and clamped her arms around them. "My mother often had to work. There wasn't much for me to do while she was gone but watch television. I guess," Blaine scrambled for some kind of memory, "I do remember watching all the Christmas cartoons like Rudolph, Frosty...you know, the originals."

"Why do you hate watching movies so much now?" Callie asked.

"I guess because that's all I ever did as a child. The television was my babysitter. Even while living with my aunt. I don't know how much trouble I would have gotten into if I wouldn't have had it." Memories began to fill Blaine's heart as if she'd turned on a spigot in her heart. "I can remember one time, we could never afford a

Christmas tree. Not even a fake one. One year my aunt had been lucky enough to have a boyfriend. He was one of the good ones."

"Where shall we put this amazing, one-of-a-kind tree, little Blaine?"

Blaine could hardly contain her excitement. Her aunt's boyfriend, Bob, had brought home a Christmas tree for them. It wasn't much to look at. Part of one side had hardly any needles, but it was a tree and Blaine didn't care. Charlie Brown had a tree like it. "In the corner." Blaine stood on the couch and pointed to the far corner of the room. She'd always imagined a tree in that corner, lit-up with colored light bulbs and silver tinsel. She could hardly contain her excitement and starting jumping on the couch.

"Blaine, stop jumping." Her aunt yelled from across the room. "You'll break a spring in that couch and then I'll have to pay the landlord for it."

Blaine knew money was tight, so she jumped to the floor and proceeded to let out her excitement by twirling about the room. "Where are the lights?" She'd so longed for the colored ones after seeing them on a tree at school.

"Lights?" Bob rubbed his chin. "Not sure I have any of those."

"Why don't we make popcorn and we can make strings for our tree?" Her aunt came in from the kitchen, wiping off her hands from making their dinner.

Blaine screamed along with the other kids, "Yes, yes, let's do it."

"Then stop twirling about and go find the popcorn popper."

Blaine scurried into the kitchen, sliding the last portion on her knees to the cupboard door containing the air popper. Pulling out the machine, she accidentally spilled a bag of kernels across the floor. She used her hands to scoop it up and put it back into the bag.

Her aunt must have heard the bag spill because soon she was back in the kitchen assessing the mess. "Blaine!" Words her mother used to use frequently came out; words that Blaine often got into trouble for repeating at school. "Why aren't you more careful? Stop being so hyper."

Blaine nodded and backed away from the mess.

"Pick up the popper. We can still use these kernels for our tree. We won't be eating them." Her aunt went for her broom and a using a dustpan, picked up most of Blaine's mess.

"What else can we put on the tree to make it pretty?" Blaine held up the bowl as the popcorn popper began to distribute fresh kernels into it. Blaine loved popcorn.

"Do you have any of that paper left from your Thanksgiving projects at school?"

It was rare for there to be any construction paper in the house, but because of Bob and his kindness, there were red, orange, and bright green turkeys still affixed to the front of the refrigerator. Blaine bounced to the door and pulled them off. "What about these?"

Bob came into the room. Wiping his hands off from putting up the tree, "I hate sap. Makes my hands sticky."

Blaine placed her turkeys on the table and began tracing out hearts and hand patterns on a few of them. The other children joined her.

"Where are the scissors?"

Her aunt brought the scissors while Bob chased her around the room with his sticky hands. They laughed and laughed. Blaine knew that if they got happy enough, they'd both start drinking and that's when the laughter would subside.

Blaine was right. As soon as her aunt had begun to string popcorn, she popped the tab on a beer. Bob asked Blaine to get him one out of the refrigerator. She liked Bob so she slipped out of her chair and brought him a beer from the refrigerator.

Bob patted her on the head, "Good girl. Thank you, honey."

Blaine smiled. She liked pleasing at least one of her Aunt's boyfriends. It was better than being hit like her Mother's boyfriends often did.

Soon Blaine was the only one left making decorations to put on the tree. Her aunt had long given up on the popcorn string. Her cousins were now in bed. Being older, she could stay up longer. She'd finished a bit of it, but not nearly enough for the whole tree. Blaine put the last finishing touches on her handmade ornaments. "Do we have any ribbon?"

Her mother hiccupped and shook her head. "I need sleep. I gotta work tomorrow." Bob followed her aunt into her bedroom and shut the door behind them.

Blaine didn't have ribbon for her ornaments. How would she put them on the tree? She decided the best thing to do was just put them on the tree anyway.

It didn't take her long. She'd only been able to make four or five ornaments from her leftover turkeys. She placed them into the tree. Proud of her work, she scurried back into the kitchen for the threaded popcorn garland. Being careful to not let any slip off the thread, she carried it gently into the living room, weaving it around the tree.

Standing back, she assessed her decorations. It looked nothing like the decorated Christmas trees at school. Even her friend, Suzie, across the street had a tree with lights.

Feeling defeat, Blaine sat back on the couch and admired the small, bedraggled tree in the corner. She'd done the best she could. It wasn't perfect, or even that beautiful, but she had a Christmas tree.

Now if only Santa knew and brought her presents this year. The song said he would. The one she'd learned to sing with the other kids at school. She'd been trying to not cry all season. She'd not been as successful to not pout. Because, as the song said, Santa was coming to town.

She must not do a very good job of being good, because Santa rarely came to visit her. She hoped this year was different.

"Did you get presents that year?" Mason reached over and patted her knee.

Blaine nodded. "A few. Bob was a good guy, but my aunt never quite knew how to hang on to the good ones. They always left."

"I'm sorry your childhood was so hard, Blaine. I wish somehow the rest of your life could be better."

Blaine nodded. She hoped so, too.

Callie's family had so many good memories. Not all were good, but this family had lived much differently than her. Why had God allowed Callie's family to enjoy life so much and her life to be completely haunted by her mother's actions? Her aunt and grandmother's frustrations with her? What kind of God would allow anyone to live as she had?

Why would she desire to have a personal relationship with a God like that?

Chapter 14

"Hey Blaine, wanna take a walk?"

"It's almost midnight." Callie scolded Mason.

"I'm tired of doing this puzzle, but I'm not ready for bed yet. I'm like Gramps, I want to take a walk." Mason held his hand out to Blaine. "Want to come?"

Blaine seemed a bit reluctant, but only when she removed her warm blanket. "Okay." Before heading for her coat she placed some of the empty cocoa mugs on the kitchen counter. She slipped into her boots and coat by the back door.

"We won't be long," Mason called into the living room.

"I'm heading to bed." Callie harrumphed. "Kids! It's barely twenty degrees out there."

They hesitated to leave the warmth of Nana's house, through her garage and out onto the front yard. Mason reacted with a, "Whoa, it's cold out here." Bending down, he scooped up a wad of snow. He thought Blaine hadn't noticed.

"What do you think you're doing?"

Mason tossed the wad in her direction. The snowball hit her boot.

She chided. "Mason!"

"What?" He grinned at her. "C'mon, let's go." Mason stuffed his hands in his pockets and headed down the sidewalk. "I'm glad you came with me."

Blaine looked over at him. "You know it's like sub-zero out here," stuffing her hands into her pockets. She shivered.

"Yeah, but look up."

They tilted their heads back. The sky was dark.

"What are we looking for?" Blaine seemed irritated.

"Stars."

"There aren't any."

Mason sighed. "What are stars for anyway? I just needed some fresh air."

Blaine started down the sidewalk, "Then, let's go."

Mason wasn't sure how much longer he could stay awake and he wanted to have some quiet time with Blaine. He thought the cold air would help, before he could stop himself, he yawned. "Ahhh, sorry."

"When did your train leave Chicago?"

The cold soon penetrated his coat and Mason shivered. "Before lunch. I guess I was excited to get here and got up earlier than I normally do."

Mason had noticed Blaine's demeanor around his mother. He loved his mother, but she could be critical at times. "You're not worried about my parents being here, are you?"

Blaine averted her eyes to the sidewalk again. "It must seem odd finding a stranger here caring for her mother."

Mason added, "Give her time. She's really accepting of most people, but super critical when it comes to Nana."

Blaine seemed to understand. "You come home and find a stranger caring for your mother. Who wouldn't be paranoid?"

Mason adjusted his mittens tighter on his hands. "It's great to have them home. It'll be good for Nana and them. Mom always hates being away when Nana gets sick."

Blaine nodded.

"So, how's it been?" Mason motioned to the houses nearby. "Being here with her. It's not Chicago."

"I need a Starbucks in my life."

Mason laughed. "Right. I totally agree." Mason stopped and scuffed his toe at a piece of ice on the sidewalk. "Are you still okay," catching up to Blaine. "By being here?" Mason pointed to her house behind them. "With her?"

"Of course. She's the best, but..." Blaine hesitated.

"But what?"

"I'm not very good at this. I mean, I've worked lots of jobs, but nothing like this. It's different than waiting on tables or mixing drinks at a bar. I don't want to mess it up. What if I hurt her or something?"

"Nana? I doubt it. She's tough."

"Do you have any idea how lucky you are?"

"Lucky?"

"Yeah. I don't think you even realize it. Most people like you don't."

"Don't realize they're lucky?"

"Yeah. Life happens and they completely ignore the fact they have parents." Blaine held up two gloved fingers, "A father. Mother. Grandparents. A home," Blaine pointed back at Callie's house, "to return to, at Christmas."

It wasn't hard for Mason to agree. "Yeah, I am lucky. Although, I think *blessed* is better."

"Blessed. Lucky. I'd give anything for parents who are still married. A grandmother like Callie. Having the opportunity to spend Christmas with family."

Mason grinned again. "Even when they're crazy."

"Especially then."

Mason grew quiet, contemplating his next question. "Blaine? Will you tell me more about your life?"

Blaine shook her head. "You don't want to know."

"I asked, didn't I?"

Blaine stopped to kick a brown leaf off the sidewalk. She bit her bottom lip.

Mason wasn't sure whether to tell her 'never mind,' but his curiosity grew.

Blaine spewed, as if saying it brought her some relief. "I grew up in a horrible home. I didn't know my father. My mother was mixed up. She battled-what did Callie call it? *Demons* in her head. She tried to commit suicide until, one day, it finally worked. We then went to live with my aunt. When I was a teenager, instead of dropping me into foster care, a social worker convinced my grandmother to take me in until I turned eighteen. I was not a nice teenager."

"You have siblings?"

"A brother. But he didn't stay long. My brother left home after graduation and my grandmother died right after I graduated. And...that's about it."

Mason rubbed his forehead with his gloved hand. "Where is he now?"

"No clue. I haven't seen or heard from him."

"What brought you to Chicago? That's where you're from, right?"

"I've lived there all my life. Lately, with Kyle."

Mason wanted to ask more. Was she still in love with him? Why had she left him? Especially at Christmas? But he kept his thoughts to himself.

"Don't worry. He's a jerk, but I didn't completely realize it until I met Callie on the train and she told me her love story. I began to see that life really could be different."

"Let's keep walking..." Mason knew he was cold, Blaine must feel the same way. "Is it over with him?"

"I think so. More so, after the train ride. All of my things are still at his apartment, but it's fine. None of it is important. I can buy new things. I needed a break. He asked me to do something..."

Mason wanted to ask what, but Blaine kept talking before he could.

"Do you like children, Mason?"

That seemed a random thing to ask. "Of course. I love kids."

"Yeah. He hates kids."

Mason stopped, "Our country is screwed up."

"Our country?"

"You've seen it, right? Children are no longer a treasured possession. Life has been devalued."

"Because of abortion?"

"Not totally. Life itself needs to be defended. Not just babies, the elderly, but even children with Down syndrome, too." Mason felt his voice get more intense, "life in itself is important and should be cherished." Mason looked over at her, "You want children, right?"

"Of course." She shoved her hands into her pockets, looked down at her feet and shivered. "Yes."

"I was an only child. I hated growing up without brothers or sisters. If I have my way, I want lots of children. But I guess that would depend on my wife. I mean, she would be the one to go through all that pain and watching her body metamorphosis into something she's never seen before."

"So would you give the woman options?"

"Options?"

"I mean, it is her body."

Mason stopped walking. He stopped Blaine. "I wouldn't marry someone who thought that abortion was right if that's what you're getting at." Mason threw his hands up in a gesture of surrender. "I'm a Christian and I do believe we have the responsibility to give babies a voice, too."

"I've been feeling the same way lately."

Mason started walking again. "I've realized, for a while now, I can't change a woman's mind about stuff like that. I want nothing more than to defend life," Mason put imaginary quotes in the air, "I understand the, 'It's your choice' thing, but I want to defend the innocent being inside. They have no choice. They're a separate soul from their mother. That's the part that makes me want to defend them. If their own mothers won't, who will?"

"To be honest, that's the part that I get stuck on, too."

"So you're more conservative than most."

Blaine smiled, "I guess I am." She shuffled, "I mean...until just a little while ago, I wasn't sure where I stood and I guess I assumed it should be the mother's choice, but all of nature protects their children, right? I've heard story after story of animals protecting their babies." Blaine laughed. "Kyle loved watching nature documentaries. Have you ever heard how an alligator takes care of its eggs and babies?"

Mason shook his head. "I don't think so."

"An alligator will use that enormous mouth of hers to shake her eggs. If they hear movement inside, and their other eggs are hatching, they'll use that mouth full of teeth and strength to gently rip off the egg, allowing the baby alligator to escape. The eggs are even healthy for an alligator. If there is no movement, and presumably the baby hasn't formed or is dead, the alligator will eat the egg for special nutrition. Did you know that?"

"That's amazing. See, I believe, God created us to protect our young. Protect the child within a woman. That's why he so beautifully created her to carry and cherish that baby for nine long months before giving birth. The baby can't live without the mother for those nine months."

"I wish other people felt the way you do."

Mason seemed to have pounced upon something sensitive. "Children are fearfully and wonderfully made. The world has cast such a dark cloak over that. Like I said, many devalue human life, not just in abortion. Not in every case, but sometimes I wonder how many decisions, especially about abortion, are for convenience or selfish motives."

"You're right Mason. We can be a selfish generation. I'm often offended by how my own gender regards children. I've heard too many horror stories from friends who have gone through abortions. It changes you. It affects more than any woman cares to think or believe. I do believe we have a right to control our own bodies, but not at the cost of taking a child's life to do so." Blake took a deep breath. "I often wonder what made my mother decide to have me. I made her life rough, yet she did her best to still defend me. Protect me, despite the fact that she wasn't a very good mother."

Mason stopped again. "She must have loved you."

Blaine looked away. "I've always wanted to believe that."

Mason wasn't sure if he should push the subject more. Something seemed to be bothering Blaine.

"Are you cold?"

Blaine nodded. "I like talking with you, but yes. I'm freezing."

"Let's head back inside then."

Just then, Mason's phone rang. As he pulled it from his pocket, it slipped from his hand and fell onto the sidewalk. Screen side up. Megan's name flashed across the screen. "I don't have to get that right now."

Blaine turned on her heel and headed back toward Nana's house. She seemed upset. Mason was confused.

"Is everything okay, Blaine?"

Blaine waved over her shoulder, but scurried into Nana's garage and he heard the door click shut.

Chapter 15

She didn't see that one coming. Blaine felt like a fool again. Mason had never mentioned anyone named Megan. Was she a friend? A girlfriend? Why did she even believe that a great guy like Mason would want to have any kind of relationship with someone like her? Blaine went to her room. The walls and closed door could protect her.

Her thoughts were interrupted by a tap, tap on her door and Mason whispering her name. She ignored it. She couldn't talk to him now. What if she had imagined Mason's interest? Could she endure another let-down? The only thing she knew for sure was, she wasn't going to fall for it again. Maybe Kyle was the only kind of guy she deserved.

Sitting on Nana's couch, Mason went over in his head their conversation. Had he said something to upset her? Reaching into his pocket, he pulled out his phone. What in the world would Megan want from him on Christmas Eve? It was pretty obvious that Blaine saw who called him. Realization came like a Michigan weather change in January. One moment it was thirty degrees and sunny...the next it was snowing like Alaska.

Sitting back on the couch, he pulled off his shoes, and removed his coat. Leave it to Megan to interrupt such a special moment with Blaine. Mason snickered to think that somehow she'd planned the whole thing from her condo in Chicago. As if she knew what was happening at that moment.

It was Christmas Eve and all Mason had tried to do was get to know Blaine. What was she like? What made her so timid around everyone? Who had she left in Chicago and did she still love him? So many questions and so little time to find out the answers he wanted and needed.

Mason went to Nana's closet for blankets. He needed a pillow. He wondered if his parents were asleep yet. They had to be. He couldn't bother them. Piling up the couch pillows, he did his best to make up a bed on the couch.

Nana's couch bed looked as uncomfortable as how he now felt. He'd never been good at sizing up a woman. He was pretty sure that most men saw women as distractions. He'd often find himself, lately, considering the possibilities of settling down soon, find a woman he could share his life. But somehow it seemed to make his life more complicated. Would the hassles be worth it when the right one came along?

Plopping down on the couch, he tried to adjust the blankets for some kind of comfort. Not one of them was long enough to reach his chin and, at the same time, cover his feet. So he did his best to pull one up and the other down. Rolling over, all the blankets shifted, exposing his feet to the chilly room.

Tossing and turning he realized his exhaustion was almost greater than his ability to go to sleep. Closing his eyes, he thought about that moment when he gazed into Blaine's amazing blue eyes. She made his heart race and it caught his breath every time she looked at him. He thought back to the moment of seeing her waiting for him at the depot. As tired as he was, his mind wouldn't shut down. He'd always loved to sit in the glow of the tree's Christmas lights. This year they seemed extra special. He was back at his Nana's house for Christmas.

He'd been so busy over the last two years at his job that he hadn't taken the time to visit Nana during the holidays. She'd always come to see him in December. He imagined, she probably wouldn't be able to do that next year. Right then he determined in his heart to not miss another Christmas with her. No matter how much it set him back at work. Since her heart surgery, he'd realized how frail she had become. He needed to make more of an effort to be with her more.

What could he do to make tomorrow special for Blaine? He wanted to show her how memorable a family holiday could be. What little he now knew about Blaine's previous life, it was obvious she needed love, real love. Maybe not the romantic love that Mason desired, but a true love of a family. His life needed to reflect God's love before his own.

It was the least he could do for her and her recent desire to help Nana. You could see how hard she'd been working to make this holiday nice for the family. Glancing around the room, he noticed how clean the room was since the last time he'd seen it. Nana's table, by her chair, wasn't piled high with magazines and books. The tree looked more beautiful than it ever had. His Nana wouldn't have been able to do all this preparation for Christmas after her recent surgery and ailments. Blaine had worked hours to make it nice for them. He noticed.

Mason yawned, his last thought before sleep finally came, being...tomorrow was Christmas morning, he would make sure to tell Blaine about Megan. As awkward as that might turn out to be.

How would he show this young girl what real love was without getting tangled up in a romantic relationship? He needed to be careful. There was only one way to get an answer to his question. He sought out the advice of the One who could help.

Blaine woke with a headache. Darkness consumed the room. The walk, Mason and Megan swirled in her thoughts. She instantly thought about the night before and buried her head in the pillow. Perhaps the softness would stop the pounding, but she had to use the bathroom.

Perhaps she needed to leave Callie's house, but she remembered, today was Christmas.

Callie had looked forward to this day for the past two weeks. All of their preparations and work had gone into the planning of it. Callie wanted, with all her heart, for this day to be special.

When was the last time she'd looked forward to Christmas morning? Had she ever? The best part of this day was going to be, she wasn't alone. What if she'd put all her efforts toward making it a memorable day for Mason's family, but then couldn't enjoy it with them?

She rose slowly, her head still pounding like the times when Kyle and she had too much to drink the night before. She sat on the edge of her bed and listened for Callie. There wasn't a sound. For the first time in days, she wasn't all that sick to her stomach.

She thought back to Mason's phone call. Perhaps Megan was a neighbor of Mason, back in Chicago? Or a co-worker? Maybe she'd jumped to conclusions too fast. Reacted too quickly? She chided herself for a lifelong problem she had of doing that.

Listening for other movement, she heard only the creaks and groans of a winter wind buffeting the house. Pulling a sweatshirt over her head, she tiptoed to the bathroom. Upon entering the bathroom, she realized she ached all over. Perhaps she done too much yesterday to prepare for today.

Leaving the bathroom a few minutes later, she found Mason curled in a fetal position with one leg hanging off the edge of the couch and another foot sticking out of the blankets covering him. He looked so uncomfortable, yet so adorable. The tree lights were lit and bright in the darkness. More presents were under the tree. The scene brought a strange feeling of comfort. She had no clue what time it was, but she knew she didn't want to be the first one up.

Crawling back into her still warm bed, she glanced at the clock. Dawn would soon be brightening her room. Despite the headache still throbbing at her temples, she drew the comforter close and under her chin. Whoever this Megan was, Blaine now realized she might have to prove herself. Yet how would she do that, with a past like hers?

A knock at the door startled Blaine awake. She answered, "Just a second." Glancing at the clock, she realized it was more than two hours since she'd last looked. She scrambled out of bed, picked up a hairbrush, and twisted her hair into a bun at the back of her head. Standing at the mirror, her face looked flushed and her body aches hadn't gone away. She wiped yesterday's mascara from her eyes with a make-up wipe and then reapplied a little color to her face.

She headed for the bathroom to at least brush her teeth and smacked right into Mason leaving the room. He smelled like the cologne section at a retail store, fresh from a shower. She didn't want to talk to him until she at least brushed her teeth.

While in the bathroom, she realized her headache had dissipated with that last two hours of sleep. Thankfully, she wouldn't have to endure it all morning. Perhaps she could take some medicine to ward off the body aches. She adjusted the wild hair bun and headed out to start work on the delicious breakfast they'd planned for the day.

She saw Callie still in her robe and slippers at the end of the hallway.

"Good morning, sunshine. Merry Christmas."

"Merry Christmas, Callie." Callie opened her arms and pulled Blaine close.

"I'm so happy you are with us today." Callie kissed her cheek. "Let's make it a good day."

"I'll get breakfast going."

Mason was in the kitchen fixing himself a cup of coffee. Blaine knew she only wanted to do one thing. She did as Callie had done to her and opened her arms. "Merry Christmas, Mason."

He smiled and hugged her. "Merry Christmas!"

"How was the couch?"

Mason stirred his cup, "Hard! And short!"

He was sleeping on the couch because of her. She had the only other spare bedroom in the house. Guilt filled her heart until Mason said, "But I was too tired to care."

"Let's have breakfast. Then we can open presents." Nana scooted her walker into the kitchen. "I'm starving."

Mason grabbed his Nana and hugged tight. "Merry Christmas Nana." His Nana's ninety-year-old eyes were as bright as a young child.

Mason wondered why his parents weren't up yet, he went to check on them. He bumped into his father in the hallway.

"Merry Christmas, kid." He patted Mason on the back.

Mason laughed, "Merry Christmas Dad."

"What did Santa bring you?"

"Nana's excitement. I'm glad we get to make her happy today," Mason replied, thinking of Nana's face.

"That's a great start to a day. God is with us."

It was a constant reminder from his Dad almost every Christmas morning. A reason for celebration. Christmas was a celebration of Christ's birth. When in a moment of time, God decided to transcend to earth to become our Savior, in human form. He endured life as a human, transforming himself into man who felt, suffered, and endured life. So that He knew the experience of being human and could relate to mankind for years to come.

Mason's mother followed behind his father. "Merry Christmas, sweetheart."

"Merry Christmas, Mom."

Mason loved being with and seeing his parents on this special day. He'd never imagined they'd be together this year, so this added blessing would transform the day into an even better one.

Callie called for them from the dining room. "C'mon you people. Blaine and I have planned a wonderful day which includes a full and delicious breakfast." Nana waved her family to flip pancakes, slice up fruit, and warm up cinnamon rolls. Everyone pitched in to help, breakfast was soon on the table.

Soon they were all enjoying the prepared breakfast which included Mason's favorite. Bacon.

As they finished their meal, Nana handed Mason's father her Bible. "Chuck? Will you read us the Christmas story?"

"I'd be honored."

Mason wondered what Blaine thought of their customs. She sat quietly on the opposite side of the table. Mason had a hard time taking his eyes off of her. Her eyes sparkled like they had the night before on their walk in the snow. He needed to concentrate on his father's words, averting his eyes to his lap.

His father began to read, "In those days Ceasar Augustus issued a decree that a census should be taken..."

Mason had heard the words so many times, he nearly had the whole passage memorized.

"Everyone went to their own town to register. So Joseph also went up from the town of Nazareth in Galilee to Judea, to Bethlehem the town of David, because he belonged to the house and line of David."

Mason closed his eyes. Distractions had always been a problem for him. And Blaine was even more of a distraction on this Christmas morning. His father's rich baritone voice filled the air with the story of Jesus' birth.

"While they were there, the time came for the baby to be born and she gave birth to her firstborn son. She wrapped him in clothes and placed him in a manger, because there was no guest room available for them."

Mason did his best to listen, but with those words he thought of Blaine again. She had Nana's guest room. She was lost. After hearing some of her story last night, he realized how much Blaine needed his Nana and her love. He opened his eyes to see Blaine who appeared enamored by Chuck's recitation of the Christmas story.

"And there were shepherds living out in the fields nearby, keeping watch over their flocks at night. An angel of the Lord appeared to them, and the glory of the Lord shone around them, and they were terrified."

Mason closed his eyes again. Terrified. The shepherds were finally having the opportunity to see for themselves the gift of Jesus to the world and yet, they feared it. They were afraid of not only the angels, but perhaps the message of an odd birth.

"Don't be afraid. I bring you good news that will cause great joy for all the people."

At this moment Mason knew that it may be the same with Blaine. She was afraid of all that Nana and his family were offering her. Perhaps because she didn't know. Didn't realize that they were only offering her love. Real love. And they were showing it through Christ's love and his commandments to 'love one another.'

Nana was wise. That was why she had pushed to have Blaine be her caregiver. Not because Blaine had any experience or even that

Nana really needed her. They could have hired someone to come help her. She had many friends in the community and even a church family who could help in her recovery, but she'd chosen Blaine. It all made sense now.

"Today in the town of David a Savior has been born to you; he is the Messiah, the Lord."

Good news. Good news that many didn't realize was the fruition of what the Israelites had been watching to come from years before. They didn't know. They didn't realize. Many, until it was too late.

"Suddenly a great company of the heavenly host appeared with the angel, praising God and saying, Glory to God in the highest heaven, and on earth peace to those on whom his favor rests."

But the angels knew. They knew who Jesus was and celebrated His birth with singing and praising to God.

Mason felt an overwhelming sense of gratitude. Not only for listening to his father's reading of the Christmas story, but in God's goodness. Blaine was much more than a caregiver. He wondered how long Nana would need her.

Mason looked up at Blaine. She ignored his gaze, so he kept staring. He couldn't stop himself.

"When they had seen Jesus, the shepherds spread the word concerning what had been told them about this child, and all who heard it were amazed at what the shepherds said to them."

What would it be like to spread the word about Jesus' birth? But then, Mason realized. They still had that opportunity. He'd not done enough to share it with those around him. He also knew that the girl who he couldn't take his eyes off of needed to hear about Jesus as well.

"But Mary treasured up all these things and pondered them in her heart."

Mason's father sat back in his chair and shook his head, "It doesn't matter how many Christmas mornings I read this, it still amazes me. God sent us His Son to change the world, but He didn't come on a throne or even in abundant fanfare. He came quietly, silently, and anonymously to the world, even though...they were watching for Him. Isn't that just like God? His ways are so different than our own. His plans so much better."

Everyone murmured, "Amen."

Blaine had never heard anyone read from the Bible before. It was mesmerizing. She'd never heard about Jesus' birth in such detail. She'd studied about different religions in high school, but never heard anyone actually read the words. She sensed this family regarded it as true and they really did believe in a story from so long ago.

As she looked around the table, each person appeared to feel the same way. The words seemed comforting to them. Chuck said he had heard the words many times before, yet they still brought joy to him. How could mere words do this? Words that were probably written thousands of years ago.

Suddenly, she realized Mason was staring at her. His gaze pierced her heart. He smiled. She smiled back.

Callie scooted her chair back and distracted her. She stood, closed her eyes, and started to pray. Blaine watched as each one at the table bowed their heads.

"Dear God. Thank you for sending us your Son. For sending Him to us in such a simple, special way. We pray that on this day we will show all those around us His love."

Blaine realized she hadn't closed her eyes. She bowed her head.

"We didn't deserve your gift. We still don't because every single day we sin against you and your Son. Please take away our sins. Guide our words and thoughts to remember these words today and always freely share them with others. Give us the love we need to love others. Give us the hearts to reach out to those in need of your gift as we give gifts to each other today. Thank you for my family." Callie chocked up for a moment and couldn't speak.

Blaine couldn't help herself. She opened her eyes and gazed at Callie. Why had she stopped? Was she all right?

Callie wiped her cheek with the back of her hand. Then continued, "Thank you for bringing them all home to me to share in this day. Thank you for healing my body."

Blaine heard others say amen to Callie's words.

"Thank you for your goodness. Your salvation. Help us to make it real to everyone we meet. Everyone needs to hear. Everyone needs the opportunity to choose for themselves to either accept or reject your Son. May this not stop us from telling everyone about You. In Jesus name."

Everyone mumbled more 'Amen's.'

Blaine wasn't sure if God liked that she hadn't closed her eyes for the whole prayer. Callie's prayer caught her by surprise. Were they revealing their personal relationships to a God they couldn't see? She'd envisioned religion in many ways, but she'd never seen it like this. She wondered if she could ever feel as they did.

Callie backed away from the table and clapped her hands. "Let's open presents now," she added with the gleeful anticipation of a child. Blaine giggled at her enthusiasm.

Mason came toward her with his plate, adding hers to his. "Let me get that for you, Blaine."

"I can get it." Blaine stood to help.

"I know. But I want to get it for you." Mason placed her plate on top of his and stacked the plates by the sink.

Amy asked, "Shouldn't we get cleaned up first, Mother?"

"No," Callie emphatically added. "I want to open presents like we used to do when you were a child. Your Dad loved this moment."

Amy tilted her head as if remembering something special, "Yes he did."

Chuck added, "I think he was more excited for Christmas presents than anyone I ever knew."

Callie laughed, "Ridiculously so!"

Everyone moved into the living room. Mason sat on the couch and Blaine sat next to him. Chuck and Amy sat together on the love seat. Callie settled in the recliner.

"Mason. Are you going to be Santa?"

Mason laughed. "I guess. C'mon Blaine, help me."

Blaine didn't know what being Santa meant, but soon Mason was picking up gifts, reading the tags, and handing them out to each recipient. She followed his example.

When all the gifts were distributed, she sat down to find presents for herself. She blushed. Who had gotten her gifts?

Each one took a turn opening one gift. Blaine had never experienced something so wonderful. She opened one box that held a beautiful lavender robe. It was soft. She rubbed the plush fabric against her cheek. "This is so soft." How had Callie been able to buy it? Another gift held slippers to match. Chuck and Amy had gotten her body wash, some after-shower spray, and a Starbuck's gift card. The gift card made everyone laugh when she opened it.

Chuck announced, "We found a Starbuck's about twenty minutes from here. One morning, when we're desperate, we'll all go."

Mason seemed to love his gifts, too. Callie had told Blaine she often bought presents throughout the year, knowing it would be difficult, with her budget, to purchase them all weeks before Christmas.

After the gifts, each one sat back and admired the tree, sipping on coffee. Blaine had never experienced something so memorable or special. She never remembered a nicer Christmas morning. Last year they'd gone out for breakfast. That was all.

On this Christmas morning, no one had received elaborate or expensive gifts. They were simple and most were things they needed, but each one brought joy to the receiver as well as the giver. Callie's smile as each one opened their gifts made that obvious. If nothing else, Blaine had done her best to help make the day special for Callie. Each day she grew more and more thankful she'd taken the time to help Callie to the train. She never imagined that one act of kindness would produce such extraordinary memories for her to cherish.

Blaine's first Christmas with Callie and her family just got better. They had a wonderful dinner complete with all the fixings of turkey, stuffing, mashed potatoes, and gravy. Amy had helped by making pumpkin pie the afternoon before.

Blaine continued to not feel well. She had picked at her dinner. It surprised her that none of the food made her nauseous. Her body aches grew worse. She wondered if she was coming down with the flu.

After the meal, Chuck and Amy worked on the puzzle in the living room while Callie lay down for a nap. Blaine finished most of the dinner dishes while Mason dried them. While standing by the sink, Blaine began to experience cramping. As soon as the last dish was done, she excused herself to use the bathroom. She just didn't feel right.

Blaine didn't know what to do. She was spotting. She'd brought her phone into the bathroom with her and now searched the internet for her symptoms. It assured her it was normal to have spotting in the early weeks of pregnancy. She probably just had a bug of some sort. She relaxed a bit.

Despite the fact that this pregnancy wasn't in her or Kyle's plans, she'd imagined herself with this baby now for over eight weeks. Even though it had sent fear through every part of her to envision going through all of this alone, she knew she loved the baby way before she'd actually realized it.

At this moment, all she could do was think of protecting it. Cherish the fact that she was carrying a child. She'd already determined to carry it to term, even if she had to do it alone. It would be her family. The start of a new life for her. She wanted nothing more than to have it. At this moment, she realized that for the first time since taking the pregnancy test.

Returning to the living room she announced to the group, "I don't mean to sound ungrateful or wanting to ignore any of you tonight, but I'm not feeling very well. I think, Callie, if it's okay with you, I'm going to head to bed." She fought back tears for she wanted nothing more than to sit with the family for the rest of the evening. "I'm sorry."

Callie looked concerned, "Can we do anything for you? Is it your stomach again?"

Blaine shook her head. "I feel feverish and as if I'm coming down with the flu. I know I've probably infected all of you today, I'd just as soon just go to bed, if that's okay?"

Everyone commented that it was fine, and each one told her they hoped she felt better.

"I think a bit of sleep might help. Good night."

Callie watched the young girl head to her bedroom and quietly shut the door. "Something isn't right."

"What's wrong, Nana?" Mason got up from the couch and went to her chair.

"I'm not sure. I think something is up that is bigger than Blaine not feeling well."

"Can we help?" Chuck added from his corner of the puzzle table.

Callie shook her head. "I don't know."

"What are you worried about, Mother?" Amy asked.

"I can't say for sure because I've only been guessing something about Blaine since she came to stay with me. I don't want to say something that isn't true." Callie sighed. "Let's see how Blaine feels in the morning."

"Should we be concerned, Nana?"

Nana patted Mason's hand now on her shoulder. "I hope not, honey. I surely hope not."

It had been such a wonderful day. Blaine recalled all the surprises, food, and stories from the day. She never had such an amazing Christmas. She snuggled down deeper into her bed. Maybe she just needed sleep. She hadn't had a day off since she'd started to work for Callie. This pregnancy had made her exhausted almost beyond belief on some days. Perhaps that was all this was.

Blaine dozed off for an hour or so and woke up to a knock at her door. She sat up in bed and answered, "Yes."

Mason called, "I've brought you some Vernors? Might settle your stomach. Can I bring it in?"

Blaine plumped up the pillows behind her and answered, "Sure. I'm awake."

Mason brought in a tray with a mug and a small portion of the food they'd warmed up from dinner. "Not sure if you're hungry, but we all had a snack and I thought maybe you'd like something, too."

Blaine smiled, "Thank you. I am a little hungry."

"The pop might settle your stomach. It always does mine." Mason set the tray on her lap. "Can I sit with you for a while?"

Blaine sipped the drink. "This is warm."

"Nana and my mom always heat it up. They say it is easier on an upset stomach."

Blaine grimaced.

Mason laughed, "I agree. I prefer it cold." Mason grabbed the chair next to the dresser and placed it beside Blaine's bed. "What did you think of your first McAnder Christmas?"

Blaine burst forth with her answer. "Quite the experience."

"Good, I hope?"

"Of course." Blaine took a small bite of the food. "Mason, who's Megan?"

"She's a co-worker."

Blaine hesitated, "Okay."

Mason pulled at his sweater's collar. "If you don't mind, I'm going to take off this sweater and remove the tag on it. It has bothered me all day. I hate tags on my clothes." He quickly removed the sweater and ripped the tag off the back collar. "There." He slipped the sweater back on. "I need to donate this. It's getting too short anyway." He then sat back down.

"Is she your girlfriend?"

"We've had a few dates."

Blaine hated to hear the words. She didn't know much about Mason, but she was pretty sure he wouldn't lie to her.

"I hadn't quite made a decision about whether I liked her all that much yet. I like to take my time getting to know a girl."

"Well, it sounds like you have some decisions to make."

Mason stuffed his hands into his pockets. "I don't know yet. I'm sure you know what I'm talking about. We're just in the beginning phases of getting to know each other. Kinda like you and I."

Blaine took another bite of food. "I did have a great day today. You are all so kind to me. I love my gifts." She hated to change the subject, but it was obvious, Mason didn't quite know what to say.

"Your family, Callie, and you, are different than anyone I've ever met. Your faith seems so important to you. For some reason, that shocks me. I've never seen anything quite like it."

"Thank you. I think that's a nice compliment. We aren't perfect, but our faith is important to us. I hope you can see that."

Blaine shifted on her pillows and repositioned her tray. "Thank you for this, but I guess I'm still not very hungry." Blaine looked up at Mason, resting her head back on a close pillow. "I'm sorry Mason."

Mason got up and took the tray off her lap. "Do you want to keep your drink? I can set it here beside you on the bed stand."

Blaine took the cup from off the tray. "Better yet, let me hold it. But Mason, will you please sit and talk a little more?"

Mason placed the tray on the dresser and sat back down.

"What kind of relationship do you want with Megan? Can I ask?"

"I take relationships very seriously. I don't jump until I'm absolutely sure something is right. Does that make sense?"

Blaine took another sip of her warm drink. It was making her feel better. "I've never met a guy quite like you, Mason. You're kind. I can see it is important for you to hold back until you're sure about something."

"I prayed your day would be good Blaine."

"You prayed that I would have a good day? Why would God care about stuff like that?"

"He cares about everything. Even the little things and you've done so much to help Nana make it a great day for all of us."

"Thanks for being honest with me about Megan. I hope it works out for you."

"I'm not sure that she's what I'm looking for as a girlfriend, but I always want to be honest. I hope you're able to do the same with me."

"I'll try. I have to be honest even about that, I'm not. I've had to lie so much in my lifetime that I forget to tell the truth sometimes. I know that probably makes no sense to you."

"Do you have a boyfriend? Did you leave him in Chicago?"

Now it was Blaine's turn to confess. "His name is Kyle. We've been dating for over a year now, living together for the past four months." Blaine looked at Mason for a reaction. He just leaned forward in the chair.

"And? What happened? Why were you on that train that day?"

It was too soon. He couldn't tell Mason why she'd left Kyle that day. She needed to be careful, but she wanted to try hard to tell the truth. "We had a big fight. He asked me to do something that I didn't want to do. I knew if I stayed, he might scare me into doing it anyway."

Mason tapped his mouth with a finger. "Scare you? Why would he do that?"

Blaine shook her head. "It's complicated."

"Can I ask one thing?"

Blaine cringed to think about what he was going to ask. Without realizing it, she must have closed her eyes.

"Have you broke it off with him then?"

Blaine opened her eyes in relief. "Not officially. But I will. I'm going to." Blaine took another sip. "I can't be with someone like that."

Blaine grew sleepy again. All she wanted to do was close her eyes. "I'm sorry Mason. Thank you for the food and this 'delicious drink,'" they both laughed, "but I'm really tired."

Mason stood. "Of course. No problem." He took the tray of food. "Please try and get some sleep. Thanks for the talk." He turned to leave the room.

"Thanks for being patient, Mason."

He nodded and then left, shutting the door slowly behind him.

Mason took the tray to the kitchen. Nana called to him from the other room, "How is she, Mason?"

Mason washed his hands and then went to tell Nana she wasn't feeling much better. "Let's hope a good night's rest helps her."

Everyone agreed.

Chapter 16

"I don't like this." Amy was undressing to get into her pajamas. "Not at all."

"Your gift? I thought you like pink pajamas." Chuck got under the covers and scooted himself down. "These beds are so nice compared to our beds in Africa."

"No Chuck, Mason and that girl."

Chuck burrowed into the comfort, turned to fluff his pillow, and then lay back. "Her name is Blaine, Amy."

"I know what her name is."

Chuck put his hand under his head, "I think she's sweet."

Amy pulled her top over her head and took off her earrings laying them on the table beside their bed. "We know nothing about her background. For heaven's sake, even Mom doesn't know much about her."

"They've lived together for the past two weeks. I'm sure she knows something..."

"That's another thing. There's something strange about her? Like she has this deep dark secret that no one is allowed to know. She's just suspicious."

"I don't know if we could actually still call her a stranger..."

"And you've seen your son." Amy slipped her pajama top over her head, pulled back the covers on the bed and slipped in beside her husband.

"What? Seen him do what?"

Amy shivered in the coolness of the bed. "I think he might like her."

"It's too soon for that. Trust Mason. He goes slow with things like that." Chuck scooted closer to her, "Amy, don't you remember when we were going through that? How long did it take you to fall in love with me?" He grinned at her like the Cheshire Cat.

"Do you think he loves her? Oh Chuck!" She leaned toward him. "And we were different?"

Chuck laughed and kissed his wife's cheek, "How?"

"We were too young to know better." Amy fluffed her own pillow and then sat up in bed instead of lying down. She grabbed a bottle of lotion and began her nightly ritual of lathering it on. "Michigan makes my hands so dry."

"How do you know what's best for Mason?"

Amy stopped rubbing her hands together with lotion, "What? I'm his mother. I know what type of girl will be good for him."

"Really. Wow. You better let God know."

Amy turned off the light.

"By the way, what did He say?"

Amy shut her eyes, "Nothing."

Silence filled the room.

Amy couldn't help herself, she added, "Yet."

Chapter 17

Chuck could hear the soft, yet significant snores of his wife as he pulled back the covers. He needed coffee. He couldn't wait to try the Chicago brand Mason had given them for Christmas instead of the instant, generic brand Callie had on hand.

Pushing into his slippers by the bed, he pulled on his robe and headed down the hallway. A small light reflected off the walls in the dining room. He found Mason with his Bible propped open on the table.

He felt bad to interrupt such a moment, but thankful that he saw it. "Good morning, buddy!"

Mason's face brightened into a smile. "Hey Dad. Good morning."

"You can't make coffee so early in the morning without me. I sure miss this rich American stuff in the Congo. I'm so glad you brought it with you from Chicago. Nana's instant stuff was making me crazy."

"Fer sure," Mason picked up his own mug and took a long swig. "Best thing about the states. And that coffee maker for Nana as a gift, best idea ever."

Both men laughed.

"Best thing?" Chuck filled a large mug and poured in some creamer. "Do you miss Africa at all?"

Mason nodded. "Of course." He sat back in the dining room chair and looked out onto Callie's back yard. "I miss those odd bird calls in the morning. The ones that wake you up out of a sound sleep with their sharp, shrill chirps, and scolding of the other birds around them. I miss the humidity that seems to hang in the air and the soft beat of raindrops on the tin roof during the rainy season. But most of all, I miss all the natural, earthy smells."

"The smells?" Chuck sat down across from Mason.

"You know the ones. Mom cooking flap jacks from the other room. The smell of dampness and that deep musk scent of animals close by."

Chuck nodded. "Everything seems so quiet here when we come home in winter. With the windows closed, I miss that open, airy feel."

"It's hard to get used to some days, especially in the middle of January and February. There are some nights I wish I could just open my window to hear Africa." Mason took a long swig of his coffee. "I also love how you can go out your front door and so many people are there to greet you, asking you what your plans are for the day. Chicago is nothing like that."

Chuck took a sip. "Will you ever come back?"

Mason sat back and blinked, "Um, I don't know. Do any of us know God's plans ahead of time?"

"I know how much you like it here. I don't blame you. But aren't there moments when you wish to go back?"

"Please don't be upset, but right now, I think my place is here."

As hard as it was to hear, in his heart he seemed to know the answer before Mason even said it. He'd said the same thing to his father about living in the states when he was Mason's age. His father could never fully comprehend why Chuck wanted to live on the other side of the world. "God places us where He wants us to be. If you feel that He has led you to Chicago then...who am I to question God." He smiled at Mason over his coffee cup. "It's all good."

"Dad, can I ask you a question?"

"Ah, hum."

Mason whispered, "Do you think Blaine is hard to read?"

"I think she's *very* pretty."

"Obviously."

"To be honest, I haven't met a woman yet who isn't hard to figure out."

"She seems to be hiding some dark secret." Mason sighed. "Her past seems to haunt her. Like it's a dark cloud over her head that isn't going away and she has no capable way of getting out from under it."

"Yes. I agree." Chuck swallowed another swig of his coffee. "We all have dark secrets we don't want others to see. We often mask, hide, or allow them to cover us. Some use dark secrets as protection."

"Protection?"

"Blaine seems to have lots of sadness in her past. Almost like dark shadows over her soul. Sometimes those dark things control all our future decisions or choices. For example..."

Mason leaned back in his chair and folded his arms.

"There is a man in Africa who I have been counseling lately. He was horribly beaten as a child. There are scars across his face. He allows those horrifying memories to define who he thinks he can be as a husband and father. Often, he believes he can't get past them. It haunts him. He has a bad temper just like his father. He fears that he will beat his wife? Mistreat his children? Many men, and women, feel they're somehow chained to their past. They have to somehow appease the shadows by trying to fix everything from this day forward. I think some people even feel guilty for their pasts, even when they aren't responsible for any of it.

"I've seen people who constantly seek out ways to make their lives better, but the past still haunts them so much they can't move on. The man I counsel is fearful to be alone with his children, so much so that he almost ignores them. He often tells his wife that she would be better off without him. Like so many, he can't seem to get around the sins of others who have harmed him."

Mason nodded.

"Perhaps Blaine has something similar. She's trying so hard to get away from her past that she makes decisions based on it. From what we've heard from her, she has had a past similar to my African friend. It's haunting her so much she can't seem to move on. That's dangerous."

"How so?" Mason leaned forward.

"People in that mindset can believe they don't have the ability to do better. And in actuality, if they depend on themselves to do better, it might not work. It's their past. It's how they were raised. They really don't know any better. Satan works hard at scoffing and mocking them with ideas that they will never be worth anything. All they know is how to hurt because for some, they've never seen how great it is to love or to be loved. Love is almost blind to them."

"That's hard."

"It's horrible. Satan convinces them they aren't worthy of love. Especially," Chuck held up a finger, "God's love. If you can't be convinced God loves you, then you won't believe anyone else can love you, either."

"So, how do we help someone like that?" Mason held up his hands as if in surrender.

Chuck smiled, "We can't, son. We have to love them yes, but we also have to allow God to work. We pray for their peace. We pray that Satan is defeated and the past can be set free. We show love, but it has to be God's love. And I'm sorry Mason, but that doesn't include a romantic kind of love. Blaine doesn't need that now. She needs to accept God's love and His worth for her first."

Mason nodded. "I know."

"Do you look at Blaine in that way?"

Mason's looked down at his hands. "I'm trying not to rush anything. I am just trying to be her friend."

"Good. That will bring great relief to your mother."

Mason shook his head, but smiled. "But what about grace? God's mercy?"

"Mercy is God not punishing us as our sins deserve and grace is God blessing us in spite of the fact that we do not deserve it. And he does this for all of us. Our sins aren't any different than a person like Blaine. Our sins cause us to not deserve his mercy, but God blesses us with His grace. All of us. We just have to make that choice to accept it, admit we need it because of our sin, and then live as though it was the greatest blessing He's done for us, because it is.

"Blaine deserves the same mercy that He's given to us. Everyone does, but each person needs to accept it personally. That's where the rub comes in, Blaine doesn't feel worthy. Most people aren't that way. Many don't believe they need God's grace. Good people base their salvation on their goodness. And unfortunately, they live good lives. They help their neighbors, feeding the homeless, they're good parents, they love their children. Shoot, some even love their enemies. But you know what God says about that?"

"It's Satan's best lie to mankind."

"Yes it is, Mason. People rely on their goodness when the only good One is God. But that's a whole 'nother tangent. As far as Blaine goes, we need to concentrate on showing her God's love right now. That works better than anything else we can do. Callie is very, very good at doing that."

Mason nodded.

"Let's give mother the chance to try and let's support her in doing it, too."

Mason finished up the coffee in his mug. "I will try hard to help. And I'll also back off in showing any romantic love, but I have to admit it..."

Chuck looked at his son with compassion. He knew what he was about to say. "You like her, don't you? Because she's so pretty, or for what you find within?"

"I'll have to look harder."

Chuck nodded emphatically, "Exactly. Don't get ahead of the process. Share your faith with her. Then wait for Blaine's response."

"Many a woman, or even man for that matter, have changed their hearts and have the opportunity to experience God's grace fully. But we want Blaine to do it for herself, not just to have a chance to have a romantic relationship with a nice, good-looking guy."

Grinning for a moment, Mason's face turned serious. "I want that, too."

"Then start praying. It's so amazing to see God work in a person's life. She was at that train station in Chicago at just the right time, mother needed help, she had a heart attack on a train all alone...we all know those were not coincidences. Don't we? Mother is old enough to see how God works and she's confident in the process. Let's follow her example and trust God for the outcome."

Later that day, Callie called Blaine into her bedroom to comb out her hair. Blaine was good at fixing her hair. Amy had helped her wash it that morning, but as usual, it was unruly. No hairdresser would be open the week between Christmas and New Year in the small town.

Blaine had some hair products to tame Callie's frizzy hair. They hadn't been able to talk in privacy since Amy had arrived. Callie could also ask how she was feeling. It could be serious and Callie wanted to be prepared to help her.

Blaine tugged at her hair.

"Are you sure you're feeling up to helping me this morning?" Callie could see Blaine's expression in the mirror.

"I do feel a bit better." Blaine sighed. "I'm sure everything is fine."

Callie wanted to pursue that subject further, but hesitated. "Did you have a good Christmas, Blaine?" Callie had prayed hard that the day would be something special for her house guest. She didn't think of Blaine as her employee. In fact, she was pretty sure she'd never call her that.

She smiled, "You and your family have been so kind to me. I can't believe you even bought me presents." Blaine pulled a bit harder on the back of her head with her brush. "Callie, these curls are so stubborn."

"Yes dear, they are. Always have been." Callie jumped right in. "Like my soul."

"Callie, you're not stubborn."

Callie wanted to jerk around to tell Blaine the truth with her eyes, but she knew it wouldn't probably be a good idea with her curl entwined in a brush. "I've got you fooled, girl."

"I'm the stubborn one. I like my own way."

"We all do."

"I don't believe that about you or anyone in this family, Callie."

Callie couldn't help it. She turned in her chair. "This family isn't perfect. If we've given you that impression, we're not being honest."

"You all seem perfect to me." Blaine sat on the edge of the bed behind her. "Everyone's nice. I mean, you pray. You listen to nice music. You're kind to me. I'm a stranger but that doesn't mean you didn't include me on your family Christmas."

Callie needed to fix this issue. "We're far from perfect"

Blaine's eyes filled with tears, "I've never been around a family like yours, Callie. You've given me a job. Been very kind to me. Why would you do such a thing? Why would you find a stranger on a train and bring her into your home under the circumstances that you did for me?"

Here it was. It was the truth of why Callie had done it. "I'm going to tell you the reason, Blaine. The exact reason I plucked you from that train and brought you home from the hospital. I think God allowed me to be an invalid on that train for you, Blaine."

"For me? Why would God want you sick? For me?"

Callie squeezed the girl's hands. Blaine resembled a lost, lonely, and sad child. "Blaine, I think he prepared us to meet that day."

"Who?"

"God. Because if I hadn't gotten sick, in need of your help, I would have never met you."

Callie could see that Blaine was processing what she had said. "I guess you're right. Once you started talking to me, I did think about finding another seat on the train. I was so frustrated that day over Kyle. But Callie, I don't understand. Why would God make you sick on purpose?"

Callie smiled, "I don't know if God made me sick on purpose. Earth has been good to me, but I'm old. Getting older every day. I'm not even sure that I'll be here for another Christmas."

"Don't say that."

"But it could be true. You heard the doctor. My heart is getting tired. Worn out. I don't say that I know God's decisions. I'm not sure why I had a heart attack on that train, far away from my family, but I do know that if it weren't for that, you wouldn't be here now."

Blaine seemed to listen intently. "Maybe."

"Blaine. What were you running away from? Kyle? Or something more?"

Blaine's eyes glassed over, she seemed startled, not sure how to answer. "Why?"

"What was it that he wanted you to do?" Callie pleaded. She remembered the moment she'd heard the conversation between Blaine and Kyle at Union Station.

Should she tell Callie? What would her reaction be? Would she kick her out on the street? If Callie didn't, Blaine was pretty sure Amy would. Panic seized her heart. Whenever that happened, Blaine felt the only option was to lie.

"He wanted me to get fixed."

"What?"

"He wanted me to have my tubes tied or even better, have a hysterectomy. Although, I was pretty sure that a normal, regular doctor wouldn't do that to a healthy woman, especially my age, but who knows. Crazier things are done these days."

Callie kept prodding, "What did you think about that?"

Tears began streaming down Blaine's cheeks. "I didn't like it, but I didn't know what to do. Kyle was the only person in the world to care about me. I thought maybe it would be better if I did. But I couldn't believe he would ask me to do something so permanent.

He said he knew a doctor who would do it for me. For us? When I began questioning his motives, I suddenly realized how selfish it was on his part to ask me to do something like that. Why couldn't he do it? If he didn't want children, why couldn't he have it done? Right?"

"Absolutely." Callie reached behind her for a tissue from her vanity.

Callie reached up and pushed a piece hair off Blaine's face, tucking it behind one of her ears. "Sweet girl. You are so right."

"That's what he was asking of me when he dropped me off at the train station. I told him I had to go away to see family for Christmas, but I needed to leave him. Get away from him. The only way I could do that was to run. Does that make sense?" Blaine knew it didn't make sense, but Callie seemed to believe her. Guilt pierced her heart as she thought back to how many times she'd rehearsed this lie to assuage Callie.

Callie wasn't judging her. She could tell by the pity in her eyes.

"You were there. Right when I needed someone to take me in, because I have something else to confess to you."

"Go ahead, honey."

Should she add onto the story or be up front? "I have no one. I don't have family in Lapeer, like I told you on the train. I don't have a new nephew. The photo I showed you was from a friend of somebody I work with." Blaine took a deep breath. "I had nowhere else to turn. No place to go. No one to run to."

Callie handed Blaine a tissue. "Blaine?"

"Yes."

"You're not alone anymore. You have me. Chuck. Amy. And Mason."

Blaine wiped her eyes, but as the waves of cramps continued even after resting all night, her tears were real. She wondered if she should have told Callie everything, but lying had always been easier.

Mason had walked down the hallway to get something out of his father's suitcase. As he did, he heard Blaine pleading with Callie. She sounded emotional and very upset.

Stopping at Callie's bedroom door, he tried to listen, but could only hear muffled voices. Every once in a while he heard the name, *Kyle*.

He wanted to open the door. Why were they talking about him? What was it that bothered Blaine so much?

His hand went to the doorknob. He jumped when his dad put his hand on his shoulder.

"Mason. Let Nana handle this, okay?"

Mason sighed. Then nodded.

Chapter 18

Blaine came into the kitchen as Amy was setting the table for lunch.

"Can I help you?"

"Sure honey," Amy answered. She saw the redness around Blaine's eyes. "How are you feeling this morning, Blaine?"

Blaine turned from her, "Better."

Amy took a deep breath. Where was her mother?

"I think we'll need these smaller plates." She told Blaine as she went to the cupboards for dishes. "I'm still stuffed from yesterday, how about you?"

Blaine nodded, but said nothing.

Amy excused herself for a moment and went to the bedroom to find her mother.

She opened the door to her mother's room to find her leaning forward in her chair, with her head bowed. Her mother looked up startled. "Oh mother, I'm so sorry. Lunch is about ready."

Callie spoke softly, "I'll be there soon."

Amy nodded, letting the door shut slowly. Something must have happened with Blaine and her mother. Amy was beginning to like Blaine. She seemed to be a hard worker, and had tried hard to make it a nice Christmas for the family.

Amy had always been quick in being defensive when it came to her mother. It didn't help that her home was around the world from her. She never wanted anyone like Blaine to take advantage of her mother's kindness. Perhaps that's why she'd been so up front and cold toward Blaine.

It was wrong. She'd begun to see the subtle ways her mother influenced people and she always had admired her for it. Amy was so intent on helping her recover from her surgery, she'd forgotten the importance of her mother's usefulness.

She needed to change her attitude.

Chuck and Amy grew agitated with each other over the puzzle later that night. Blaine and Mason had driven into town.

"Why can't you share those pieces over there with me?" Amy pleaded.

Chuck sat up straight in his chair, "Cause I'm working on that section. It's my special project."

Amy rolled her eyes at him.

Callie felt a growing sense of need to share with them what Blaine had told her that day. She wanted them to know the desperation the woman felt and how important their family must be to her right now.

"Do you think he meant her to really have that kind of procedure done?" Amy couldn't be more incredulous.

"That's what I'm questioning. Why would a young man, Blaine's age, ask her to do something like that?"

Chuck seemed to not be listening, but concentrated on his little project until he added, "I believe it. The world has gone crazy. There are worse things happening around us than we could ever imagine."

Both woman agreed.

"I always thought the barbaric issues of where we live were harsh. There are things happening, here in the states, that are much worse. I'm not surprised at anything anymore."

"What do we do to help her?" Amy's eyes now showed the compassion Callie knew existed in her daughter's heart.

"Right now, we love her. I believe the child is an adult orphan, if that's even a term we can use. She's all alone. No one calls her. Have either of you heard her phone ring?"

Both Chuck and Amy shook their heads. "Only when Mason called her," added Amy. "Are you sure she has no family?"

"Pretty sure," Callie adjusted her knitting closer on her lap. "It makes me so sad. Can you imagine being that age and not having anyone in your life? I'm sure this Kyle fellow fills that need."

"I'm sorry, mother. I need to do better. Chuck said Mason realizes it now, too. Let's do our best to show her God's love. Sometimes it takes me longer than most to figure things out."

Callie smiled at her daughter. "Let's all pray and watch God work. I don't know the answer to any of this, but He does. Also, I'm not completely convinced that this is what that young man asked Blaine to do to make her run away from him. Something doesn't add up."

Blaine's pain was growing worse. She didn't know what was wrong. Thankfully, Mason had driven them into town. "Mason, I'm not feeling well. Can you drive us home?"

Mason was standing in front of the ice cream display in the frozen food section. He'd been asking her what flavor she wanted, mint chocolate or chocolate. "Um...sure."

As Blaine turned toward the exit, she felt pressure and much more pain. She leaned forward.

"Blaine, what's wrong?"

Squeezing her eyes shut, she held on to Mason and waited for the wave of pain to pass. "I'm okay. I just need to get back to Callie's."

Mason placed the items they were going to buy on a nearby shelf. "C'mon let's go." He seemed to understand something was wrong.

Blaine moved slow, not letting go of Mason's jacket. "Here, let me help you." Mason grabbed her arm.

She nodded.

Mason put his arm around the back of her waist and supported her. "Lean on me."

At that moment, Blaine was thankful he was beside her. The pain was growing more intense. What was happening? Something was definitely wrong.

Mason helped her into the passenger seat. He rushed back to the driver's side, fumbling with the keys in his hand. After starting it, being in a rush, the car lurched backward out of the space.

Blaine winced.

"I'm sorry, Blaine. I'll get you home."

The store was just blocks from Callie's house. The pain had subsided, but as Blaine tried to relax, something began to soak through her jeans. She could feel it. Had she wet her pants? What would she do now? Her face grew flush.

"Mason, please hurry."

"I am, Blaine. Almost there."

As soon as Mason put the car into park in Callie's driveway, he jumped out and approached Blaine's side of the car.

Blaine responded with embarrassment as he helped her out of the car. "I think I've made a mess in the seat."

Mason didn't know what to say. "It's okay. Let's get you into the house."

As they entered the back door, Mason steadied Blaine. Each step seemed to put her in more pain. She almost completely stopped walking as they crept up the sidewalk. Mason didn't know what else to do, but screamed for his Dad.

The closed windows and door brought no help. Blaine continued to gradually make it to the door inside the garage. "Almost there."

As he stepped back to allow Blaine through the door first, he yelled for his Dad again. This time brought his father running through the kitchen. "Dad, where's Mom?"

Chuck yelled over his shoulder for Amy. Blaine stood at the back door, bent over in pain.

"Something's terribly wrong, she seems to be in a lot of pain."

Amy came around the corner and immediately went to Blaine. "Honey, what's wrong?" Placing her arm around her waist as Mason had done, Blaine leaned into her.

"I'm sorry. Something's very wrong."

Chuck was the first to speak. "Let's get you to your room."

"I think I need to use-" Blaine moaned.

"Get her into the bathroom!" Amy stepped back as Chuck picked up Blaine and began rushing down the hallway.

Mason came around behind them. Callie gave him a scared look from her chair. "Mason?"

"I don't know what's wrong, Nana. She said she wasn't feeling well at the store. We were choosing a flavor of ice cream and then she could barely stand."

As they rushed Blaine down the hallway, Mason looked at his Nana. Tears filled her eyes. "I think she might be having a miscarriage."

Mason looked at his nana. "What?"

Blaine had never felt such excruciating pain. As she leaned against the sink she felt more pressure. Looking up at Amy she knew she had to tell her the secret.

Amy's eyes didn't reveal shock. She nodded, "You're pregnant, aren't you honey?"

Blaine started to sob. "Yes."

"It's okay," Amy rubbed her back. "I'm here. I've been through this. I won't leave you." Amy held her hand through every wave of pain. She rubbed her back. Chuck handed her a blanket she'd asked him to bring and Amy wrapped her in it, but didn't leave her side. As the pain increased, Amy did her best to talk her through it all. "Blaine, I'm pretty sure you're having a miscarriage."

Blaine began to cry harder. "No. I don't want to lose this baby."

"I'm sorry, Blaine. I'll be right here with you, if you want me to."

Blaine was so afraid. Her legs shook, her body soaked with sweat. She nodded. "I'm sorry."

"It's not your fault. Everything will be okay."

"Don't leave me," Blaine pleaded.

"I promise you, I won't." Amy kept assuring her with kind words and assurance. There were even moments that she could overhear Amy pray. Prayers for comfort, strength, and even that she'd be able to help Blaine. Everything seemed to go in slow motion. The pain grew in intensity. Minutes passed, then perhaps hours. Blaine knew that she'd never experienced anything so painful.

Callie or Chuck would tap on the door and ask if they needed anything. Whenever Amy asked for something, it would soon be handed to her, then the door would shut again.

At one point, Chuck whispered something to Amy. Amy shook her head. She smiled down at Blaine. "Let's keep her comfortable. As soon as it's over and if needed, we'll get her to a hospital."

Hours later, the pain began to subside. Amy hadn't left her alone. She'd been beside her the entire time. She wiped off Blaine's forehead and helped her take a shower. At first, Blaine was embarrassed but the pain had been so bad, she was thankful Amy hadn't left her side.

As the hot water spilled over her body she realized that now everyone knew. The agony in her body was replaced by shock, and even disappointment. She wanted nothing more than to protect and love this child. It would have been something for her to cherish. Despite the fact that she would have been alone with no way to support a child, Blaine wanted someone to love and to love her back. And look what happened, she couldn't even do that right.

Chapter 19

The next morning, the house was quiet. Everyone was sleeping late. Blaine had been put to bed after two in the morning, everyone was exhausted and had headed to bed without much conversation. From the couch, Mason heard his mother check on Blaine throughout the rest of the night.

The remnants of the night's chaos were strewn through the kitchen as Mason got up around ten to make himself coffee. Cups filled with cold coffee and half empty water bottles were everywhere. Piles of towels had been placed in laundry baskets at the top of the stairs.

Mason was in shock. He had no clue Blaine was hiding this secret from everyone, but Nana knew. Why hadn't she told anyone?

There were so many questions. So much to think about. What would happen today? Would Blaine stay with them?

He began to get food out of the refrigerator. Everyone would need a good breakfast. He was good at making scrambled eggs. Searching through Nana's freezer, he found some bacon. He could fix food. He pulled out the toaster and a loaf of bread as Chuck walked into the kitchen.

"Good morning."

All he could do was nod. Chuck came up from behind him and patted his shoulder. "We didn't know, Mason."

Mason turned, "Nana knew. Why didn't she tell us?"

Chuck shrugged. "I don't know, but I'm sure she had her reasons."

"I'll help you with breakfast."

Amy woke up shortly before noon. Going in to check on Blaine, she found her still sleeping. It was a good sign. Callie was knitting in a chair beside her bed.

They whispered good morning to each other.

"I'll stay here and knit today. Go get yourself something to eat." Callie spoke softly.

Heading into the kitchen, Chuck greeted her with a kiss and a hug.

Amy topped Mason's head with a kiss as she sat down at the table with them.

"I made you a plate, Mom. Want me to warm it up?"

Amy nodded. She was hungry.

Mason delivered a steaming plate and placed it in front of her. She thanked him.

As she bowed her head to pray, she thanked God for the provisions of the day and even through the night. As she opened her eyes, both men asked her almost simultaneously, "What now?"

She dug her fork into the yellow pile of eggs. "I don't know. We'll watch her today. If the pain starts up again, we'll probably need to get her to a hospital."

Both men nodded.

"I'm sorry, Mom. I'm sure this isn't quite what you had in mind when you returned home."

Amy smiled, "It's okay. I'm happy God had me home to help her. She had a hard time. What if it had been just Mother and her? Mother would have been beside herself."

Both men agreed.

"Mother was right."

Chuck added, "Blaine needs us."

Amy smiled. "Yes she does. I'm thankful God allowed me to help her."

Blaine opened her eyes to see Callie in the chair of her room, busy knitting. Reality of what had happened the night before struck her with force. She felt so empty. "Callie, what are you doing here?"

Callie stopped knitting, "Good morning."

"How long have you been here?"

"Just a few hours."

"Hours?" Blaine tried to set up in the bed, but her body protested.

"Are you hungry? Are you in any pain?"

The pain from the night before haunted her. She'd never felt such horrible pain. "I'm just sore."

"That's normal. Blaine..." tears filled Callie's eyes, "...I'm so sorry, honey."

"Are you mad that I didn't tell you?"

Callie set her knitting aside, gradually got to her feet with the help of her walker and came to Blaine's side. Picking up her hand, Callie rubbed it. "I knew."

Blaine was shocked, "What?"

"I knew you were pregnant. Or I guess, I suspected it."

"How?"

"Trips to the bathroom. The morning we were making that grocery list and I heard you throwing up. I'd put all the subtle hints together and I knew." Callie took her hand and wiped Blaine's cheek with the back of it. "It doesn't really matter, does it?"

Tears now filled Blaine's eyes. "I'm sorry. I should have told you."

"Like I said, it doesn't matter. You didn't hurt me by not telling me. It's okay."

Blaine relaxed into her bed. "You've been so good to me. I don't deserve you."

Without hesitation, Callie responded with tears streaming down her wrinkled cheeks, "We love you, Blaine. God has taught me to love each one he puts in my path. This was your turn and I'm so happy He allowed me to do it."

Blaine did her best to eat the meal brought to her that evening, but she just wasn't hungry. She hated to not eat any of it, as if she were ungrateful.

Soon Amy came in for the tray of dishes. Looking at the uneaten food, she asked Blaine. "Are you okay, honey? You didn't eat anything."

Blaine lowered her eyes. "I'm sorry, Mrs. McAnder. My stomach is still a bit upset. I'm not very hungry."

Amy took the tray and placed it on the dresser behind her. She reached for the chair beside Blaine's bed and asked, "Blaine, can I sit with you for a bit."

Blaine didn't know what to say, but she nodded. She didn't really feel like talking and she was a bit embarrassed over the intimate moments Amy and she had shared the night before.

Amy sat down. "Last night was so hard for you. I'm so sorry you had to go through that."

Blaine scooted up higher in her bed, "I'm sorry you had to be the one to help me. I'm sure it was as uncomfortable for you as it was for me."

"But I'm very happy I could be here to help you. Mother would have been a frantic mess and if it were just Mason..." Amy looked out the window. "Let's just say, God planned it to happen and for me to be here when it did."

Amy looked at her with loving eyes. "I know I haven't been that nice to you while you've been staying with mother and I really want to apologize for that."

Blaine started to protest, but Amy stopped her.

"No...please give me a chance to apologize. I didn't realize the condition you were in and mother didn't even tell me she knew. If I'd have known I would have realized why you needed her. Why you needed a safe place to be. I'm so happy mother followed God's leading to have you spend Christmas with us. You're a sweet girl and I am sorry you had to go through a miscarriage. It's a hard time in a woman's life and often we just don't understand the reasons why it has to happen."

Blaine shook her head. "I don't. I wanted this baby. I know I'm not married and that it probably wasn't the best time to have one, but it happened. One of the main reasons I left Chicago was because my boyfriend wasn't as excited as I was."

Amy took Blaine's hand in her own. "I can't imagine feeling so alone at a time like this."

"Why are you all so nice? I'm not a good person. I don't deserve you being so kind to me."

"None of us deserve anything we get. I don't deserve my mother who loves me. A husband who supports me, or a son who is one of the best a mother could ask for. But you, my precious girl, deserves kindness. From all of us. And again, I apologize for my actions."

Amy scooted her chair away. "Blaine, it is hard to lose a baby. I've been through it. It's sad, hard, and the ache goes on until God allows another small child to fill your lonely arms. I pray that God will allow you the opportunity to have another child again. Someday." Amy stood to leave. "It's okay to be angry at the situation. It's okay to hurt. If you need to talk about it, please ask me. I'll listen. I promise. And without any kind of judgment. Okay?"

Tears filled Blaine's eyes, but she nodded. "Okay."

Mason had to get on his computer and check out the latest accounts he'd failed to finish before heading home for Christmas. He could only do this without interruptions and as everyone napped that afternoon, he found his chance.

"Work?" Nana had asked him out of frustration. "You're on vacation."

"I didn't get all my accounts completed before leaving town on Saturday. I'm sorry Nana. I'll finish it as quickly as I can." Mason patted Nana's wrinkled hand. Now she was in her chair in the living room resting, too.

His mother had been busy all morning washing linens and towels. As she came through the kitchen she found Mason and his computer at the table.

Mason smiled at her. "Are you almost finished?"

She placed the basket at her feet, sat down and began folding laundry at the kitchen table. "Just about. One more load to finish drying." Pulling a towel out of the basket, she snapped it in place, ready to fold.

"I shouldn't do this here, you need to work."

Mason chided her, "It's fine. But you should be taking a nap, too."

She shook her head. "I'll catch up tonight."

"I'm sure Blaine really appreciates all your help."

"She did all the hard part, I just helped her."

"I'm sure it was hard to watch her go through it."

His mother picked up another towel and folded it, "It's never a pleasant thing to watch. Life is leaving a woman's body. For whatever reason, God knows what is best. Sometimes the baby isn't forming well or could have major health complications. It's another reminder for us that God is in control of death and life."

"Well I know one thing that's for sure." Mason typed in a few more numbers.

"What's that, sweetheart."

"I'm glad I'm a man."

Mason's mother giggled. He'd always loved hearing his mother laugh. Life had been too difficult in the past twenty-four hours.

"What are we going to do now?" Mason stopped his typing.

"About?"

"Blaine. Who will take care of Nana now?"

"It won't take long for Blaine to recover. We'll be here another week or two and can help mother until then."

Mason nodded.

"I'm much more confident about Blaine's caregiving abilities. She was a good choice, Mason, despite what I first thought. She seems to care for your Nana and that's a blessing."

"But what about after that? Do you think Blaine will continue to stay with her?"

His mother put the last folded towel on the pile she now had made on the table. "I don't know, Mason. We'll have to wait and see." Picking up the folded towels she added, "I'm gonna check in on Blaine now. You get back to work."

Mason nodded and dug into the other file waiting to be processed.

Chapter 20

That evening, everyone gathered in the living room. Nana had gone back into Blaine's room and was helping her to get comfortable for the night.

Mason's dad was back at working on the family puzzle. They had nearly finished it the evening before. It had been better than pacing the hallway.

Mason brought up the subject of Nana's care. "She's not young. She's struggles getting around the house. I knew this day would be coming but now, it's here. I guess I was one of those who thought she was invincible, but these past weeks have proven she isn't."

His dad fumbled with a puzzle piece, holding it up to the light. "They don't stay young forever. We've been considering the options at our end, too, Mason. Perhaps we need to take a leave for a bit. Stay here instead of going back."

"That's not an option. You've got too many things happening at the mission base right now. You need to be there." Mason knew it wouldn't be popular, but he'd been thinking about his decision ever since he'd left Nana at the hospital right after her heart attack. "I need to go back to Chicago for a bit. If you guys can stay with Nana for a few more days, I need to take care of some business."

"What business?" His dad looked up.

Mason leaned forward. "I'm unhappy at work. I've been that way for a while. I work long hours. Most of them I don't get paid for because I'm salary. I'm not ungrateful, but there isn't anyone above me that plans on retiring anytime soon. This is a dead-end job. I can see it clearly now. I'm not sure about my decision yet, but I want to head back to Chicago to check on a few things."

Mason's mother seemed about to speak, but when her husband covered her hand with his own, she went back to finding a puzzle piece. "We trust you and your decisions, Mason. Just don't do anything in a hurry. Pray about all your moves."

Mason nodded. "I know, Dad. I will."

Mason went to Blaine's room that night. Softly knocking, he found her fiddling with her phone. "Want some company?"

She blushed, but scooted up in the bed and nodded.

"How are you feeling tonight?"

"Tired, but better."

"I'm sorry you had to go through that. I'm also...," Mason took a deep breath, "sorry about the baby."

Blaine's eyes grew moist, "Thank you. I'm sorry I didn't tell anyone."

Mason waved at her, "It really wasn't any of our business." Mason pulled up a chair and sat beside the bed. "I came in tonight to tell you that I'm headed back to Chicago tomorrow."

Blaine scooted higher in the bed, "Tomorrow? Why? I thought you had the whole week off."

"I do. That's why I need to head back. I've got some things I need to do."

"Okay."

"My parents are going to stay here for a few more weeks to help Nana until you feel up to getting around better. Mom said you should be up and about in a few days."

Blaine rubbed her forehead. "I feel like such a burden."

Mason fumbled with a part of the blanket. "You're not a burden, Blaine. I hope you know that by now."

"I'm a stranger to all of you, yet you've all been so kind."

Mason grew nervous. "I know we don't know you very well, but Nana loves you. She cares about you. I know that seems a bit foreign or odd, but my Nana doesn't take things like this lightly."

"Mason?"

Blaine hesitated as if unsure of what she wanted to say. "I've felt compelled to tell you why I decided to take up Callie's offer to become her caregiver. Can I do that?"

Mason nodded.

"Remember how I told you about living with my grandmother when I was a teenager?"

"Yes."

Blaine took a deep breath, "I was a horrible teenager. I was dumped into her lap when my aunt decided she didn't want me influencing her kids. My grandmother didn't have a choice, but took me in to live with her. She resented it from the first moment." Blaine waved the thought away, like it wasn't important. "My life has always been hard. My mother tried to live a normal life, but that wasn't who she was or even could try to be. In spite of her efforts to keep us normal, we weren't. My life was never like yours." Blaine wiped her eyes with a tissue. "I haven't told many people about my life growing up. I often went hungry. My clothes..." Blaine's hand moved down the front of her shirt, "...were always dirty. If it hadn't been for my grandmother, I wouldn't probably be here at all.

"She stepped in when she knew my mother couldn't. For some reason, she felt responsible for me," Blaine blew her nose. "Other people don't realize the heartache of living in a dysfunctional family. You have no idea what it's like."

"You're right, I don't."

"On the days when Mom would bring home strangers, usually men, I'd have to cower or hide in a bedroom. If they found me, she'd distract, kiss, or prod them to follow her. I didn't realize it at the time, but being a little girl, I assumed she didn't want to be around me. Now I believe it was her way of protecting me. If nothing else, it helps me cope with my childhood."

Blaine met Mason's eyes, "I made up stories about my life so people wouldn't realize I was poor. I envisioned a normal life and my lies made it almost believable."

Mason couldn't take his eyes off Blaine.

"I'm a liar." Blaine took a huge breath. "I lie to have people see me in a different light. It got me the attention I wanted and sometimes needed. That's been my normal for so long, I have a hard time seeing reality."

Mason took her hand. He wanted to tell her how sorry he was and to make it better for Blaine, but her life held more heartache than he'd experienced in his life.

Blaine pulled her hand away. "I know you're thinking that I'm this nice person who only wanted to help Callie at a train station and for once, that's true, but Mason I've done some pretty horrible things in my life.

"One of them included neglecting my grandmother at the end of her life. She put up with me as a teenager and all I wanted to do was run away. I've spent times in homeless shelters, at the city's rescue mission, on the streets. Then one day, while waitressing, I met Kyle. He soon asked me to live with him." Blaine shrugged. "I know that it's not the right thing to do, but it was a roof over my head. I knew he didn't really love me because he always wanted to change me.

"I was in a bad way when Callie found me." Blaine now had tears streaming down her face. "Pregnant. He told me that we could make it work and for a while I believed him...until...I realized he was doing his best to convince me to have an abortion."

Blaine looked at Mason for a reaction. All Mason could do was shake his head.

"He told me it was the best thing for us. We could do it over a weekend and by Monday...everything would be normal again. Just like before." Blaine wiped her eyes. "But I felt protective. For once, I felt like my mother, doing her best to keep me safe. But Mason, I did consider it. I really did."

Mason nodded.

"Then as Christmas approached, I just couldn't. He'd convinced me to go that next weekend and have it done. I was close to six weeks along." Blaine twisted the tissue in her hands. "He was right. We could do it and just go on with life, but that's when I decided to get away. Run. I had to think and I knew I couldn't do that staying with Kyle. He'd almost convinced me to go through with his plan. But Mason...after I met Callie and she told me her story about Miles, I realized something.

"They loved each other with a love that I'd never heard of and amazingly, they survived some hard things. I wanted to get to know Callie more and what had driven her to love a broken man and to be faithful to him for so many years. He wasn't good to her for a while, yet she still hung on and loved him through his difficult years after the war. What kind of love is that?" Blaine questioned Mason through a lost look in her eyes.

She continued as if her life depended on him knowing everything about her. "I'm not sure what you want from me and I know you're expecting me to be something that I'm not. But what I really am is a thief and a liar. I've done things I'm ashamed of, but at the time, I didn't realize they were wrong. Sometimes it was just to find shelter at someone's house, or a little money in my wallet.

"I'm telling you all of this because I want to be here for Callie. As long as she needs me. If only to ease the ache in my heart of neglecting my own grandmother. She died two months after I left her. She died alone. I never spoke to her again."

Blaine turned back to Mason, "I didn't even go back when a friend told me she'd died. I'm not even sure how she was buried, or even if anyone was there to attend a funeral. You would never do that to your nana, Mason."

Mason had no words and a lump in his throat. He couldn't relate to it or understand a life like she'd lived.

Blaine pushed her hair back, tucking it under her head, "I'd hoped I could make Callie's life easier. I could somehow make it up to my own grandmother by taking care of her." Blaine shifted in bed, "I just needed you to know all of that. I'm tired of lying. Pretending. But when it comes to Callie I'm very serious. I want to take care of her, Mason. Will you and your parents still let me do that?"

"I can't answer for my parents, Blaine, but I think Nana would like nothing better than to have you stay here."

"Like I said, I'm tired of lying, but more than anything I'm tired of running away. I want to stop."

All Mason could do was nod.

When Mason left her room, Blaine felt a rush of relief. She'd been truthful. She wasn't sure what Mason thought of her, but for once in her life, she'd shared something important to someone who cared about her. It was an amazing new moment for Blaine, yet no one else would probably understand.

Blaine hoped the family would allow her to continue to care for Callie. The act might not redeem her, but it would bring her a sense of finally growing up. She did not want to live a life like her mother or grandmother, she wanted something more.

Callie had gone to bed a little early to catch up on some reading. The night before had tired her out and she knew if she relaxed a bit before bed, she'd fall asleep easier. Someone knocked on her door.

"Nana, are you awake?"

Callie heard Mason from the doorway and stirred, "I'm awake, come in sweetheart."

Her grandson came toward the bed.

Callie tried to push herself up to a seated position. "Is everything okay? I saw you were in talking to Blaine. Sit down here beside me."

Callie scooted over as Mason crawled in beside her. Mason had done this for years, she loved it. Even at his age.

"What's on your mind?" Callie picked up Mason's hand and held it. There were so many times this had happened in their life together. Oh how she loved this boy who was now a man!

"Nana. I'm not here to ask your permission, but I have something to tell you."

Callie took a swig of water from a glass on her night stand. This conversation could get dicey. To add to the thought she said, "Do I need something stronger than water."

Mason's laughed, "Like what?"

"Orange juice or some of that punch your Mother made us on Christmas day."

"It was just orange juice and Vernors."

"I know, but punch none the less." She winked at him.

"Okay, now try to be serious. I've made a decision."

Sighing, Callie knew it must include her somehow. He wasn't as open about his life, unless somehow it included her.

"I'm moving back to Michigan. Until I find a place of my own, can I live here with you for just a while?"

"What?" Callie wasn't sure if she heard him right, "Why?"

"You need me."

"I do not..." even before she could add the rest, Mason put his finger to her lips.

"I told you, I wasn't asking your permission."

"Mason, are you sure? What about your job? Your life there?"

"Life is wherever your loved ones are."

Callie knew she should put up a fuss. Stop him. Ridicule him for even thinking about doing something so unselfish, but as she looked into the eyes of the young man who most resembled Miles, she knew better than to even try.

"As far as Blaine goes, she needs you Nana."

Callie smiled. "I know honey."

"More than ever now. She thinks because we all know the truth about her life now, that somehow we won't want her staying here to take care of you. You still want her here, don't you?"

Callie had been contemplating the answer for a long time, but now knew she needed to confide in her grandson. "To be honest, I wasn't sure she would even want to stay."

Mason put his hand underneath his head, so he could see Nana's face better. "Because of her circumstances?"

"More than that, she hid the truth from us. It's hard to trust someone like that."

Mason agreed. "Are you afraid of her?"

"No," Callie thought through her response carefully. "I just need to be able to trust her. Do you think I can do that?"

After his recent discussion with Blaine, he was pretty sure she would be trying harder to not lie. "I'm pretty sure she will be better about being more honest, after this."

"I need to pray about it some more. And as for you coming back here to live near me, I couldn't be happier, but please, please don't do it just for me. Seek out what God wants for your life, Mason."

"I already have." Mason leaned over and kissed her cheek.

Chapter 21

Mason worked long into the night. He'd been able to finish the last account before leaving for Chicago.

He thought again about the decision he'd made that afternoon. Nana would need a family member closer than Chicago. His lease was almost up on his apartment. He could easily move his stuff back to Michigan and live with Nana for a while until he could find a job closer. There really wasn't anything tying him to Chicago. Yes, he liked it there, but there had to be other jobs closer to Nana.

He thought of Miguel and his comment at the hot dog stand back in Chicago. He'd ask him about the possible job connection. Perhaps that was where he could start.

As he shut down his computer and slipped it into its leather case, his mother strolled into the kitchen tying her robe around her waist.

"Mom. What are you doing awake?"

"Oh you know." She pulled a chair out from the table and sat down across from Mason. "I have this insatiable urge to fix everything for God." She gave him an embarrassed expression and shrugged her shoulders.

"I wouldn't be trying that if I were you."

"Oh how I know that," she rubbed her eyes, "but if I don't try, He'd wonder what had finally snapped in me to believe that He is able to manage all of my problems as well as the entire world...all by Himself. I thought maybe a couple of ibuprofen tablets would help me sleep so my imagination would stop stomping through my brain." She tapped the top of his leather computer bag, "Are you all done? It's..." picking up Mason's phone she thumbed the button, "two a.m."

"I'm done, but could you talk something through with me?"

She tipped her chin up, "Is something wrong?"

"I've been thinking it might be a good idea if I quit my job in Chicago."

That seemed to get her attention. "Mason, why would you do something like that?" His mother gave him an incredulous stare. "Hold that thought for a moment. I need a glass of water and these two tablets." Mason watched his mother get some water and gulp down the medicine. "What's brought about this decision?"

Mason leaned back in the kitchen chair and crossed his arms, "I don't know. Nana needs me. I've been thinking about it before I came home for Christmas."

His mother took a sip of her water. "I thought you loved Chicago."

"Yeah, I do. But I also like the hometown feel here. With Nana."

"Well Mason, good jobs are hard to find."

"I know, but it isn't far to Flint or even Lansing. I could find another job closer. I'm sure. In my line of work, jobs are easy to find."

"I hate to have you throw out this past year's efforts."

"Yeah, I know. But like I said, I'm not really sure it's getting me anywhere. My boss continues to give me more and more work that I can't possibly finish in a normal forty-hour work week. There are many assignments he could be helping me with, but instead he places them all in my lap and if I don't come through and meet his deadlines, well then, I'm not pulling my weight."

"Okay, well I have to ask this."

Mason leaned forward. "What?"

His mother squinted at him. Whenever she did that, he knew she was trying to come up with the best question to ask.

"Just say it, Mom."

"This doesn't have to do anything with Blaine, does it?"

"Blaine?"

His mother lowered her glasses on her nose, "Mason?"

"No." He raised his hands in defense.

"If she stays here with mother, you'll be closer to her."

"I was trying to decide about it while Nana was visiting me in Chicago before Christmas. Even before Blaine was on the scene. She seemed extra frail and I knew that she would soon be needing my help. Although," Mason leaned back in his chair again. "I didn't think it would be as soon as right now, but that's life, right?"

"Are you leveling with me?"

Mason knew he couldn't hold back anything from his mother. "Life is fragile. Just like what happened to Blaine last night. We won't have Nana with us forever and I want to be able to enjoy helping her as long as I can. I can't do that living and working in Chicago."

"Truly?"

Mason raised his right hand, showing three fingers. "Scout's honor."

His mother shook her head, "We want you to choose wisely. I mean, really, do we know that much about Blaine yet?"

Mason agreed. They hadn't known her long. "But she's so pretty, Mom."

Mason's mother shook her head, "Mason!"

Mason smirked. "Sorry, I knew that one would get you."

"I trust your judgment about your job. It's your life, not mine. But Blaine. You need to be careful. Don't toy with her heart."

Mason picked up a pen and scribbled on a note pad beside his computer. "I know, Mom, I know. Also, I'll be talking to Blaine later this afternoon, she wants to stay here and help Nana. Are you willing to allow her to do that?" Before she could answer, Mason continued. "She seems to have come out of some kind of horrific relationship in Chicago. I now know why she left him. I agree more than ever Nana was right, she needs us.

"Lately, I've thought life is confusing, but Blaine's life has revealed to me that I've taken my own life for granted. I haven't had a hard life. I'm thankful for your influence, but also Nana's."

"I'm not sure it's up to us. It's Nana's decision, but I'll talk to your Dad." His mother stood up and placed her empty glass on the counter. "Now let me get back to bed. God and I have more things to sort out before I can get some sleep."

Blaine was up and dressed the next day. Everyone seemed thrilled to have her back up and eating at the table with them.

She was glad to be out of bed. Still sore, her pain had gone away, but her heart still ached from the loss. How could she be so attached to a child she'd never seen? It seemed crazy, yet she couldn't convince her heart. She felt like crying. All the time.

"I hope the weather stays good for your travels, Mason." Chuck said as he scraped his bowl of oatmeal clean.

Blaine's fears were confirmed. Mason's leaving this week seemed odd to her. Why was he returning to Chicago so soon? Was it the other girl? He hadn't said anything more about her. Perhaps she shouldn't have told him some of her life's story. Her emotions were in turmoil. Yet, she knew she'd finally done something right. She'd been honest and if that meant Mason was convinced to go back to Chicago, perhaps that was for the best.

Callie grabbed Blaine's hand, "As soon as you are up to it, let's rethink this caregiving situation."

Blaine held her breath.

"I think I need a companion more than a caregiver. Do you still want to stay here with me?"

Releasing her breath, Blaine relaxed. "I would like nothing better, Callie."

Mason smiled across the table at her.

Chapter 22

Mason decided to head back to Chicago early the next morning. He wanted to get some things packed up and give his notice. Nana protested a bit; but she also was thankful.

He also had asked everyone to keep it a secret from Blaine. He wanted to tell her himself once it was all over and solidified. If she knew, she might think he was returning home to take over her job.

Chuck and Amy had a few people they wanted to visit that afternoon after dropping Mason off at the train station. Blaine got settled in the living room with Callie. They were both enjoying the quietness and comfort of warm blankets.

"Blaine, you're so quiet. You know how I like to talk." She smiled at the subdued woman across the room.

"Just tired, I guess."

"Blaine, can I ask you something?"

Blaine's face went pale, taking a deep breath.

"I don't mean to be nosey or anything, but what are your dreams in life? What do you want to do?"

"Why do you want to know?"

"Most young women your age know exactly what they want. Don't they?"

Blaine shook her head. "Callie, I'm not like others. What is there to look forward to? Lately, life just makes me tired. And now, after losing the baby..." Blaine began to cry.

Callie knew this moment would come. She knew Blaine needed to talk through her grief. "It's okay, honey. Tell me what you're thinking about."

Blaine wiped her face with the edge of her blanket. "I'm sorry Callie. All I want to do is cry."

"It's perfectly normal. You've just suffered a great loss. You need time to deal with it."

"How can some women so easily cast it off as nothing?"

Callie shook her head. "I don't know."

"As odd as it seems, I wanted that baby." Blaine cried some more. "I wanted it so bad."

"Can you tell me why?"

"It would have been mine. All mine. I would have had someone to love and someone to love me back. That isn't too hard to understand, is it?"

Callie shook her head. "Not at all, Blaine. That's very understandable."

"I'm sorry I didn't tell you about it. I truly am."

"Blaine, if you're going to be staying here with me, I need you to know that it is okay to tell me the truth. I need to know the truth about you."

Blaine nodded, "I know Callie. I'm so sorry I didn't tell you that I was pregnant."

"Not so much that, but about your life. I want to share in your life. That's why I don't want you to think of yourself as a caregiver anymore. My employee. I want to be your friend. Even more than that, I want you to feel like I'm your nana, too. Do you think we can get to that point?"

Blaine stopped crying and looked at Callie. "Are you serious?"

"Very." Callie got up from her chair and sat on the couch next to Blaine. "Honey, more than anything I want you to know how much I care about you."

"But you don't even know me."

"I know, because you won't let me get to know you."

Blaine seemed to think about that for a while.

"Please be honest. Don't hold anything back. We want to love you Blaine, whoever you are. We don't care what you've been through or what you have done in the past. We want to be close to you, but you have to let us."

Blaine leaned into Callie. No one had ever asked her to do that before. She was shocked.

Callie took Blaine's hand in her own and patted it, "I knew it the moment you descended the stairs at Union Station. Your heart is so hurt and it seems you just can't look beyond tomorrow. Why won't you let me help you?"

Blaine couldn't look at Callie. Did she really want Callie's help? She was an old woman. "I don't know. You don't understand my life." She pulled her hand from Callie's. "Why do you get the impression that I even need your help?"

"I'm sure you don't need me at all, but I do want to help."

Callie wasn't going to back off. Even though, that's all Blaine wanted her to do, yet her thoughts tormented her. Could she share with Callie how she was really feeling?

"Callie, I've lived my whole life alone. Sure, I had people around me, but no one cared about me. Do you know that this is the first Christmas I asked for a present and got what I asked for? I'm twenty-two years old. Before you, no one bothered to ask me what I wanted for Christmas. What does that say about my life?"

Callie interrupted her. "It says you've had to live a very sad, hard life."

Blaine covered her face with her hands. "You want me to be completely honest. That's very hard for me. I'm sorry, I'm used to lying. It's what I do."

"Let's start there then, can you tell me what you want for your life? What is one of your biggest dreams?"

Blaine lowered her hands and looked at the woman who seemed to really care about her. She thought a moment about what to say. She decided to do exactly what Callie wanted. "I want to meet a man like Mason. I want nothing more than to find someone who can truly love me for who I am and then I want to have children."

Callie didn't hesitate, "That's a wonderful dream. There is nothing wrong with a dream like that."

"Except one thing."

Callie cocked her head, "What?"

"I'm not worthy of someone like Mason or anyone for that matter. I'm damaged goods. I don't deserve happiness like that. You have no idea what I'm really like. Until this Christmas, I didn't know what it was like to even see a man who might be good for me, let alone good to me. I didn't even know how to look for one. I've never done anything that I'm even slightly proud of. Ever."

"Well, perhaps now is a good time to start." Callie took her hand again and squeezed it. "You know, when I saw you in the station God placed you not only in my life, but on my heart. He encouraged me to talk to you. Do you know that you were the absolute first person I ever told my love story to? Why would I do that to a stranger? Yet I couldn't stop myself. It just all spilled out. Every single wonderful thing, but also...the bad. Miles wasn't a perfect man when I married him, but neither was I...a perfect woman. It took us over sixty years to become even fit for each other. That's a long time of changing, adjusting, and becoming accustomed to loving a person.

"The movies have it all wrong. Women don't just find a cute guy and fall in love. Falling in love takes a lifetime. It doesn't happen in the first month, year, or sometimes in the first five years. It takes nights of pacing the floor wondering if they'll come home after an argument. It includes those fights that neither one changes the other's mind about regarding finances, food, or even how to raise a child. It's the trips to the emergency room in a panic, the worry of having a medical test go wrong, it's in the little things like sleeping with them when they snore. All of that happens and before you know it, you realize that you don't want to live without that person. He becomes a part of you. So tight that no one can pull you apart. That's what love is." Callie sighed, "Hallmark has it all wrong."

Blaine smirked, yet tears trickled down her cheeks.

"Blaine, I'm not sure if your dream will come true. Only God knows that." Callie waved her finger, "I do have a feeling you want to change, if you want to start anew, today is the day to do it. You don't have to live like you have in the past. You can change, Blaine. You can change as Miles did so long ago. Remember?"

"Yes."

"And you know what will come with that change?"

Blaine shrugged.

"A new way to look at things. A new perspective. And better yet, good choices. Choices that will make you happier and stop the cycle of abuse and frustration you've had your whole life. Does that make sense?"

"I don't know if I have it in me."

251

"You probably don't." Callie sat back in her chair.

"That's harsh!"

"You can't change so drastically without help."

Standing up, Callie shuffled to her table and picked up her Bible from the table beside it and walked back. "See how far I just walked. On my own." The old woman sat down again. "Can I read to you some verses?"

Before Blaine could answer, Callie added. "Listen to this."

Callie began to read things like *'becoming a new creature'* and *'behold all things will become new.'* Then she added things like, *'God is love,' 'God so loved you,'* and *'He cares for you.'*

Blaine had never heard words like that. She was skeptical. She'd never thought about God or what He thought about her. She never really cared. But she did know one thing to be sure, Callie believed every word. She'd watched her read the words and smile. As if it brought her some kind of comfort. Peace. Help.

"Blaine, I don't know if you want to begin a new life. It's your choice, but why wouldn't you want to continue your future knowing that a God who created the universe and millions of stars in the sky, loves you and will love you for eternity. If you're tired of how your life has been, wouldn't you want it to change from this point?" Callie wasn't about to stop. "I've lived a long life. I've tested God over and over and He's always been faithful to me. Despite what people tell you. He is real and alive and wants nothing more than to have a personal relationship with you. Why would anyone want to reject that?"

"How does that work? Have a relationship with someone you can't even see?"

Callie's eyes lit up as she answered. "You talk to Him. Pray. You read what He wants you to know, in the Bible. You listen to His leading by reading His words. There isn't a day that goes by that I don't speak to Him and ask Him what my next step in my life will be. And amazingly, He tells me. Just like when He told me to talk to you that day in the train station."

"He told you to talk to me?"

"Not in an audible voice, but it was like a nudge. You caught my eye and I knew you were in trouble. Then, he told me to tell you something I'd never told another living soul."

"I don't know, Callie." Even as the words left her mouth, she hoped Callie was right. A tiny sliver of hope built in her heart. She did need a life change. She didn't want to end up like her mother or her grandmother. "If I were to decide to have a personal relationship with God, what would I need to do first?"

Callie took her hand, "Realize you need Him?"

"I need something, Callie."

"We all do, Blaine. We're sinful people. His love, guidance, and instruction are so helpful, but we need Him to change our hearts. Change what's broken into something new and the only way to do this is to accept what Jesus did for us on the cross. He died to take away all our sin. That's why He was born. And that's why Christmas brings us so much hope."

At that statement, something began to make sense in Blaine's heart. "I want to change. I want to believe. Can you read more about how much He loves us?"

Callie opened to another page in her big worn Bible. "Oh Blaine, it would be my pleasure."

Wringing his hands, Mason entered his boss's office and shut the door behind him. He'd never quit a job in his life. He almost felt guilty doing it. Was he giving up too easily? Ending something that God had blessed him with, but before he could freak out, he blurted out the speech he'd practiced in his head all the way back to Chicago.

"What do you mean?" His boss stopped drumming the table with his fingers and now seemed concentrated on Mason's words.

"I'd like to put in my two weeks. I'm resigning from my position here." Mason felt as if a boulder had dropped off his shoulders. He took a deep breath.

"But why?"

Mason sat down. "There are many reasons. Two weeks ought to be enough to show Miguel how to finish up my files." Mason knew Miguel had a family to support and he hoped his boss would move him up. "Miguel will do a great job for you."

The boss looked up from Mason's resignation letter and shook his head, "You're making a huge mistake, Mason. This could have been an awesome position for you in the future. We had plans for you."

Mason couldn't stop now. "I'm sure, but I'm not sure I want to wait that long to find out what those will be."

The boss tossed his letter to a pile on his desk. "You're insane. All for a sick grandmother!"

"I wanted nothing more than a job in Chicago. A good one. But not at the cost of never having a spare second to even tour Chicago. Do you know I've never been to the aquarium downtown?"

"What?"

"I've been working so hard and been so busy in the last year that I haven't had any time to stroll to the edge of Lake Michigan and see the dolphins at the aquarium. Not once. I've also wanted to go to the top of Willis Tower. I love this city. I always will, but I don't love this job enough to waste every second of my day slaving over it. I'm sorry. I'm sure you'll find another who might want to give away his life like that. There are a million guys here in Chicago that will jump at the chance. But it isn't for me. Thank you for this opportunity..."

"Get out!" His boss stood up. "Pack up your belongings and get out."

Mason stood and as every other time, he did as his boss asked.

"Leave your accounts on your desk. I'll have Megan find another employee to take them over."

"I'd be more than happy to stay for the next two weeks..."

"You're finished here."

Mason left the office and went back to his desk. Packed up his belongings as the entire office staff watched.

He was pretty sure he'd done the right thing, but those around him were murmuring. Some probably assumed he'd been fired. He couldn't be sure what the boss would tell them. As he pulled things out of his drawers and stuffed them into his backpack, he pulled out a slip of paper and wrote on it. Quickly, he slipped it onto Miguel's desk. He read it and nodded.

He took his key to the office out of his pocket and removed it from the key chain. Holding it up, he caught Megan's eye and placed it into her hand. "Mason, what are you doing?"

Mason didn't want to talk in the office. "Meet me outside." Megan nodded.

Out on the sidewalk he glanced up at the enormous building he'd left and those surrounding it. He remembered the first day he'd walked into the building. It was a week after he'd graduated from college and his first job interview. He couldn't believe how fast he'd landed a job in Chicago. Who wouldn't be thrilled to have a job here? Despite that fond memory, he still felt great relief to be leaving.

Suddenly, he felt someone grab his arm from behind. He turned to find Megan slipping into her coat.

"What in the world happened, Mason?"

Mason grabbed her arm, pulling her toward him. "C'mon with me. I'm going to get pizza."

"A pizza? What?" Megan folded her arms and she shivered. "Did that idiot fire you?"

"No, I quit."

"Why?"

"I've had enough, Megan. I'll find a new job. I'm totally happy with my decision."

Megan gripped her arms. "I don't understand."

Her reaction made Mason laugh out loud. "Megan, you see how they treat me. Do you remember the last time I got to go out for lunch? It's been months." Mason pointed to the office above their head, "That guy almost made me work through Christmas."

Megan began to shake, "But that's no reason to quit."

"So you're upset that I'm leaving?"

"I just can't imagine you'd quit such a great job to do what? Go search for another one. Why? It seems insane."

"Well insane or not, I'm going for pizza."

"I gotta get back to work." Megan walked backwards for a few steps and then turned. A few steps from him, she turned back, "Mason, why? Tell me the real reason."

"I'm moving to my nana's house. She needs me right now."

"To Michigan?"

"Yup."

Megan turned on her heel. "I hope whatever is there makes you happy." Megan just waved over her shoulder, "Have a good life."

Mason stood on the sidewalk and watched her walk away. He was a bit confused. What did Megan want from him? She was obviously not happy about his decision. Perhaps all she wanted was someone who was up and rising in Chicago. Someone to make her look good.

Mason turned. He wondered if he should have sausage or bacon on his pizza and if he'd find the aquarium open this afternoon.

After his Chicago pizza lunch, Mason headed for his landlord's office to see if he could extend his lease for another two weeks so that he could get a moving van to pick up his things and deliver them to Nana's house. Thankfully, she had room in her basement to store them until Mason could find another job and a new place to live. This would also keep Mason available for a little while to watch over her. Perhaps Blaine would change her mind, if not, they could care for Nana together.

Nana needed him and in this season of her life, he could do nothing more than to be there for her so his parents could return to the mission field.

He'd called to make an appointment with the landlord, and was assured that he could talk to him today. Mason wanted to be sure to return to Nana's house sooner rather than later.

Snow began to fall. The temperature hovered under twenty degrees. The sharp air made his ears hurt as he made his way down to the landlord's office. People were back to work in Chicago, now that it was after Christmas. The city never slept.

Mason turned a corner at State and Jackson street and headed west. The smell of gourmet popcorn permeated the otherwise stale Chicago city air. Glancing in the window, Mason saw the counter filled with all the delicious mounds of popcorn that made this shop a great place to visit on a shopping trip to the city. Mason thought back to the surprise his father had as he opened the special popcorn from his favorite shop on Christmas morning. He smiled and stuffed his hands deeper into his pockets to ward off the cold air skimming the sides of the buildings on each side of him. Chicago in the winter was brutal with the never ending gusts off Lake Michigan.

Past the popcorn shop was a jewelry store. Mason had often wondered if he would one day purchase a ring in the store for someone special. At that moment, he thought of Blaine.

Mason wasn't sure why but he stopped to glance into the store's display window which contained sparkling diamond jewelry. As Mason glanced up he saw tall, young man holding what appeared to be a ring. Two women were helping the young man as he set that ring down to pick up another. Mason hoped, as he turned away from the window, that one day he'd have the opportunity to spoil a young woman like this man was doing right now. As he often did, Mason prayed he would find the right one who he could not only love, but also share a whole lifetime of memories.

Walking away, he wondered who God had for him. How much longer would he have to wait?

Chapter 23

Blaine wasn't sure what to believe about Callie's God. Why had God chosen her to have an absent father, a drug addicted mother, and a grandmother who had only taken her in because she had no one else? Blaine couldn't understand that kind of love. Why hadn't God ever placed someone in her life to love her?

All these thoughts flittered through Blaine's thoughts as she began to take down Callie's Christmas tree the next day. She had been feeling much better. Callie sat on the couch behind her.

"You need to pull off the tinsel first?"

The strong static electricity in the room caused every strand to stick to Blaine's shirt. She kept pulling it off the tree and then off the front of her. "Sticky stuff."

Callie laughed. "Yes it is. But look what a single strand can do."

"What? Stick to you." Blaine picked pieces off her sweater.

"Well yes, that, but see that strand up there by that blue light?"

Blaine stooped to pick a few strands off the floor and looked at the spot where Callie pointed. "That one?"

"Yes. Look at how it reflects the light so beautifully."

Blaine laughed. "Callie. Only you could see the beauty in a tiny strand of silver."

"It took me ninety years to be this observant. But sometimes when I lay here on the couch, I gaze at the tree. I've done that a lot this time. I've tried to soak up every single moment of this holiday. I noticed how reflective a piece of tinsel can be. It reflects the lights of the tree and even the sunshine as it beams through the window. It never stops shimmering when it's hit by light."

Blaine nodded as she grew intent on gaining the same perspective about the clingy decoration. It did reflect many facets of light.

"The whole thing reminds me of our life in Christ."

Blaine continued to pluck off the strands and placed them across her hand. "How so?"

"When we have the light of Christ in our lives, it needs to reflect to others. Somehow it resonates to those around us. Either in our demeanor as we go through a day knowing He is close and watching or in how we kindly and lovingly treat others. People notice. I love it when I find someone who appears to have the weight of the world on their shoulders and I simply smile. That gesture shows them and reminds me of all the good ways God has blessed me. Somehow, as I reflect His goodness to me, I reflect His love to others."

"Kinda like you've done for me?"

"Yes. I've tried to share Christ's light with you. He has given me so much. Why wouldn't I want to share it with you and others."

As Blaine removed the remaining strands of tinsel, she understood a little more.

Callie held out her hand so Blaine could place the silver strands across it. "Here, let me put that away for you."

"Do you save it every year?"

"Sometimes. It gets frail after a couple of years. It is annoying to get back into a container and separate it for the next year. Depends on my mood."

Blaine understood that as she fought the same issue.

"Hand me the ornaments as you take them off the tree, Blaine. I want to dust off each one before we put them back into boxes."

Blaine carefully removed a tiny angel and handed it to Callie. "Why do you dust them now?"

"So next year, they'll be clean and ready to put on the tree."

Blaine didn't know there were so many aspects of taking down a tree before she'd met Callie.

"Look at this one, Blaine. Miles gave this one to me after one of my miscarriages. It helped me to remember that our baby might not be with us, but she or he was with God now. We don't turn into angels when we die, but angels protect us. They're amazing creatures that God has made for us."

Blaine stopped working. "In heaven? Do you think...?"

Before she could finish her question, Callie was nodding. "Your baby is there too, Blaine."

"My baby probably isn't there, Callie."

"Why would you say that?"

Blaine didn't know for sure, but why would God love her baby like He loved Callie's baby? "Just because..."

"All babies are made in the image of God, Blaine. Each one. They are precious and cherished by the God who created them. He loved your baby just as much as he loved mine."

Blaine had never considered that fact. For some reason, it made her heart feel better to know that God was taking care of her baby at that very moment. That He cared enough to do that for her.

"See the football player?" Callie pointed to a blue and yellow ornament at the side of the tree.

Blaine pulled the little player off a branch and put the hook in a tiny box and handed the ornament to Callie.

"Miles loved this one." Callie gently wiped off the player with a cloth. "He never would believe that I've allowed Chuck to put green ornaments on my tree. I'm sure I'll hear about it someday in heaven, where I'll get to see him again."

"I've never heard stories attached to ornaments."

Callie laughed. "I suppose not. But when you've lived as long as I have, it happens." Callie placed a bulb into a nearby box. "I'm sorry, I'm probably boring you with all this chatter."

"You don't have to apologize."

"It's funny. I've been taking down these ornaments for so many years. They seem a part of me, almost a recitation of my life in Christmas ornaments. Each one has a meaning. Each one a story."

Blaine sighed. Who was she to take away memories from simple ornaments?

"See this one?"

Blaine had just taken it off the tree. A paper clip was attached to a green sheet of paper shaped like a heart. "Amy made this when she was in second grade. See?" Callie turned the ornament over and saw a date and Amy's name. "I miss all those homemade paper decorations coming home from school each year."

Blaine turned again to her job, "I can't believe you've kept *all* of these."

"I know. I am a bit of a pack rat." Callie sighed, "Okay, I keep many strange things. But look at the love put into this one." She held up the misshapen heart. "She couldn't even cut straight."

"Maybe you should get a few new ones. Some of these are showing their age or..." Blaine handed Callie one that had lost almost all of its glitter and had tape over one side of it, "get rid of a few and buy new."

Callie shook her head. "Never! I made this one for my Daddy about eighty years ago."

Blaine wrinkled her nose, "No way!"

"Yup. I even remember the day I brought it home from school for him. See?" Callie pointed to the small wooden soldier etched out on red, now faded hardened clay. "He was a soldier in World War one. He was proud to be a fighter for his country. I was proud of him, too."

Blaine noticed how Callie's face glowed as she held it up and it twirled in a circle. She thought about how wonderful it would be to have Christmas ornaments to put on a tree from a lifetime of memories. In a society of throw-away items, it had to be as rare as Callie.

"He's missing his hat though. That fell off when I let Amy decorate the tree when she was little." Callie grimaced. "Every year I imagine this will be my last Christmas to hold the ornaments and know the story behind each one. Amy and Chuck or even Mason won't remember the story behind each one.

"When it comes time to go through my things one day, they'll probably toss half of these because they won't mean anything to them. But they hold precious memories for me. I hope you can do the same one day, Blaine. I hope you'll have memories to share with your grandchildren that can help to shape their journey and teach them to remember their blessings. Even a paper ornament made by a child."

She'd lost almost twenty-three years' worth of memories so far. After hearing many of the stories, she hated to remove the last ornament, "What's the memory behind this one?" The tiny crown was gold and had been painted with lots of color.

"Oh that is one of my favorites. Look at the wonderful paint job on it."

Blaine shook her head, "I'm sorry Callie but that's the absolute worst painting I've ever seen."

"Not if it was done by a preschooler."

"Who?"

"My favorite grandson painted this and gave it to me to represent the crown all of us will receive when we meet the Lord."

"Mason made it?"

"Yes, he was four." Callie actually kissed the ornament. "It has always reminded me that even when life gets hard. When trials come, in the end, special things will follow. The Bible says we'll all receive a crown for the things we were able to do for Him while on earth. But the best part is, we don't get to keep them. God says we'll be able to present them to Jesus one day. The giver of eternal life. The One who provided our way. I can hardly wait!" Tears filled Callie's eyes.

Blaine hoped that someday she would like to start her own collection of ornaments. But how was that possible after missing so many years all ready.

Almost as if she sensed Blaine's thoughts, Callie said, "I'd like you to keep this one."

Blaine shook her head as Callie held up the baby angel. "No Callie. This is from Miles. I couldn't possibly take this one."

"I insist." Callie waved her hand over the now-filled boxes beside her on the couch.

Blaine wanted nothing more than to have the tiny angel, but she also knew how much it meant to Callie. She couldn't possibly be so selfish as to take it away from her, but Callie held it out to her. "Always remember that your angel is in heaven."

"C'mon, take it. I insist. Like I said, the memories are all mine. Amy won't ever remember me having it. Perhaps this will be the start of your own memorable collection."

Tears filled Blaine's eyes as she took the ornament from Callie. "Thank you." It was another way that this unselfish woman had loved on Blaine in the past few weeks. "I will remember."

"Now keep her safe. Every time you place her on your Christmas tree, you'll remember this time you shared with me. I'm so glad you decided to come home to be with me, Blaine."

Tears now spilled down Blaine's cheeks. Is this what real love was like? Despite her burning a few meals, sleeping so hard she didn't hear Callie at night, or having a frustrating attitude with Callie, Callie had done nothing but show her love. For once, Blaine felt she could really believe that this woman loved her unconditionally. She'd never felt it before. Ever. But with Callie, it felt almost silly and unreal to not believe her. She managed to reflect that special kind of love to others, exactly like the tinsel on her tree. Blaine was continually amazed by Callie's solid faith.

"Well, that's about it. Let's put these boxes in their totes and we'll be done for the day. I'm hankering for some hot chocolate. How about you?"

Blaine longed for something to drink, too.

"Here," Callie held up a small box. "Will your angel fit into this? It will keep her protected for years."

"Perfectly."

"Write on the box. Put today's year and every single time you open it up, you'll remember me."

Blaine would never lose it and at that moment she realized she didn't have a single possession in her life as wonderful as this ornament. It was given in true love. She took it to her room and placed it on her bed stand. She'd probably not pack it away but she'd look at it every single time she needed to remember that someone loved her.

Mason returned to Nana's house later that evening. He'd gotten his extension on his apartment's lease. Snow was falling as he got off the train. His dad was there to pick him up.

"Well?"

Mason shrugged, "It's over. I got that extended lease on my apartment that I asked for."

Chuck slapped his back, as they made their way to Nana's car off the parking lot of the depot. "You're a wise young man. I trust your judgment. It's a scary thing to stand up for something you think is important."

"I couldn't work for a company that cared more about the bottom line, than about their employees. Now I can be closer to Nana. Help out more."

"Will you miss Chicago?" Chuck opened the driver's door and slid into the car. Mason threw his backpack in the back seat and sat in the passenger side.

"Yeah, but it's only a four-hour trip and I'll have to return for your favorite caramel corn." He buckled his seat belt. "I feel relieved. But Dad, let's not tell Blaine yet."

"Why not?"

"I don't want her to think that I quit because I was afraid she'd leave Nana soon. I want her to still feel wanted."

Chuck patted him on the back. "You'll find another job soon. You're doing an admirable thing. It will be a relief to your mom knowing you're here with Callie."

"Thanks Dad." Mason hoped he could find another job quickly. "Let's go home."

Blaine was putting supper on the table when Chuck and Mason arrived. She was surprised seeing him come in with Chuck. No one had told her how long he'd be gone.

"I can't believe it's time to put all the decorations away. The house looks so bare again without them." Mason picked up a bowl of rice and handed it to Callie.

"I hate it, too, but it's time. Blaine and I worked all day. We had a nice afternoon."

Blaine agreed with a nod.

Chatter filled the room as Chuck and Amy filled everyone in on their visits to friends over the past few days. They talked about seeing people that Callie knew and about how good it was to catch up with old friends.

Mason seemed relieved about something. He wasn't quite as frustrated with life as before he left. Perhaps something had happened in Chicago to make him happier. Blaine wondered about Megan.

Clearing dishes from the table after the meal, Mason wanted to go on another walk with Blaine. He wondered if she were up to it.

As they wiped dishes, the others went into the living room to talk a bit more about Chuck and Amy's time away, leaving Blaine and him alone to clean up the kitchen. Mason was so relieved to be home and have the job issue behind him.

"So...," Mason picked up a dish and wiped it dry, "You had a good day with Nana?"

"She's so full of stories. Memories."

"That she is."

"Did you know there is a story with almost every ornament on her tree?"

Mason nodded, "That there is. Kind of a long production to take down the tree, isn't it?"

"That's for sure."

"I tend to take it for granted," Blaine could feel his eyes on her. "I need to do better."

"She showed me your preschool crown."

Mason put his face in his hand. "Oh no. The one with the awful paint job."

"Yes, but Callie saw it through different eyes. It wasn't a horrible paint job done by an inept child. It was a masterpiece, made by you."

Shaking his head, Mason wiped another plate. "Pretty pitiful, right?"

"Mason, I don't know if I've said this before, but don't take all of this for granted." Blaine's motioned around them as soap suds dripped from her hand. "I have nothing from my life to share with anyone. I've moved so many times and left so many treasures behind. I have nothing to show for my past twenty-two years on earth. You have an ornament you made as a child. How special is that?"

"I often wonder why Nana doesn't buy new ones."

"Those ornaments hold a lifetime of treasures for her."

Mason placed his hand on Blaine's back. "I'm sorry Blaine. I need to be more grateful. I didn't realize that something I find mundane and ritualistic could mean so much to someone else."

"Think of me the next time you forget that."

Mason felt chastised for not thinking of Blaine's feelings. "When we finish up these dishes, will you go on another walk with me?"

"Okay." Blaine seemed hesitant.

He hoped she hadn't changed her mind about staying with Nana.

They ventured out into another cold, snowy night. Before she lost her nerve, she asked, "Mason, why did you go to Chicago so quickly?"

Pulling up the hood on his jacket, Mason plunged his hands in his pockets. "I had something important to do."

It wasn't the answer she wanted. She plunged ahead, "You seem relieved."

"In the past few weeks, work has been hard. You saw over Christmas, I had work to do, instead of being with my family. I needed to change my priorities. Family is important. Nana might not be with us much longer."

"That's an awful thing to say." Blaine zipped her coat up higher.

"I'm sorry, but you've seen how frail she's been since her surgery. Nana is a strong woman. But we have to face reality. I want to be here for her when she needs me."

Blaine stopped. "So, what does that mean?"

Mason turned toward her. His nose beginning to turn red from the cold. "Blaine. I quit my job."

Blaine gasped. "What?"

"Not only for Nana. There are other things going on, too."

"Are you gonna tell me what?" Blaine knew if she didn't ask now, she'd regret it later.

"A few days ago the boss asked me to do something that I just wasn't comfortable doing. He'd asked me to change some figures on an account to help our customer get a tax break. I couldn't consciously change numbers like that without it being accurate. I can't be dishonest and the boss wasn't taking my 'no' as an answer."

"So your trip back to Chicago had nothing to do with that girl?"

"Who?"

"Megan?"

"Oh her. She wanted someone who would never be me."

Relief filled Blaine's heart. Her shoulders relaxed. "So it's over!"

"My job? Yes."

"No!"

Mason turned to her. "I'm confused."

Blaine grew frustrated. Even though she really didn't want to hear the answer, she had to know. "Megan?"

"Blaine, there was never anything to be over with that. She wants a boyfriend who will become a Chicago multi-millionaire. Her priorities aren't anything like mine."

Blaine felt herself grow warm, despite the cold temperatures. If this Megan girl was not an item anymore, Mason would be free to date other people. Blaine wasn't sure she wanted to dwell on it. For in her heart, she knew for a fact that Mason would want to fall in love with someone that shared his faith, matched his goodness, and Blaine wasn't anything like what Mason deserved. "I'm getting tired and cold, can we go back inside?"

Mason seemed surprised, but he nodded, "Of course. Let's go."

Chapter 24

Crawling deep into her covers, she pulled them up to her nose and ducked down. For some reason she couldn't get warm after her walk outside with Mason. Doubts about the last few days flooded her heart. Perhaps she shouldn't stay at Callie's any longer. She wasn't sure why she felt so lost all of a sudden.

If her life proved only one thing to Blaine, if something was happening to her that was too good to be true, it usually ended up badly. She wanted to store away the treasures and good things that had happened at Callie's and let nothing change them. If she were to stay any longer, perhaps something would happen to ruin all of that.

What if Mason had quit his job because the family had suggested to him that Blaine wasn't fit to take care of Callie? What if all of this was a ruse, and they didn't really like her at all? She'd felt this way before. Old thoughts and memories tormented her soul.

No one had ever really wanted Blaine. Despite all of Callie's kind words, what if she didn't mean any of them? Surely Amy and Chuck didn't want her living in the same house with Mason.

Blaine felt bombarded by her fears. Despite being deep under the covers of Callie's warm blankets, she felt like she had no protection from the darts slipping deep into her heart. *They don't really want you. No one has ever really wanted you.* Something convinced Blaine while she lay there that she needed to make a new plan. She needed an escape route. But for once, she had no idea what that would be.

The family prepared for a New Year celebration at church the next day. Callie hadn't been able to attend for a while and she was excited to attend church to celebrate the incoming year.

They'd asked Blaine to go with them. She'd never thought about being in church for New Year's Eve. Kyle and she had usually celebrated the night by getting drunk, partying too late into the night and starting off the New Year with an explosive headache.

She mulled over the decision whether to go or not. Callie asked her again by mid-afternoon.

"Blaine, would you like to join us for the service tonight?"

Blaine shrugged. "I don't know Callie. I'm not religious like you."

"That shouldn't prevent you from going to church. I want to introduce you to my friends."

Blaine sighed. How could she turn Callie down? Even if she'd done this whole thing with Blaine for a reason, she wouldn't hurt Callie's feelings for anything.

She'd actually thought about packing up her stuff and leaving quickly. Slip away. That would be the best way. Especially for Callie.

At dinner that evening, they talked about the service. It did sound odd, but Blaine's curiosity got the best of her. Perhaps she should go. What could it hurt?

She would tell them her decision right after dinner, but as they finished up the meal, Callie's doorbell rang.

"I'll get it." Mason scooted his chair back from the table and wiped his mouth.

Callie voiced her concern, "I can't imagine who it could be. Anyone from church would be heading to there soon."

"Perhaps it's Christmas carolers." Chuck chimed in.

"Shouldn't they come before Christmas?"

Mason reached for the door handle. A young man stood at the door with a determined expression.

"Hey. Is this..." the young man spouted off Callie's address.

Mason nodded, "Yes."

"Where is she?"

Mason shrugged. "I'm sorry? Who?"

"Blaine."

Mason's hand dropped off the doorknob. As he looked a little closer and his eyes focused, he knew who this was. He'd seen him in the jewelry store, a few days before, shopping for a ring.

Chapter 25

Blaine recognized the voice. It was Kyle. Blaine stood up, nearly knocking her chair to floor.

"Blaine!"

Blaine heard Callie call for her, but she needed to see if it really was Kyle. As she looked past Mason, she saw him. How had he found her? "Kyle, what are you doing here?"

Mason blocked the space between them.

"What are *you* doing here?" Kyle asked her in a matter-of-fact tone.

"I work here." Blaine pushed hair back from her face. She looked at Mason who still stood between her and Kyle still on the front porch.

"Can I come in?" Kyle asked and pushed the door open with his hand.

"Sure." Mason backed away from the door but he still didn't move. He kept himself in front of Kyle.

Kyle pushed further into the room. Blaine knew Chuck came up right behind her, she saw his reflection in the front window. It was as if both McAnder men were protecting her.

Kyle reached out his hand to Chuck, but not Mason. "Hello, my name is Kyle. I'm Blaine's boyfriend. From Chicago."

Chuck extended his hand and shook Kyle's. "Uh...welcome. I didn't know Blaine..."

"It's her boyfriend." Mason added, but didn't move.

"Boyfriend?" Chuck apologized. "I didn't know."

"Can I hug you?" Kyle tried to push past Mason. Mason looked at Blaine. His eyes questioning. He didn't smile. He stared at her.

She waved Mason off, "It's okay. But how did you find me?"

Kyle held up his phone. He'd tracked her.

They all stood in silence for a moment. Kyle seemed happy. Unusually nice. "I've missed you and I've been worried."

"Worried?" Blaine smirked, "Why?" Even though she was shivering. She assumed it was from the open door, but she wasn't sure.

"You didn't call me? In fact, it was as if you'd dropped off the face of the earth."

Blaine's thoughts whirled. Did he care about her? Should she trust him? What if by leaving him, he'd had a chance to rethink their situation?

Kyle pushed past Mason and took her in his arms. "I can't believe you left like that. Honey, why would you do something like that? Especially now."

Blaine felt odd as Kyle continued to hug her tight.

He whispered in her ear. "Are you in some kind of trouble?"

"I'm fine."

Kyle took her hand and held tight. "Well now that I've found you, who are these people?"

He seemed happy. Charming even.

He went toward Callie who stood with Amy in the archway of the dining room. Amy had her arms wrapped around her mother who looked scared and worried. It was a stark difference to the people who had been relaxed and enjoying their dinner.

"Who is this beautiful lady?"

Callie stuck out her hand, "I'm Callie. I saw you at the train station. With Blaine."

"I'm sorry," Kyle took her hand and held it for a while. "I don't remember you."

"We didn't formally meet," Callie nodded, "But Blaine and I became friends after you left her."

Kyle grimaced. "I hated leaving her that day. She was upset, yet I knew she needed some time to think things through."

He then dropped Callie's hand and turned back to Blaine and wrapped his arm around her shoulders, "I guess I didn't realize you wanted this much space, with the baby coming and all."

Blaine scanned the faces in the room. She needed to get Kyle out of there and soon. He needed to find out what happened.

"Can we go outside? Talk a moment."

Kyle gave her the sweetest, most tender look. "Sure."

"Let me get my coat."

"Good, good," Kyle said as he stood in the living room waiting for her.

Blaine pulled her coat off a hanger in the closet. "We'll...I mean I'll...be right back."

She'd never seen such sober faces around her. It seemed as if the joy had been sucked out of the room by Callie's vacuum. Mason's eyes left her and returned to Kyle.

"I'm so happy to have found her safe. Thank you for allowing her to stay with you." Kyle took Blaine's hand. She felt the tight grip he had on it. For a moment, she gasped. Then the grip loosened a bit. She had to know why he'd followed her here. What did he want? "I'll be back soon."

Before she left, she looked at Mason. She wasn't sure what he was thinking, but he seemed to be perturbed. Annoyed. Was it directed at her or at Kyle?

Amy was the first to speak. "Do you think she'll tell him about the baby?"

"I hope so," Callie responded. "He needs to know."

Everyone nodded.

"I'm shocked that he came," Mason added. He went to the living room window and looked out at the car in the driveway.

Walking outside, the night wasn't as cold as it had been in the last few nights. Kyle still had a tight hold on her hand. He pulled her down the sidewalk and into what appeared to be a rental car. She'd never seen it before. He opened her door and pushed on her shoulder to get into the car.

Fear filled Blaine's heart. Would he leave with her? What could she do if he did? When he shut her door, she felt for the lock switch and flipped it to open. She wanted to be sure she could leave quickly, if she needed to.

Kyle went around the front of the car, then slid in beside her. "Blaine. I've missed you so much." He took her hand again, but it was a gentle touch. "I can't believe I finally found you."

"How did you...,"

"Don't worry about that now. I just did. I've been so wrong. I knew the moment I left you at the train station that day that you misunderstood me. Didn't understand what I wanted you to do?"

"You wanted me to have an abortion. It was clear."

Kyle bowed his head. "I know. That was lame. I was in shock. We've discussed this scenario before, I thought I made it fairly clear how I stood on the problem."

"Kyle, the baby wasn't the problem."

"Of course it was. We would never be the same as a couple. But I thought about it long and hard. I think we can still make it work."

Kyle reached into his pocket and pulled out a box. He tilted the top of it back to reveal the most magnificent diamond ring that Blaine had ever seen.

She gasped. "Kyle? What are you doing?"

"It's the best I could find. I think it's time. Blaine, will you marry me?"

Kyle picked up her left hand and slipped the ring onto her finger. Was he serious? Did he really want to marry her? She thought this moment would never happen between her and Kyle. It was the last thing she ever suspected he would do.

As she gazed at the large diamond on her finger, despite the doubts flooding common sense, she knew this was best. Perhaps the situation would now change, but how could she know for sure.

"Kyle, it's beautiful, but I need to tell you something." Kyle had the resources to give her a good life. Should she tell him now? She knew if she didn't, she wouldn't be faithful in keeping her promise to not lie anymore. Tears of fear pricked her eyes.

"Don't you like it?"

Like it? Of course, she'd never seen anything so bright and pretty. He'd outdone himself. "Yes, it's very pretty."

"Well then. What do you say?"

Blaine looked at him. It was now or never. "Kyle, I lost the baby."

Kyle stammered, "What did you say?"

"Last week. I had a miscarriage."

Kyle's demeanor disappeared like the air out of a balloon. He put his hand over his face and wiped it as if to erase her words. "Wow. I never thought that would happen. Are you sure?"

"Completely." Blaine pulled off the ring and held it out to Kyle. "I'm sure you want this back now."

Kyle took it from her hand, reached for her left hand and slipped it back onto her finger. "No way. I mean," Kyle stammered again, "I don't quite know what to say. I'm sure you're disappointed, but Blaine think of it...we can be just like we were before. We'll go back to being the same. This changes everything, but I think we should still get engaged." He took a deep breath, "I'm sorry Blaine. I've been an idiot. I should have never asked you to do something so harmful to the baby. We need to regroup, rethink, and figure out our next steps, but how about it. Will you still accept this ring from me?"

Blaine was pretty sure he'd lost his mind.

Mason stood at the doorway.

"What do you think he wants?" Chuck asked.

Callie began to cry. "How did he find her? If he knew where she was, why didn't he come earlier?"

Amy consoled her mother. "Don't worry, Mother. Maybe it's for the best."

Callie wiped her eyes with the back of her hand, "No. You're wrong. It can't be good."

Chuck stood beside Mason at the door and said, "Should we shut the door?"

Mason's voice quivered. "No."

"Are you worried about her safety, you two?"

Mason and Callie said in unison, "Yes!"

"Mother, please sit down." Amy added, "You're shaking."

Callie went to the closest chair and fell into it. "Mason, do not leave that doorway?"

"No way, Nana."

"Do you think we should call the police, Mason?"

"Let's wait a bit. If they back out, then yes." He turned a bit and motioned to his mother. "Mom, go get some paper and write this number down."

Amy ran for paper, then rummaged through her purse, taking out a pen.

While she did that, Chuck stooped beside Callie on the floor and took her hand in his and began to rub it.

Amy came to the door with Mason. "It's a black BMW. Four door. Chrome wheels. The license plate is 871BGW." Amy wrote it all down.

The car lights turned on. Mason opened the screen door. He wasn't sure what to do. He didn't want Blaine going with this guy.

He started out on the sidewalk and as soon as he did, the passenger door opened. Blaine got out. She shut the door and walked toward Mason. Her gloves were off and she was holding her left hand up.

Mason knew what was on her finger.

Blaine was smiling as the car drove off.

Chapter 26

Blaine came back into the house and went to Callie who was wiping her eyes with a tissue Amy had brought her. She knelt in front of her chair. "Callie, look! He bought me a ring. He wants to get married."

Callie didn't know what to say. She took Blaine's hand in her own and caressed it. "Blaine, are you sure?"

"Yes. He's changed his mind, Callie. Look at the ring he got me." He would never do this if he wasn't serious.

Blaine held her hand up for Callie to see. Callie knew she had to think with wisdom and discern her next words. She did the only thing that kept her in tune with the correct words. The only three words that helped her in an intense and stressful situations: *God help me.* "Blaine, it's lovely." She knew in her heart, she needed to be happy for the girl. If she didn't, she might lose her completely.

"I can't believe it. I never imagined this is what he'd do." Blaine shook her head, "I'm in shock."

Callie looked past Blaine to Mason standing by the door. Despite the temperatures outside, he wiped sweat off his forehead with the back of his hand. His look seemed defeated, let down.

Blaine continued to stay kneeled in front of Callie gazing at the diamond ring on her finger. It was a large diamond, surrounded by smaller ones.

"What did he say?"

"He said he's been worried sick about me. That he missed me and wanted me to come home with him."

Callie couldn't help herself. "When?"

"Tomorrow. He wanted me to go with him tonight, but I told him I needed to pack my stuff. He said he would be back in the morning to take me home. Back to Chicago."

Callie heard Mason sigh. She looked up at Amy and then back to Blaine, "Honey, are you sure about all this? This is awful sudden."

"I think so." Blaine looked back over her shoulder at Mason. "The only thing he could think of was to give me a ring and ask me to marry him." Blaine sat back on her heels and gazed at the ring. "I just can't believe it."

Callie knew what to say now. Her short prayer had worked, "Are you *sure*?"

Callie's voice made Blaine turn back to her. "This is for the best."

"Are you sure this is what you want?" Callie's voice made Blaine turn back to her. "It's my dream, Callie, remember?"

"If this is what you want."

Blaine stood up. "I need to pack," and left for her room.

Mason was in shock. "I need some air." He went for his coat in the closet and left out the front door. Out on the sidewalk he paced. What had just happened? She'd even told Nana that this is what she'd dreamed would happen.

He should be thrilled for her. If this is what she wanted and she was happy about it, why shouldn't he be? It wasn't like she was his girlfriend. She didn't believe the way he did. There wasn't any reason for her to tell Kyle no.

Blaine had been doing her best to be honest with him, now he had to be honest with himself. He was jealous of the man who had just left.

Callie wasn't quite sure what to do. Blaine was right. This was her dream coming true, but did she really like this Kyle fellow all that much. He'd asked her to do some crazy things. Why had he returned now? The whole thing was odd.

Callie watched Mason outside pacing. What was bothering him?

Oh God, what should we do? Should we try to stop her from leaving with Kyle? Surely this isn't what You want for Blaine. What would he do to her? Please give us wisdom and guidance. She's so young and naïve. Please help our attempts at reflecting You to her and that what we've done the last few weeks is not in vain. Oh God, help her to want to still go to church with us tonight. Don't take her from us yet. She not only needs us, more importantly, she needs You. Amen.

Chapter 27

Mason wrestled with disturbing thoughts as he went back and forth on Nana's front sidewalk. He wasn't sure what to do. He'd held himself in check as best as he could, but to see that man come for Blaine ripped his good intentions to pieces. He'd been having so many emotions concerning Blaine. God had tried to instill in him to be cautious. Reflect only love. He'd been faithful to do that, but look what it had gotten him.

As he paced, Mason struggled with how to react. What to think. Tears slipped down his cheeks. Getting through this would be hard, but more than anything he worried about Blaine's life. She'd had such a hard time, was God really going to allow Kyle to now take her away from them. She also realized that it was Blaine's choice. She seemed thrilled with the idea. Who was he to try to stop her?

Why was she returning to someone that she didn't seem to love? Did she feel that Kyle was her only option?

A cold wind made his wet cheeks grow numb. He hadn't noticed it until his fingers began to tingle. Blowing on his cold hands, he decided instead of being out here without any gloves, he'd better head back inside. Perhaps Callie would know what to do or perhaps she'd know for sure why Blaine would make such a drastic decision so fast.

Before he did, he prayed. Like he'd never prayed before; begging God for His protection over Blaine. As the numbness grew in his hands and feet, he felt a chill enter his heart.

Callie had been diligently praying. All they needed to do was somehow get Blaine to church that night. Surely there would be something said or someone who could change her mind about returning to Chicago with Kyle.

Mason came in and threw his coat on the couch, sitting down opposite of her. As Callie saw the sorrow in his face, for a moment she thought maybe she'd done the wrong thing asking Blaine to live with her. Doubts began to seep into her thoughts. What had she done?

He got down on his knees, kneeling beside her chair, whispering, "Nana, what do we do? Is it safe for Blaine to be with this guy?"

Callie shook her head, "I don't know for sure. Something isn't quite right? I can't imagine him changing his mind so quickly. It's only been about a month since Blaine left him at the station. Miraculous things do happen, but..."

"Why do you think he'd make a move like this?"

Men often do odd things when they struggle for control. "I think he's desperate."

Mason nodded, "Yeah. He wants her back. I saw him in the jewelry store looking at rings before I left Chicago. I've never seen him before, and I watched him purchase that ring for her. Isn't that weird that God allowed me to see that?"

"God often does things in ways we can never imagine. Look at me; I'm ninety years old. That alone is miraculous," Callie fought back tears, "but something needs to happen in Blaine's heart. We've done our best to show her love. God's love. You've done the same. We need to pray, that it's enough."

Chuck entered the room. "What can we do to encourage her to come to church with us?"

"I don't know, but I'm with you Chuck, that's the only way." Callie wrung her hands in her lap. "We do need to remember it's in God's hands. He always knows what's best. We've done all that He's asked of us, now perhaps he wants us to trust Him."

The tiny family knelt by Callie's chair to pray. They prayed for guidance and direction. Their prayer was also that Blaine would see truth and God's love before going back to Chicago with Kyle. When they finished, Blaine came out of her room.

"Good, I'm glad you're all here. I know I promised to go to church with you tonight, but I'm tired. This whole thing has caught me off guard, and I'd really appreciate some quiet moments alone tonight. Is it okay if I stay here, while you all go?"

Instantly, Callie fought for something to say to change her mind. What could she say? Nothing came. Somehow she knew trying to convince Blaine otherwise would probably be useless. They'd prayed for God to work, now they needed to do something that took each of them more courage than pushing her to go to church.

Callie spoke first, "If that's what you think is best, Blaine."

Mason shot her a skeptical look.

"We'd love for you to go with us to church. It's supposed to be a very nice service. Ringing in the New Year like this, at church, has always been a favorite of mine." She knew she'd spoken from wisdom and guidance. God had never failed her yet.

Callie watched Blaine avoid looking at Mason. "I think I'll stay here, if that's okay."

There had to be something to convince this young woman to do otherwise. To join them. *Attend church with us, Blaine. It might change your life forever.* Yet Callie knew she couldn't control Blaine. As much as she wanted to treat her as a child, explain to her how necessary it was to try...she knew it was hopeless.

The sighs from the others sounded like everyone felt the same way. Callie reached down and patted Mason on the shoulder, and answered Blaine. "Okay, sweetheart. As much as we'd love to have you join our family...we understand."

Mason was quiet in the car all the way to church. He sat in the back seat with Callie.

She reached out and took his hand in her own, "God does work but always in His time. Now is the time to trust." She saw the young man bow his head, "Don't give up. Keep praying."

As they got out of the car at church, Callie asked Amy to get her Bible from the back seat.

Amy peered in through the back window, "It's not here, Mother."

"Oh darn, I must have left it at home. Why am I so forgetful?"

Chuck took her by the arm, "I'll share mine."

Blaine shoved the rest of her clothes into her suitcase. Some of them needed to be washed, but she could do that as soon as she returned to Chicago and Kyle's apartment.

She couldn't believe how the night had turned out. It was obvious that Kyle loved her. She admired the ring on her finger and twirled it around. The light above reflecting on the oval. It was bright, big, and pretty. She'd never imagined Kyle would give her something so incredible. She recalled his words in the car.

"So what do you say? Will you marry me?"

This was crazy. The whole moment. Why would Kyle just show up like this? Not only that, but want to marry her. Maybe he'd come to his senses.

How could Blaine say no? Why would anyone say no? Kyle was a good catch. She knew she'd never measure up to Mason's perfection, but she fit in Kyle's world. They knew how to deal with each other. They'd known each other for years.

"So come home with me. We'll leave in the morning." Kyle pulled tickets out of his coat pocket, "Here they are, tickets for home. Are you coming with me?"

At that moment, Blaine remembered the ornament Callie gave her, tucked safely in its box beside her bed. "I need to pack. Why don't you come back for me in the morning?"

"Oh c'mon." Kyle begged, even with his cute bottom lip stuck out. That often worked with her, but not tonight. "No stop. Let me pack." Then to be sure he was sincere she asked, "Can we set a date soon?"

Kyle laughed, "Don't be in such a hurry, dear one. We'll set a date soon enough."

He'd kissed her, and the answer to her question went away like a gust of Michigan winter wind. He agreed to let her stay but that he'd pick her up in the morning before the nine o'clock train. "Be ready by eight thirty. You know how I hate to be late."

His traits weren't perfect like Mason. He still was rough around the edges. But they could now be a family. Something Blaine could finally cling to and feel like she belonged. It was something she'd dreamed of, her whole life.

Finishing up packing, Blaine wondered if everyone had left for church. She hoped so, especially Mason.

The house was quiet. She'd forgotten how nice it was to be home. Alone. Strolling through the kitchen she saw that Callie had put out two cookies on a plate for her. They were some that they'd made together. Blaine smiled at the thought. Who'd have imagined the fun she would have with a ninety-year-old, making cookies.

Glancing around brought back the memories of spending the last few weeks with Callie, Mason and their family. The meals they'd shared around the table. Putting together a puzzle with Chuck. Washing dishes with Mason. She'd remember all of them.

Soon she'd be headed back to Chicago. She'd missed the city. Glancing out the living room window, she noticed the lights glowing from across the street. She remembered her first night at Callie's house and how hard it had been to be in a town without a coffee shop on every corner. She couldn't wait to get back to Chicago and have coffee, even late at night.

The thought of Chicago coffee made her thirst for a cup at that moment. Returning to the kitchen Blaine opened Callie's coffee canister, as she did she realized she'd actually grown accustomed to her instant coffee. It wasn't all that bad. She remembered Callie's laughter as she relayed the fact that it was so much worse than the coffee she was used to. And then when Chuck made the comment about it, she remembered how he'd said the same thing. But for some reason tonight, Blaine wanted nothing more than a cup of Callie's instant coffee.

Shuffling through the mugs, she found her favorite one. Sitting down at the table with it, she thought over all the times the family had sat around the table. Laughing, showing photos of Africa and the experiences there. Blaine smiled. She'd felt so out of place when she first arrived, but Chuck and Amy, as well as Callie had taken away her reluctance bit by bit. Even though she'd felt like an outsider, Callie's family had done nothing but show her how she fit well into their mix. Even Amy's reluctance was pushed aside with all the help she gave Blaine on the day of her miscarriage. So why did she still feel like an outsider?

As her eyes passed over where Mason usually sat, her heart began to hurt. She'd miss him the most. She loved Callie and her talks, but Mason. She'd never forget him. His kindness and gentle ways. The way he made her feel. She felt pretty around him, all the time. Not just because he'd tell her, but because he showed it in his actions. Never once had he tried to seduce her or convince her that he needed her. Her decision would make it easier for Mason to find someone else to love. Someone who deserved his love. For some reason, that made her sad.

As she sipped her hot drink, she listened to the furnace sounds give way to other familiar sounds of Callie's house. Gazing around the room, she remembered the way the house felt when she'd first entered it. Strange, but oddly warm. Inviting. The whole house had an aura of warmth and that feeling of being home. She'd miss that in Kyle's austere, modern apartment.

She'd grown comfortable here. Every object in Callie's home held special meaning to the elderly woman. As every single ornament on her Christmas tree, each item held a memory of her life. From the family photos to the objects handed down through a generation of mothers, the items brought remembrances of special occasions. Each one significant, in its own way.

Blaine decided it would be better for her to get a shower tonight instead of trying get one and still be ready on time in the morning when Kyle arrived. She finished her coffee and headed to the bathroom.

That room reminded Blaine of the hard moments of being at Callie's house. She also remembered the pain, shedding tears from the loss, yet the comforting ways Amy had cared for her when she needed her the most. At first, she didn't think Amy liked her at all and now, she seemed as kind as Callie had been to her from the very beginning.

Blaine let the water drip over her body. As she reached for the shampoo, her ring reflected off the light above. It took her breath away each time she looked at it. She'd never imagined having something so amazing on her finger, especially from Kyle. It's diamonds glistened in the water. If he could give her a ring like this, something must have changed his mind. In a dramatic way. Perhaps leaving him had been the best decision. He'd finally come to his senses.

As she got out of the shower she glanced at herself in the mirror. Life would be different from this point. Her worries about her future, were now something of the past. Kyle wanted to marry her. All would be well. Her dreams were finally coming true.

Rummaging in her cosmetic bag, Blaine pulled out her tweezers. She hadn't spent much time lately on making herself presentable. She'd miss the moments when she could whip up her hair and not worry about styling it. Being with Kyle would be different. She decided she'd better style it nicely tonight so it would be pretty enough for him the next day. What about the days when she wanted to wear a pony tail, like she'd been doing regularly at Callie's house? Would Kyle allow her to style it the way she wanted after she became his wife?

Once she packed, she went into Callie's living room and sat on the couch. The hours had passed quickly and soon it would be a New Year. She decided to sit in the silence of Callie's home to celebrate. This year would bring challenges, but she'd be a bride and soon a wife. She wondered if Kyle would allow her to purchase a wedding gown from downtown. She'd admired one in a Chicago store for years. She knew exactly the style she'd chosen for her special day.

What kind of wedding did she want? Kyle would probably prefer a quiet ceremony down by the lake. They hadn't talked about a wedding, but he'd mentioned the frivolity of one they'd attended together last spring. She'd always dreamed of a church wedding, but who did they know that would even attend.

Would Kyle allow Callie to come to the wedding? She'd love to have her there. In fact, she didn't know what she'd do without the elderly woman in her life. Wrapping her new bathrobe tighter around her shoulders, she remembered the moment she got to open her gift on Christmas morning. What a special morning that had been.

Soon the ball would drop in New York City to herald a new year. What was Callie's family doing in church? Was the service as special as Callie made it out to be? She thought back to all the prayers she'd heard in Callie's house over the past few weeks. They talked to God like he was in the next room. He was important to all of them.

They trusted Him for everything. From thanking Him for the food they ate, to protecting them on the roads. They asked Him for guidance and to help them remember hope in scary situations. It was odd at first, but thinking back to all their words and actions, Blaine realized how genuine and real their faith was.

So many memories in such a few short weeks. Would she be able to remember them all in the years to come? Would it ever be the same for her? Would life change once she got back to Chicago because of her experiences here in Callie's home?

Tears began to flow. She told herself they were joyful tears, but as they fell down her cheeks and off her chin, she wondered. Glancing down at the ring on her finger, she knew life would never be the same. But how could she take Callie and the memory of these few weeks with her? Take part of Callie home with her?

Blaine grabbed the remote and turned on the television. She found the broadcast from New York just as the numbers went from ten to zero. Blaine wondered if there was something from Callie's house she could take back with her. Looking around she spotted Callie's Bible on the table beside her.

It was one of Callie's greatest treasures. She wondered why she'd left it tonight and hadn't taken it to church with her.

Blaine opened the book to find it marked with Callie's scrawled notes. Page after page covered with her thoughts. Reading a few of them, she became entranced. It was a treasure to Callie.

Tucked inside the middle section were a few sheets of paper. It was written in Callie's handwriting. The date read 'August 19, 1975.' The memory written out was about a change Callie had seen in Miles since his attempt at taking his life.

Tears came to Blaine's eyes as she read how she'd given up hope for Miles. Yet she now knew that God had changed his heart on that night. Blaine remembered Callie telling her about the change. The note read –

I can see such a difference in Miles' life. The fear is gone from his eyes and is replaced by a look of confidence. He counts on God to keep him sane and in touch with reality. The nightmares are gone. His gentle spirit is back, much like it was before the war. God has changed his heart. He now sees the importance of God in His life. He has that intimate relationship with God that I'd pray would change him. His prayers have changed. His way of loving me has changed. The way he disciplines Amy shows great love. I'm so thankful.

Blaine smiled at Callie's written words. Is that what she was missing for herself? Inside of the written pieces of paper was a small booklet. It told how to ask for that personal relationship with God.

Blaine then realized that this is what she could take from Callie's house. Perhaps when she got back to Chicago she could even find a Bible of her own and begin reading it like Callie did every day. Would that keep Callie and her love alive in her heart? She hoped so.

Following the instructions in the booklet, Blaine asked God to be real to her. She wanted a relationship like Miles had received on that August day so long ago.

Blaine had heard Callie pray dozens of times. She asked God to become real in her heart. Just like Callie seemed to do every day.

Blaine didn't know at the time if it would make a difference in her life, but she knew she now had something special from Callie to take with her forever. No one would ever be able to take it away. She knew this from something Callie had told her one day.

Placing the Bible back on the table beside her, she focused on it in silence. For some reason, she now felt drawn to read it. Opening it again, she read a bit more. As if by magic, the words made perfect sense. They seemed alive on the page. The minutes disappeared and soon she heard Callie and her family coming back into the kitchen. She placed the Bible back on the table beside the chair, wishing she had time to read more.

Chapter 28

Mason came into the living room and perched himself on the couch across from Blaine. He didn't waste any time or words. "Have you thought more about your decision to leave, Blaine?"

"Yes."

"So you're still going in the morning." Facing Mason and answering any of his questions, made Blaine uncomfortable. The words made the morning's departure seem final. She had to squelch the tug on her emotions, "Now that you plan to be here, I'm not needed." That's not anything like what she was feeling, but she knew it might appease Mason.

Mason leaned forward, placing his elbows on his knees. "No one told you that you aren't needed here anymore, did they?"

Guilt filled her heart. "No."

"Nana loves you, Blaine. She still needs you here. But I guess I understand why you want to return to Chicago." He massaged his temples, "I think." He looked up at her with pleading eyes almost as if asking her to stay. "Is there anything we can say to keep you here?"

Blaine avoided his eyes. She'd never seen him like this. What if he stood, took her into his arms, and told her she couldn't leave him, would she stay then? What if he begged; got on his knees and told her that there was no other girl but her in the whole world. Would she stay then? She knew only one thing to be true. He deserved someone better. Kyle would have to be who she deserved.

If she didn't leave the room, she'd say something she'd regret. She didn't want his sympathy or to see her so vulnerable. She stood, "I'll say goodbye in the morning. I'm going to bed."

Mason leaned back on the sofa and sighed. Putting his arm on the back of the couch, he gazed out the window. He'd been praying so hard for her all the time they were away. *Lord, help her to see truth.*

Mason knew he wouldn't be able to change her mind, though his whole being wanted to try. Perhaps he shouldn't have quit his job so soon. He might have had the chance to see her while in Chicago, but if he did see her, he'd wonder if she was happy or if Kyle was being good to her.

Rubbing his forehead, he went into the kitchen. His family stood around the kitchen holding mugs of coffee.

Mason slid into his jacket. "Did you hear her? There is nothing more we can do. If she won't stay for you, she won't stay for anyone. Sorry, Nana."

"I know, honey."

"I gotta go for a walk."

"Mason, it's so late," his mother started in and his Dad grabbed her arm.

"He'll be fine. Let him go."

The door slammed shut behind Mason. A chill filled the kitchen where Callie, Amy, and Chuck stood.

Callie shivered. "I was afraid of this."

"Me too," Amy added. "Despite how I feel about it, my heart aches for him."

"I know his heart. His heart is telling him he loves her more than his head knows he shouldn't." Callie pulled her coat off the counter and handed it to Chuck. "Hang this up for me, would you love?"

Chuck nodded and left for the side room to hang up all their coats.

Blaine needed to use the restroom before crawling into bed. While in the hallway, she overheard the discussion from the kitchen.

Had she heard Callie right? Callie always imagined things. Surely, Mason didn't love her. He had never tried to hold her hand or try to kiss her. He had never shown her physical intimacy or even hinted that he cared for her in a romantic way.

From her perspective, Mason only wanted to find someone to take care of Callie. Once finished, she carefully opened the door to the room and listened for a moment. The only sound came from the television now on in the living room.

Ready to slip under the warm covers, a figure outside caused her to pull back the sheer curtain over her window. She saw Mason facing the street with a determined stance. Hands in his pockets. He gazed at the sky.

Blaine watched him for a moment. Tears filled her eyes, but this time, she didn't try to prevent them from spilling down her cheeks. If only Mason knew how much she loved him. Would it make a difference?

Blaine allowed the curtains to fall back, hiding the scene. She would always wonder what magnificent girl would be able to return love to such a good man. Would she ever have the chance to meet her? She hoped so, but it was doubtful that she ever would.

As Callie kept so many prized possessions in her house to remember her ninety years on earth, Blaine stored memories in her heart. They were safe there. No one could take them from her or make her leave them at another abandoned house. She could carry them with her. Always.

The sight of Mason outside, staring up at the sky would follow her everywhere. As she tried to close her eyes and go to sleep, it seared into her memory bank. And for the second time that night, Blaine prayed.

God. It's me. Blaine. I'm not sure I'm doing this right, but I want you to know that I'm glad you had me sit beside Callie on the train that day. I now feel what it's like to be loved. By good people. By strangers. Thank you. And one more thing before I go to sleep, thank them for me by finding someone else who can care of Callie better than I ever could. And be with Mason. Find him a companion that deserves him.

As sleep began to creep into her thoughts, Blaine decided to try one more request. Perhaps God could help her with a bit of fear she had as she returned to Kyle. *God. One more thing. Help me to know if I'm doing the right thing.*

Blaine didn't know if God was even listening, but figured if He didn't listen to her while at Callie's home, He never would.

Chapter 29

Blaine rose early and got herself back to Kyle's standards by fixing her hair and putting on makeup. She put on her slick, black knee-high boots and her good coat. She was not only Chicago ready, but prepared to become Kyle's wife. He expected nothing less.

As she walked out into the main part of the house, she found everyone waiting in the kitchen.

"Did you guys even sleep last night?" Blaine asked as she pulled out a bottle of orange juice.

Chuck was the only one to smile, "I slept like a baby, but I always do."

Mason had dark circles under his eyes. He was still in the clothes he'd worn to church the night before. Blaine smiled at him. "Good morning."

Mason smiled back. "Good morning, Blaine." He hesitated as if he wanted to say something else. "Ready to head to the train station?"

Blaine nodded. "Soon. Kyle just texted me. He's on his way." She averted her eyes away from Mason. Blaine leaned back against the counter. "I feel like I should have a speech prepared."

Amy smiled. "We've enjoyed getting to know you, Blaine."

Callie joined in, "Blaine, you know if this young man didn't want to marry you, I wouldn't be allowing you to leave. Thank you for returning to help me get to the train in Chicago. If it weren't for you, I don't know if I'd have even survived the walk to the train that day. And ever since," With tears now coursing down the face of her friend, she gulped, "you've been a godsend to me." Callie held out her arms and Blaine curled up into the embrace of the woman she'd grown to love over the past few weeks.

"Thank you," Blaine whispered in her ear.

Chuck also pulled Blaine into an embrace. "Sweet journey, young lady."

At that moment, Blaine couldn't get over the heaviness in her heart. These people really did love her. It was evident by their embraces and words.

Blaine turned to Mason.

"Do you have anything else that you need help with?" He didn't move to hug her.

"It's all by the front door." A horn honked out front. Blaine drank the small glass of orange juice she'd poured for herself.

Callie added, "Blaine, you didn't even get to eat breakfast with us."

Blaine began putting on her coat. "I'm not all that hungry this morning."

They all accompanied her to the door.

Mason slid her duffle bag over his shoulder and pulled the suitcase out the front door to the car.

Kyle opened the back door for him. "Hey, thanks man. She always has so much crap." He didn't take the bags from Mason, but motioned him to put them in the car.

Blaine came up from behind Mason and touched his shoulder, "Thanks."

Mason nodded and shoved his hands into his jacket. "Bye Blaine. May God protect and guide you."

Blaine sighed.

Getting into the car, Blaine felt as though she was being ripped away from another home. Just as she had done with her mother and grandmother, so many times. She waved to Callie, Amy, and Chuck in the front window. Mason stood firm on the sidewalk.

Kyle smiled over at her and said, "Ready?"

She nodded. But was she? It all seemed so final. So over. Everything she'd experienced in that house. Memories of it were etched in her heart, like they'd been in the past, but would that be enough to sustain her? She did have the tiny angel tucked deep in her suitcase as a mere token of Callie's love. Surely, that wouldn't be enough. Could she really rely on this newfound personal relationship with God? Would He stand by her? Be there for her? She didn't know, but if it had worked for Callie and her family all through their lives, why couldn't it work for her?

Chapter 30

Mason didn't know what to feel. He wanted to put Blaine in God's hands. Yet as he watched the car drive away from him an intense feeling of loss overwhelmed his heart. He'd tried so hard to show Blaine God's love. So much so that the whole time he'd deny any attempt at a romantic gesture. Watching the car disappear from sight, he felt his attempts at showing her love had failed, but deep down it came down to one thing: He'd obeyed.

Would God change her heart from just the few weeks they had been able to interact with her? His whole being wanted to believe it to be true, yet his heart and head thought otherwise. By ignoring his romantic feelings, had that alienated her more?

Mason knew he had to trust God in this. It felt odd to finally realize that it wasn't up to him to know or to do everything to advance the cause of loving Blaine. All he could do was pray it was enough.

Standing alone on the sidewalk, Mason questioned many things. The doubt of it all crept slowly into his being. He hated being alone. He'd long grown tired of it.

This wasn't a new feeling to Mason. He often felt alone as he sat in his Chicago apartment, eating by himself. Being surrounded by people each day made it hard to imagine that he was ever really alone. Yet he was.

There were some nights, when the television was on, his mind would drift back to the African jungle where he often sat and wondered about his future. Back then his questions consisted of: Where would God place him? Where would he live? Would he end up staying here in the jungle or somewhere back in the states? He'd felt the need to leave Africa after he graduated from high school, but the world here in the states, was unfamiliar and scary and each time he found himself alone, he wondered. Had he chosen the right place?

At that moment, he still wasn't sure. But as he turned to see his nana staring at him from her living room window he knew that at this exact time, he was exactly where he should be. He was glad he'd taken care of quitting his job before Blaine decided to leave. If he would have waited, Callie might not be so enthusiastic about him coming back to stay with her. This way, she knew he'd done it because he wanted to.

He could use a bit of his savings to keep himself going until he could find a job. Nana wouldn't charge him rent and that would help, too.

But that didn't take away the hurt now penetrating his soul. His only consolation was that he got the chance to meet her. Be her friend. Perhaps it would be a relationship that would consist of nothing more than gratefulness that he'd been given the chance to meet her.

Stuffing his hands in his pockets, he went back into Nana's house.

Chuck met him at the door. Mason shed his coat and placed it in his Dad's opened hand. "You okay, bud?"

Mason nodded.

His mother came to the door and hugged him.

Walking past his mother, he saw Nana now in her chair. She smiled up at him. "I love you, kid."

Mason got down on the floor at her feet, leaning his back on Nana's chair. His grandmother placed her hand on his shoulder. "I have a feeling that this isn't the last we'll see of Blaine."

Mason rubbed his eyes. A headache was forming. "How can you be so sure, Nana?"

"I don't know. I have an overwhelming sense of peace about it all. Whenever God allows that to enter my heart, I feel relief and comfort. There have been so many times in my life that I can consciously say that I've done the best I can and the rest is up to God. This is one of those times. Trust can be the only thing to follow. It's a hard thing to trust, but sometimes it brings great comfort that you can."

"I'll try to do that, too." Mason leaned down and put his head in his nana's lap. She patted his cheek with her warm hand.

"But in the midst of that trust, God also has given me overwhelming promises to rely on. He'll never leave me, although people do. He'll stand with me, while I wait. And by trusting, it will never be in vain. You learn many things while you trust only in God."

"Perhaps that's why this is happening. I need to learn how to trust more." Mason added.

Callie patted his cheek some more, stroking his face with the love only a Grandmother can give a grandson. "Learn the lesson now Mason. It will only make your life on earth easier when it happens again."

Mason announced two days later that he would be returning to Chicago to pack up his things to bring back to Michigan. Nana told him about boxes she'd been storing in the basement, but Mason was taking the train and driving his own car back loaded with his belongings.

"I'll get more boxes from the grocery downtown, Nana. I don't have that much to pack up. I can use garbage bags for my bedding and clothes. Almost all my furniture will stay at the apartment. None of that is mine."

His parents had headed off, the day before, to Pennsylvania to visit friends there for the week. They knew Mason was headed back to the city and told him they'd be back before he returned.

Gathering up his things, Mason made sure that a caregiver had been in place to be with his Nana until he could return. A lady from the church had agreed to come and stay. Callie and she were good friends. She'd be fine until he returned.

"What do you want me to bring you back, Nana, on my last trip back?" Mason had always brought Callie something back. If only a bag of Chicago-made popcorn.

"You. I just want you."

Mason smiled and hugged her. "Are you sure?"

"Sure? That's an understatement. I've never been more sure. But I'm being selfish. Are you positive this is what you want?"

Mason squeezed her tight. "Of course. I love you, Nana."

Nana patted his back. "I know. I don't deserve you."

Mason left shortly after he'd prepared lunch for himself and Nana. He got her propped up on the couch and assured her that her friend, Miriam, would be there soon.

"I miss Blaine." Tears welled up in Nana's eyes.

Mason hugged her. "I know Nana. So do I. Why don't you lay down here and take a nap. It's been a busy week and a crazy few days."

Callie gave Mason an extra tight squeeze. "I love you, kid." Mason leaned down for her to place a kiss on his cheek as she patted the other cheek. "God be with you, child."

Mason stood, "He always is. And Nana, thanks for being such an awesome example to me. You reflect Christ in many ways. I learn something new every single time God allows us to be together and I'll always be thankful to you for that."

Callie exhaled, "Only by God's grace, young man. Only by God's grace."

Getting on the train that afternoon, Mason looked forward to some quiet moments to rest and think about things. This was a big change for him. He'd had a couple of companies close to Nana's house call him and next week he'd be going on some interviews. He was also going to get in contact with Miguel's friend in Lansing to see about a job there. It might be nice to be back in a small town atmosphere again.

That morning, a fresh new layer of snow covered the earth. As Mason gazed out the train window, he was reminded how snow made everything fresh and not so dreary. Once the leaves fell from the trees in the fall, the Michigan landscape always looked dull and bare. Once a snowfall came, the earth seemed quenched and refreshed again.

The wind was blowing strong today. Snow piled up against the fences bordering the tracks. Cars, at the railroad crossings, had layers of brown ice and snow encrusting on their wheel wells. He was glad he wasn't driving back to Chicago and prayed that by the time he returned, the roads would again be dry. That was unlikely during Michigan in January, but you can always ask.

As the train sped along the track, Mason leaned his head back on the head rest of his seat. He closed his eyes. There was only one person on his mind today. She haunted his thoughts. He knew the only way to know or think of her as being safe was to ask God to protect her.

Mason fell asleep praying for her.

"What are you saying?" Blaine pulled back her hair into a ponytail. They'd been home for just one night, but Blaine felt like a lifetime had passed since leaving Callie's.

"I'm telling you I want us to wait. Now that there isn't a rush for our child not to be a fatherless victim, I don't think we need to rush into marriage. Or anything, for that matter." He smiled.

He tried pulling her into an embrace, but she backed off. Was that the only reason he wanted to get married, so their baby wouldn't be illegitimate? "Seriously?"

Kyle stood with his arms folded, feet apart. "What's the matter with you? Now that we don't have a baby to worry about, why would we even consider the marriage issue further? Weren't we doing just fine before you found out you were pregnant? You weren't screaming for a ring then, were you?"

Blaine stood back, "I never screamed for you to marry me? I asked if you wanted to. I asked you to love this baby like I did, but that didn't happen. Wasn't it you who wanted me to go get an abortion?"

Turning his back on her, Kyle answered. "Yeah, that probably wasn't one of my finer moments, but I was worried. It costs so much to live in Chicago as it is. Having a baby on top of it all just made me nervous. I probably shouldn't have asked you to do that."

Blaine mellowed out a bit, "I'd have still been helping you with all the bills. Just because I was going to have a baby didn't mean I'd have stopped working."

Kyle turned to face her again, "Blaine, I'm not stupid. Do you even have a clue how much day cares charge? And then there's diapers, formula, cribs...the list goes on and on for what we'd need for the kid. And from what I hear, kids don't get any cheaper after their out of diapers."

He was right. Blaine knew the cost of having a child. Her mother had probably suffered more through having to take care of her than anyone else. Then she became a burden to her grandmother. "I know. Don't you think it scared me, too?"

Kyle pulled her into his arms. "Now we don't have to worry about it any longer. We're free from the problem."

Blaine backed away, "Is that what you thought our baby was? A problem? Do you know how much it hurt to have a miscarriage? I was miserable. For hours. The pain was beyond anything I've ever had in my whole life. Yet..." Tears filled Blaine's eyes. "All I could think about was what I was losing. It was almost like a part of me died that night. I cherished the fact that I would soon be having someone who needed me. Someone who cared whether I lived or died. That baby needed me and now..."

Kyle again tried to pull her into his arms. "I'm sorry. I guess I didn't realize how much this kid meant to you. But now, let's move on. We can go right back to being like we were before. We can go on our morning runs. We can drink. Thank God we can still do that. It'll be great. Better even."

Blaine looked down at the ring on her finger. What had she believed when Kyle put it there? Did she really believe it would change anything? "Kyle, this baby wasn't a problem to me. This baby was a relief. This baby showed me truth. The truth about my life. The truth about you." Blaine pointed to him. "I never imagined it would come to this with us."

"What are you saying? What truth about us?"

Blaine took a deep breath. "You don't love me. You never have. I'm someone to fulfill your life. Make you somehow feel like you're someone important. You never ask me if I want to go running every morning after working long into the night. I'm exhausted almost all of the time. And then, if I don't dress a certain way or put makeup on, you insist I go and fix myself up to go out on my only nights off. I want to enjoy more than one piece of pizza. If I want to scarf down six pieces, I want to do that."

"When have I ever denied you the right to eat more pizza?"

"Verbally no, but whenever you give me that look and insist I put the leftovers in the fridge, I know what you're thinking. I will not always be the skinny, model-like puppet on your string, Kyle. I refuse. I've seen what it's like on the outside, and I know that women can be treated differently."

"So," Kyle folded his arms, "what are you saying?"

"I've had a taste of what real love is and I liked it."

"What do you mean? Were you cheating on me with that other guy?"

"Mason would never do that to you or me. He's a very kind person. He's nothing like you."

"So what," Kyle held his arms up, "sounds like you're into him more than me."

Blaine wanted to tell him the truth, but even she didn't know where she stood with Mason. "This whole argument isn't about Mason. It's about our baby. This baby showed me many things and I mourn it. Every day I wonder what it would have been like to hold it. Love it." Tears now slipped down her cheeks. There were days she couldn't stop crying. Looking up at Kyle she added, "I'm sad that I will not have the opportunity to do that."

"Maybe someday, we can think about having another. Once we get established and I get a promotion. When we get older. You'll have another chance, I'm sure."

"I hope so." Blaine held up her left hand and slipped off the ring, "but I'm pretty sure it won't be with you." Picking up Kyle's hand, she placed the ring into it. "Thanks for this, but I'm sure this really wasn't something you wanted. And for that, I'm extremely thankful."

Blaine left for their bedroom. Her bags were still packed and on the bedroom floor. She wadded up a few more things from her closet and put them in the bags until she could barely zip them shut.

Kyle leaned against the door frame. "I'm sorry, Blaine. I guess I didn't realize what you wanted in life. I'm not that into kids. I mean, especially not right now."

"I'm not really ready for kids right now either and yes, this baby would have put an even more emotional strain on our relationship. I guess I didn't realize everything about our lives until I had the opportunity to see something much, much better. I think I want that now more than anything." Blaine picked up her backpack and flung it over a shoulder. "And I want something different, Kyle. I hope you find someone who can give you the things you want, but I'm pretty sure it's not going to be me."

As Blaine got on the elevator outside Kyle's apartment she started to think. Where would she go? Again she found herself alone and homeless. Perhaps she could get her old job back. Her boss had always liked her. She was efficient, a hard worker, and punctual-rare in the waitress industry these days.

She needed a plan. Why had she left Callie's? Why did she possibly think Kyle would change? At least, at Callie's, she would be warm and safe. Looking down at her phone, she realized she hadn't charged it. If she headed downtown, she could duck in the coffee shop and plug it in so at least she'd have a working cell phone. The thought put her into survival mode.

As Blaine gazed out into the cold Chicago morning, mist still clung to the air as the sun began to dissipate it with its rays. She wasn't sure where she'd stay that night, but maybe someone at work would offer her a place. She had one or two friends there who might be able to help.

She rummaged in one of her bags for her cosmetic bag. Unzipping each one, she realized she must have left it at the apartment. She didn't even have a toothbrush to her name. She hoped she could get some inexpensive items at the store to tide her over.

"You want your job back?"

Blaine nodded. Her fingers tingled with cold even still in her mittens. She was frozen from the walk to the restaurant from the café downtown. Her bags making her shoulders ache. "I'll come back at minimum wage again. If you'd just hire me back."

"You left without telling anyone." Her boss was cashing out a customer at the counter and didn't even look her way.

"I'm sorry." Blaine shifted her weight onto another foot. Her feet were freezing, she should have worn better boots.

"I don't think so Blaine. I need trustworthy employees."

"But I was trustworthy while I was working for you."

The man looked up at her. "I don't know."

Blaine hated to plead, but she needed this job. Now more than ever.

"I'll work any shift you want. I'll even take extra hours. Just let me return. I swear. I won't leave again."

Her former boss slammed the cash register door shut. "It's after Christmas. We're not as busy as we once were. We needed you then more than now."

"I know. Like I said, I'm sorry. I had to get away for a few weeks."

"Conveniently, at our busiest time. I don't know Blaine." The man wiped off the counter after placing some mugs into a nearby sink. "It wasn't easy trying to manage without you, especially during the holidays."

Blaine couldn't apologize again. She'd done enough of that in the last few days. She turned to leave.

The boss didn't call her back. She hated to think about going back out into the Chicago cold. In fact, she dreaded it, but what other choice did she have.

She felt a warm body up beside hers as the cold of the outside drifted into the warm building. Another fellow waitress pushed a note into her hand. "It's a phone number of a friend of mine. They might be hiring."

Blaine looked down at the paper and then up at her former co-worker. "Thank you."

"I hope you get something soon."

The girl was the one co-worker she thought she could ask to stay with that night, but as the girl rushed back into the restaurant, she decided she'd have to find another place to stay.

It didn't take Mason long to pack up his belongings. He labeled all his kitchen items, and the other boxes went into his bedroom to load up his clothes. Perhaps he could bag up some of his unused clothes to take down to the mission before he left. He loved that old mission and had always tried to leave clothes or donate money to help homeless people in Chicago. Many went there for warmth and a hot meal.

Stuffing clothes into a plastic garbage bag, Mason cleaned out his drawers and then went to the bathroom to finish up with a few towels and toiletry items. He was glad the apartment had been furnished when he'd rented it. He wouldn't have to be hauling furniture back to Nana's house.

In the tiny kitchen, he sat down to nuke the leftover pizza he'd purchased the night before. As he took a bite he realized how much he'd miss Chicago pizza. Even a day later, the cheese melted well and his first bite brought his famished hunger to an end. He'd been working hard and went to the fridge to grab a bottle of water. Unscrewing the lid, he took a long gulp before sitting down for a quick view of his social media page before finishing his packing.

Several co-workers had reached out to him after he'd resigned from work and many had been asking why. He didn't want to overshadow his decision on speculations and rumors, so he'd used his grandmother as his excuse to leave. It was partially true.

Miguel wanted to meet him for dinner before his final day in Chicago. They'd chosen to meet at the restaurant he and Megan had visited at Christmas. He hoped he didn't run into her again. He didn't have hard feelings against Megan, but he had no clue how she'd react after their last encounter.

That evening he packed up his final box and decided to take it down to his car before heading out to meet his friend. He hoped their conversation didn't dwell on his reasons for leaving. He worked through what he'd say to him if it did. This was a farewell dinner. That was all.

Ducking into a retail store, Blaine shivered as the door slammed behind her. Finding a cart, she stashed her bags in it and began to wander. She'd have to remember to ask if they were hiring when she checked out. For now, all she wanted was to get warm.

Memories, forgotten long ago, flooded her mind. She was little. Probably as young as four when her mother had ducked into a local hardware store to warm them both. It wasn't a store where people often found a mother with such a young child and she could remember her mother growing tense and frustrated.

A clerk asked her mother if he could be of help. She looked him up and down. It wasn't because of being unsure of what to say, but she must have been wondering how such a young man had a job and she didn't.

"We need a pipe."

"A pipe?" The young man had asked. "What kind of pipe?"

"Um, a big one."

He'd laughed. "Okay. Well. What for?"

"What are most pipes for?" Her mother had chided him about his question.

"Um," the clerk grew irritated, but kept up his effort to be a good employee. "I mean. What specific job do you need this pipe for?"

Blaine's mother had pulled a camping blanket off the shelf and placed it right on top of Blaine. "Plumbing."

The young man watched but didn't say anything. "Okay. That narrows it down." He motioned toward the back of the store. "The plumbing section is back here."

Blaine's mother had seemed relieved. She quickly reached down for the folded blanket that was in the cart, ripped apart the packaging surrounding it and placed the now open blanket over Blaine. She grew warm and her shivering began to subside.

The clerk had gone quickly. Blaine's mother followed at a snail pace. She smiled down at Blaine, but her eyes darted back and forth. "No worries, baby. We'll stay in the store as long as we can. Take a nap."

Blaine tried to close her eyes, but watched as her mother picked up several things as if to look at the prices. She'd stopped following the clerk and was now wandering in another aisle.

Blaine peered up beneath the layers of the blanket now warming her body as her mother kept evading the clerk now trying to find her again. She'd duck down one aisle and then another and, thankfully, he'd gone on to help another customer.

Her mother leaned down toward Blaine. She shut her eyes. "Baby, do you need to use the restroom?"

Blaine nodded. She'd needed it longer than she could remember.

Her mother picked her up out of the cart and escorted her to a small room at the back of the store. Looking up, Blaine saw a large man headed their way. He seemed important. Blaine's mother ducked into the small room, shut, and locked the door. "Take your time, honey. I'm gonna wash up, too."

While Blaine relieved the ache in her pee pee, her mother took off her hat, gloves, and began using the water from the faucet to wash her face. She smoothed down her hair with wet hands and also used her finger as a toothbrush.

As Blaine stood, her mother reached for her and began washing her with the towel wipes as well as the soap from the dispenser. Blaine stood there for the longest time with her pants still down and her mother washing her. Soon she pulled her pants up and her mother told her to wash her hands.

As she flushed the toilet, her mother took her time to go to the restroom. They'd been in the room for several minutes. Her mother in no hurry to leave. Soon a knock was heard on the door.

"Ma'am, is everything okay in there?"

Her mother shook her head, "Of course. Can't a customer use a restroom?"

"Um yes. I'm sorry to bother you," came the answer from a man's loud voice on the opposite side of the door.

Her mother bent down, after washing her own hands. "Feel better now, sweetie."

Blaine nodded. She'd grown much warmer and now that she didn't have to go to the bathroom, the lower front of her belly stopped hurting. Now it just grumbled.

"Just follow Momma and do what I tell you."

Blaine nodded. As a little girl she'd soon learned to do all she could to obey her mother. She trusted her. Even though they often would get into trouble, she knew her mother would never leave her alone in a store. She hoped.

Blaine's mother lifted her back into the cart and again placed the blanket over her. Blaine cuddled down into the warmth and closed her eyes. This would be a perfect place to take her nap. It had been a long, cold night.

As they came around the corner, Blaine's mother gasped. "Oh..." as she uttered a word that sounded scared and panicked.

Blaine's eyes popped open when she heard, "Um Ma'am, you need to come with us." Two men took her mother's arms and began leading her to the front entrance.

Blaine stood up in the cart and held out her arms. "Mommy."

Her mother turned toward her and told the men, "Can I pick up my child?"

The large men, with guns strapped to their hips, bright silver buttons lined down their coats, and funny hats began herding them toward the door. Blaine had reached down for the blanket after her mother picked her up. The large man who'd talked to them from the bathroom door came up and started to take the blanket Blaine now clutched in her arms.

Her mother turned just in time to see the man, "Please." Her voice shaky and tired, "She's so cold."

The owner dropped his hands and nodded. "Okay, but don't come back into my store again. Do you hear?"

Blaine's mother nodded, but added, "Thank you for the blanket."

Soon her mother and she were in the back seat of a large car with flashing lights on top. A fence kept her from getting into the front seat where all kinds of pretty lights were shining from radios. A noise was heard from one machine as another large man slipped behind the driver's seat. He picked up a small box and talked into it. "Headed downtown. Give us ten."

The radio erupted a reply, "Ten-four."

Blaine crawled close to her mother's side on the seat as she wrapped the new blanket around her shoulders and hugged her tight. Blaine was so tired she couldn't keep her eyes open much longer. She was warm and the new blanket, soft. It smelled like the hardware store's soap now making her face feel fresh and clean again.

Her mother was answering questions the big men in the front seat kept asking her. Before Blaine knew it, her world went silent.

Blaine picked up a new toothbrush and some toothpaste and placed them in her cart. She also chose a hair brush. Next she headed to the bath department and placed a towel and washcloth in her cart. She shook her head and placed the washcloth back on the shelf. She knew how to use one towel to care for herself. She'd been taught by a pro.

Stopping to count her money, she counted out one hundred and eight dollars. She wasn't sure if these kind of stores took other retail credit cards. If not, that's all she had.

Scooting to another aisle, she took this one slowly. Gazing at each item and dreaming of a day that she could pick up anything she needed and not worry about the dollars left in her wallet to pay for it. Would there ever be a day like that?

She tried hard to remember other items that would be necessary. Sweat pants, maybe some warm socks. She even tried on a few boots, but all of them were too expensive. She'd have to do with the fashion boots on her feet.

Soon she was perusing the grocery aisles. What would help her keep up her strength? What about protein bars? She reached for the heaviest box. It took her quite a while to scan each section for just the right food to buy.

As she headed to the counter to pay for her things, she hoped she had at least a twenty left over after buying her things. She quickly added the items in her cart. Two dollars and twenty-five cents plus seven dollars and a half. She'd never been good at math. She did have money left, but how long would a mere hundred plus dollars last? She'd shopped like her mother had taught her for so many years.

As she made her way toward the front of the store a soft, plush blanket was sitting in a marked-down bin. It was on sale. She looked down at her coat. If she could slip it up under her coat, she'd have enough money to purchase food for the next two days. She remembered back to the warm blanket her mother had asked to get from the owner of the store-even her mother hadn't resorted to stealing. And suddenly the thought of doing it brought her regret and a feeling of wrong. She placed it back on the shelf and then before she walked two steps, she reached back and placed that in her cart as well.

Her total came to twenty-two dollars and sixty-eight cents. She had enough for even more meals than she bargained for. She'd be fine. For at least a few days. She hoped. Shopping for necessities, on a slim budget, had always been a major part of her life.

As Blaine lingered at the door of the store, she thought of the mission downtown. It was odd that while at Callie's she reminisced about it. She wondered if it was still open to people like her. It had been a long time ago that Blaine and her mother had frequented the familiar place downtown. The police had taken them there after the incident in the hardware store.

Awakening from her sleep, Blaine found herself still in her mother's arms, but they were warm and in a building that housed several cots. Her mother placed her down on one of the cots and covered her up with her new blanket.

She lay down on a cot opposite of hers. Her eyes were red. Her face seemed calm and serene. Reaching out, she took Blaine's hand into her own. Blaine found herself with even a pillow for her head. Soon her mother's breathing slowed and her mouth opened for air.

Blaine knew she probably needed sleep, too. Getting up from under her blanket made her shiver a bit, but not as bad as she'd been doing that morning upon waking up under a tiny funnel of air coming from a metal grate in the building downtown. Blaine took hold of the blankets at her mother's feet and pulled them up and over her. She even did her best to tuck in the edges. Her mother never stirred.

She went back to sit on her cot and stared at the other people in the room. They didn't look back at her, but were busy making up their beds, gathering their belonging to stash under their cots.

Soon a large woman walked into the room. She had on a bright pink shirt, under a large, bulky black sweater. She smiled at Blaine and came closer. Blaine got off her cot and went to her mother's side. Her mother shifted and pulled the blanket over her tighter. Her eyes never opened.

"Hello sugar. What's your name?" Her black skin was plump and looked soft. She smiled down at Blaine with teeth missing.

Blaine shook her head. She'd been instructed many times, by her mother, to never talk to strangers without her in the room. She looked up at the woman who now stooped to her level and held out her hand. "Don't be afraid. I'm here to help you and your Momma. She seems awful tired."

Blaine nodded and clutched her new blanket tighter.

"Are you hungry?"

Blaine was always hungry.

"Why don't you come with me? We'll go down to the kitchen and see if we can find you some leftover breakfast food. Do you want to do that?"

Blaine knew she'd better not leave her mother, but she was so hungry. She didn't remember the last time they'd had something to eat.

"I promise. As soon as you're done we'll bring you back up to be with your Momma. Okay?"

Blaine wasn't sure what to do. "Can I take my blankie with me?"

The old woman grinned and laughed, "Of course, Sugar. I promise. We'll come right back up here when you're done putting something in that belly of yours."

Blaine took hold of the large black woman's hand.

She looked back at her mother who was still sound asleep on her cot. "She's real tired," she told the woman.

"I know she is, baby. Let's just go get you somethin' to eat and let her sleep. Okay?"

Blaine tightened her hold on the woman's hand. "I like orange juice."

The woman bent down and giggled, "Me, too. I betcha we can find some of that, just for you."

"Where am I?" Blaine asked as she descended a long stairway into what appeared to be a restaurant of sorts.

The old woman hollered, "Mabel, get this child a plate."

Another woman yelled back, "How much?"

"I think she's about four."

"Okay," came the answer from behind a counter filled with steamy hot pools of water. The noise sounded as though someone was banging on pots and pans.

"She wants some orange juice, too."

"I'll check to see if we have any left," the voice answered from farther back into the kitchen.

"Sit down here, baby. We're at the city rescue mission. Do you know what that is?"

Blaine didn't know. Sitting down, she pulled her blanket into her lap and tucked it deep there. She'd never part with the warmth of it.

The large woman sat down opposite her. "The mission is a place where people stay who don't have a place of their own. We try our best to take care of them. Help them. Little girls, boys, and even some Mommas and Daddy's come here for warmth and help."

Blaine watched another woman, slim and black, place a glass of orange juice in front of her. "How's this, sweetheart?"

Blaine couldn't wait to taste it. She hadn't had it since visiting her grandmother a few weeks before.

"We also like to talk about Jesus here. Have you ever heard about him?"

Blaine took a big gulp of her juice causing a little bit to dribble down her chin. "Is He nice?"

The old woman put her head back and let out a deep and loud laugh. "Oh baby, he's the best!"

Soon a hot plate of food was placed right in front of her.

"Now eat slow, baby. Your little tummy isn't used to all this food and you might see it again way too soon."

It was too delicious to not eat as fast as she could. What if someone changed their mind about giving it to her?

Blaine walked out into the cold, frigid air of Chicago. It was a typical January day. Full of strong winds and below zero temperatures. How long could she stand it?

Unzipping her backpack, she stuffed all her purchases inside and sat down on a curb. She reached inside her pocket and pulled out her cell phone. Luckily, it had almost thirty percent left. That would at least get her through the day. She'd stay off it and use it only for emergencies. She hated to sell it, but if she got desperate, she could.

Standing, she made her way down the street. Everyone zipping around her with things to do, places to go. No one looked her in the eye. No one knew her. No one cared about her. She headed into the wind and soon turned to head the other direction. She needed to keep the sharp, icy blast at her back.

When she did, she thought of Mason. Then Callie. Her life, a roller coaster of emotions. Why had she left them? She'd never learn.

She remembered all the things that Callie had taught about God. She knew the mission practiced the same faith. The same trust that Callie had been exhibiting for weeks. Would she find relief there again, as she'd done with her mother those long years ago? Blaine knew one thing for sure, she had no other place to go.

Chapter 31

The air of the evening was icy and sharp. The wind caught his breath. Mason wondered if he'd made the right decision to go out tonight. Perhaps if he stayed at his apartment for the evening, he'd be better off, but he wanted to see Miguel one last time. They were good friends and Mason hated to leave Chicago without saying goodbye.

Mason's thoughts drifted to Blaine. He wondered how she was doing. Upon his return to Chicago, he found himself staring at every woman on the street who resembled her. The chances of meeting her there were slim, yet perhaps God would allow him one more chance to talk to her.

He knew Blaine's coat was brown, with a fur collar surrounding the hood. Every time he saw one, he looked at the young woman's face. There were a million women like her, and a million coats the style of her coat. He always kept an eye for Kyle, too, although he was pretty sure he didn't know what he'd do if he saw him.

What would he do if he did find her? What would he say? If he could just ask her how she was doing, it would seem legitimate to talk to her if he did find her. Whatever his decision to say to her, he'd figure it out. He prayed God would allow him to see her. If he didn't, then it was God's choice.

He'd brought along the bag of clothes he'd packed to donate to the mission. It was a few blocks beyond the restaurant where his friend was waiting for him. It would be one less stop to make the next morning before heading home to Nana's.

Now he regretted it. The bag was heavy and bulky. He looked more like a homeless man carrying everything he owned. Perhaps he should get rid of it before he went into the restaurant. He was early anyway. The mission was just a few short blocks away. But the evening was so cold. Venturing a few blocks farther and then returning to the restaurant seemed ridiculous. The excuse of having to deliver it later might get him out of an uncomfortable situation conversation with Miguel about his reasons for leaving the company.

He decided to keep it with him and deliver it later. As he walked into the restaurant he found Miguel at a table at the far right side of the room. It looked as though he'd brought his wife along. Mason smiled as he approached them, he stowed the bag at his feet while he removed his coat. Shaking Miguel's hand and hugging his wife, he exclaimed his happiness at seeing them both.

"Have you ordered?" Mason picked up the menu. The efforts of carrying the bag from the apartment added to his grumbling belly.

They'd waited for him before ordering. Setting down his menu he asked, "What are you guys having?"

After ordering they asked about Nana. He told them she was healing well. "It was so good to see her." He then told them how his parents had come home for the holidays and each related their own experiences from Christmas.

Miguel told Mason how everyone had reacted to his leaving the company. He added how upset Megan was for a while.

"So," Miguel's wife Marissa smiled, "Is there someone else? We thought you kinda liked Megan."

Mason could honestly say, "Not right now." But then why couldn't he get his mind off Blaine.

"Hey dude, what's with the bag of goodies?" Miguel pointed down to Mason's bag. "Christmas is over, Santa."

"I had some extra clothes that don't fit anymore." He glanced at Marissa. "I'm taking it to the rescue mission downtown. I had an abundance of gloves for some reason. I'm sure someone there can use them instead of having them transported all the way to Nana's." Mason tossed a french fry into his mouth.

Miguel patted him on the shoulder. "That's cool, man. I'm sure they'll appreciate them. In fact," Miguel took out his wallet and handed Mason a fifty-dollar bill, "Give this to them, too."

"Thanks. I'm sure that will be put to good use, too."

"I wish it was more," he added, "but I overspent on Christmas."

Mason put the money in his shirt pocket. "Thank you. That's very generous. I'll give it to someone in charge when I get there tonight."

"It's quite a jog up there. I can drop you off on my way home. It isn't far from our house."

Mason nodded. "Hey thanks. That wind out there is pretty stiff tonight."

They all nodded. Mason didn't quite realize the extent of what he was doing until he would have to say goodbye to his Chicago friends like Miguel. He'd been a kind, supportive co-worker. He hoped eventually that Miguel would get the position he'd be leaving behind to better support his family.

Chapter 32

It was odd when Blaine thought back to her first time at the mission in Chicago. The wind kept getting colder and colder as she made her way down a back street. Perhaps she could find a building's heating system as her mother used to do, but all she found were dark, scary allies. She wouldn't be safe in those.

She had to keep walking. Stores were closing as the temperatures continued to drop. How had she gotten into this predicament? She pulled her jacket tighter around her, zipping up her collar one more time. Jerking at her mittens, she pulled them on tighter as well. Nothing was going to keep her warm tonight. She needed to do one thing and that was to find some kind of shelter. Perhaps the train station? Would it still be open?

As she headed in that direction, she passed under a glowing sign. Looking back over her shoulder, she recognized it. What if, just for tonight? She remembered the warmth. The hospitality. Even that small cup of orange juice. It was then that it suddenly hit her. She recalled her story today to remember that it wasn't the warmth of the furnace or even her blanket that had given her hope that day so long ago, it was that large black woman showing her Jesus. Just like Callie had done for the past few weeks.

She wasn't very good at praying, but Blaine stopped in her tracks and leaned against a building. Looking up she saw the dark sky. The stars. And she prayed. "God, give me that warmth again."

She looked down at her shoes which hours before had refused to warm her feet. Her feet were growing numb and hurting far more than she could even imagine. Why hadn't she pitched them and put on her warmer winter boots? She hadn't thought well about her departure from Kyle. Yet she knew, for many reasons, she couldn't spend another night in that apartment.

Tears began to slip down her cheeks. Why had she thought he would change? What had possessed her when he'd handed her that ring? She should have known better. Men like Kyle never change. She thought of Mason. Oh how she missed him.

Looking down the street again, the sign glowed in the otherwise dark street. It wouldn't hurt for one night. Would they even take women? She didn't know, but her feet would only be able to walk a bit further before she was sure frostbite would take over her toes. She needed to give it a chance.

Mason paid his bill. As they left, Miguel pointed to his car in a lot across the street. Mason threw the bag of clothes over his shoulder, as they made their way to Miguel's car.

Nearing the curb to the mission, Mason told Miguel he'd walk home from there to his apartment. "It isn't far, my friend. The wind should be at my back." He wished both Marissa and Miguel well and promised to keep in touch through emails.

Miguel slapped his shoulder, "I'll miss you, my friend." They shook hands. "Keep in touch."

Mason threw the bag of clothes over his shoulder. The mission was across the street. Watching for traffic to stall, he waited for a chance to cross the street.

As he entered the mission, a large, older black woman opened the door for him. "Need a place to stay tonight, young man?"

Mason smiled, "Thankfully, no ma'am. I'm in the process of moving and found a few things I'd like to donate." Mason lowered the bag to her feet and she smiled. A toothless grin.

"Thank you, young man."

"There are a few extra sets of gloves. My Nana swears I'm gonna freeze here in Chicago. I only need two or three pair, not twenty."

"Sounds like a good grammy to me." The woman picked up the bag and smiled, "Thank you. Have a good night. May God bless you and whatever journey you are on."

Mason saluted her. "Thank you. He already has."

Turning to leave, Mason looked into the cafeteria at the side of the open foyer of the mission. It was full. So many residents were eating a meal. "Do you need any help tonight?"

The old woman laughed. "I think we're good. We had a church from across town come to help. But I appreciate your offer."

Mason zipped up his coat higher. "Okay, then. Good night."

The old woman raised her dark hand, "God bless you young man. Stay warm."

Mason pulled on his gloves and headed back to his apartment. He couldn't imagine being outside in the cold on a night like this. Looking up, he caught a glimpse of the stars and thanked the One who enabled him to be warm and dry. He remembered Blaine's words to, *never take his blessings for granted.* Smiling, he thanked God for all the gloves he still had back at his warm and safe apartment.

The large black woman who Blaine remembered from so many years ago entered the cafeteria with a bag. It was full and she wondered what was in it.

She looked down at the mashed potatoes on her plate and again thanked God for helping her to find a warm place for the night as well as a good meal. She'd arrived just in time for an available cot. The woman who escorted her to her room was the same familiar lady. She could never forget her kind face, welcome smile, and jovial spirit. Blaine even shared the story of her past visit. The woman asked forgiveness for not remembering her, but loved on her just like she had those many years ago.

As the woman pulled open the garbage bag, she began pulling out what appeared to be men's clothes from it. The bag contained shirts, a sweater, even a light jacket, and an abundance of gloves. She laid all the items on a table by the door and announced, "If anyone needs any of these items, feel free to take them," to the group of people huddled around tables. Everyone nodded and expressed thanks with audible voices or raised hands.

The woman was older now, but she held that same wonderful, warm smile Blaine remembered from so long ago. It was hard to believe she needed her help again, but she remembered so clearly the moment that woman claimed her hand and took her for orange juice those many years before.

"Did you get enough to eat, baby?" She had looked down at Blaine as they went back upstairs to Mommy.

Blaine nodded and smiled. "My tummy feels real happy."

The woman tossed her head back and again showed her toothless, wide smile. "Good baby! Did you like the orange juice?"

Pulling her blanket closer, Blaine smiled. "Yes."

She'd taken her back to her mother who was still fast asleep on her cot. She hadn't even noticed that Blaine had been gone.

"Why don't you just sit here on this cot for a while, honey? While Momma sleeps."

Blaine crawled up onto the cot and again stuffed her new blanket in between her legs to keep it safe.

"Do you like to color?"

Blaine had nodded.

Soon the woman brought her crayon stubs and a book which had already been colored in, on a few pages. Blaine didn't care; it made her happy for hours.

As Blaine watched many men and a few women finish their dinner that night, she watched as that same old woman now stooped over to finish emptying the bag of clothes. Blaine wondered if she could find something to keep her warm outside the next day. She finished up the last sip of her milk and took her tray to be washed.

She placed her silverware into a plastic tub full of water. As she turned she realized many were already sorting through the clothes on the table. She'd better hurry to see if she could fit into anything. Perhaps even a shirt to go under her coat.

Nearing the table, there wasn't much left. She picked up a pair of gloves. Something on the edge of them caught her attention. She picked up the metal tab and examined it. That was odd. She swore Chuck had been given a pair of gloves just like this at Christmas. In fact, she was sure of it. How ironic that she were to find a similar pair at this table?

As she turned to walk away, a sweater fell to the floor as a man rummaged through the items. Blaine picked it up to put it back on the table, when it hit her. She'd seen Mason wearing a similar sweater at Christmas. She was sure of it. He'd worn it a few days before and kept pulling at the bottom of it. He kept saying it was getting too short and needed to find a new one.

Was Blaine just imagining all of this? Why would she assume that a bag of clothes, in Chicago, would have recognizable items in it? Blaine knew only one thing that might distinguish it to be something Mason would wear. She reached inside to find the tag at the neck. Mason hated tags. He'd always cut them out of his shirts. He claimed they irritated his neck.

The tag was cut. It was missing. Blaine gasped.

The old woman was out in the foyer greeting a few of the men who had just left the cafeteria and were headed upstairs to bed.

Blaine went up to the woman and asked.

"Who brought these clothes to you?"

"A mighty, handsome, young man. He just dropped them by a few minutes ago. Usually we wait and sort through the things and put them in our store, but since Christmas, it's been so full. Thought I might as well hand them out-"

Before she could finish, Blaine interrupted her. "He was just here?"

The woman seemed to sense her anxiety. "Yes honey. Is everything okay?"

Blaine handed the sweater to the old woman. "Which way did he go?"

The old woman pointed off to the left of the door. "Down that way."

Blaine grabbed for her coat and pulled it back on. "I'll be back." The door slammed behind her.

The old woman hollered after her, "Honey, I can't hold your cot if you leave."

Blaine's heart sank. What if she were wrong? She had to see if it was Mason who'd dropped off the clothing.

Mason got almost all the way down the street and remembered the money in his pocket. He grumbled to himself. *Of all the stupid things. It's so cold out here.* But instead of continuing to head for home, he turned around and stuffed his hands into his pockets. At least he didn't have to carry that bag any farther.

Heading back toward the mission, Mason ran directly into a person rushing down the street. He began to apologize, until he focused in on the person staring back at him.

Chapter 33

Blaine couldn't stop crying. She hugged Mason until she realized he hadn't said a word to her. She stepped back.

"Blaine," he looked at her as if she were a Chicago ghost haunting his imagination.

"Yes, it's me!"

"What? I mean. Where? What are you doing here?"

Blaine wiped the warm tears that now seemed to be the only thing not freezing on her face. It was as if something inside her was warming them. "Mason. I'm so happy to see you."

"Where did you come from?"

"The mission?"

Mason shook his head, "What? I mean-what were you doing there?"

Blaine wasn't sure if she should tell him, but what choice did she have. He'd find out soon enough, "I'm staying there tonight." She looked down. Relief flowed into her heart. She was so happy to see him.

"Why?" Mason now had tears in his eyes. He looked at her with sympathy and what appeared to Blaine as something way beyond what she could imagine.

"I left him, Mason. He didn't want to marry me. He wanted a person who I no longer am."

"What do you mean?" Mason held onto her arms from the hug and he wasn't letting go.

"Mason...it's crazy but I haven't been the same since leaving all of you, but it took me this long to figure it all out. I'm still unsure of many, many things, but I do know one thing for sure."

"What's that?"

"It's cold out here, can we go in and talk."

Mason nodded and took her by the hand, "C'mon. Let's go."

As they got back to the mission and came through the door the woman was standing there, as if waiting for Blaine to return. She opened the door to them. "Do you know this special young fella?" She asked Blaine as they walked in.

"Yes, I do and of all the people to find in this vast city, I never thought God would allow me to see him again. This is a miracle."

The old woman's head went back and a large toothless smile got caught up in a large, roaring laugh. "My, my, my...miracles happen around here all the time. Would you two like to talk for a little while?" She laughed as she ushered them both back into the eating area of the mission. "You take as long as you need." With that, she shut the door and Blaine saw her wink at Mason.

Blaine and Mason sat down at a table in the now nearly empty eating room. The sounds of pots and pans being washed and dried in the kitchen mingled with music playing in the background and the kitchen help singing as they worked.

"I'm confused. Why are you here?"

For once, Blaine didn't want to lie because she didn't feel like she had to. Mason would understand.

"Do you remember New Year's Eve? The night you all left me at home to go to church?"

Mason nodded.

"I did something that night and I'm not exactly sure I did it right, but I asked God if I could have a personal relationship with Him."

Mason sighed, as tears formed in his eyes. He put a hand over his eyes as if to shield them.

Blaine grew confused. Was he mad? Upset at her?

When he lowered his hand, tears fell down his cheeks.

"Mason..." Blaine grew concerned. "What's wrong? I thought you'd be happy for me."

Mason shook his head and wiped his cheeks with the back of his hands. "I'm sorry."

"Don't be sorry," Blaine took his hand, "is something wrong with Callie? Your parents? Please tell me, what's wrong."

"It's just plain shock." He took his other hand and wiped down his cheeks. He was too choked up to talk.

"Shock? Now I'm confused." Blaine began to tear up watching Mason fight for control to speak.

Mason sat for a moment. Then he looked deep into her eyes. "There are moments in my life that shock me. To the very core of my faith. I never imagined this to be how we'd end up. When you left Nana's house that night, God told me to let you go. And you see," Mason fought back some more emotions, "I didn't really want to. I wanted to run down the street after the car that was taking you away and pound on the window and beg you to come back.

"I asked God to bring you back. I begged him to allow you to finally see the truth of His love and what He can offer you. God always gives me three answers. One is yes, another is no, but sometimes He just asks me to wait. But at that very moment, I wasn't sure what He wanted me to do. I chose to wait. I didn't know how long or if I would wait for you, but He must have asked me to wait. And unbelievably, I never imagined this to be the answer. Not in a million years."

"So..." Blaine didn't know what to say. "What did you want to wait for?"

"You." Mason took her hands in his. "I wanted to wait for you. I wasn't sure he'd let me have you. I thought maybe He had someone else for me, but here you are. And you're not only Blaine, but a changed one at that and exactly what I've been looking for."

Blaine sighed. He was happy to see her. For once in her life, a dream of her own was beginning to come true.

"Come home with me. Come home to Nana's. Please."

Blaine nodded. "There's nothing I would like better."

Blaine gathered her things and packed them up in her backpack while Mason waited in the foyer for her. She couldn't believe Mason had found her. But she'd never been so thankful to see him.

As she descended the stairs she saw Mason hand the woman folded money. He smiled as he saw her approach.

The old woman looked at Blaine and smiled, "Honey, God has his eye on you, do you know that?"

Blaine smiled, "I guess I never thought of it."

"Well think about it. Remember who God is...by this moment. Nothing He does is a mistake. Don't miss out on it. Take it. Believe in Him. He is good all the time!" The woman looked up to heaven and raised both her hands. "Praise Jesus!"

Blaine smiled. It had to be God. There was no other explanation. As the old woman held out her arms, she kissed the top of her head. "Baby! Promise me one thing."

Blaine backed away, but the older woman kept her close. "What?"

"Never, ever, ever return here again! Live your life for God. Follow Him. Promise me that?"

Blaine didn't know if she could be honest with this dear woman, but she said, "I'll try."

The woman hugged her again. "Baby, you'll be secure in His love now. I never want to see you again, but honey, I hope to see you again in eternity. Where we'll always have a home. Forever!"

Blaine nodded. *A heavenly home. What would that be like?* She'd need to remember to ask Callie.

Mason put his hand at her back and escorted her toward the door.

The woman went with them to the door. "Keep her safe, young man. But you two," she wiggled her finger at them like Nana would do, "be good."

Mason whispered in Blaine's ear, "Just like Nana would say."

Blaine nodded and decided she didn't care what Mason thought. She grabbed his hand and held on tight.

Chapter 34

Mason couldn't help but smile at Blaine in the passenger seat all the way back to Nana's house the next day. She was here. With him. He was shocked to have found her. Why did God continue to surprise him like this? With such wonderful outcomes? He didn't deserve His goodness.

As they drove, Blaine told him how Kyle had treated her all the way back to Chicago. She knew almost immediately that she was in trouble when the first thing he asked her to do when they arrived home was wash the stack of dishes in the sink.

"I thought of Callie and you almost all the time and how I'd let you both down. For just a pretty ring. How bad is that? Kyle wanted the woman he'd left at Union Station, but I'm not the same woman anymore. I want a true, loving relationship with a man who can love me like Miles Reynolds. And I know only one person who could do that better than anyone else."

Mason wanted to tell her how he really felt, but he waited. He wanted to start off right and with God's blessing, yet God had allowed them to find each other. In one of the largest cities in America. How could he doubt? Yet, what were God's plans?

Callie hated having Miriam at her house to help her. She could probably have been fine without her, but on more than one occasion she realized she still needed help. She moaned to herself each time. Each time she'd feel that ache of missing Blaine. Why had God allowed her to meet her and not finish the job? At her age, she planted plenty of seeds in people's lives, but it was rare that she got to see the fruit of her efforts. She breathed a silent prayer that one day she could before He took her home.

Finishing her dinner, Miriam announced she needed to head home for an hour or so to make dinner for her husband. Callie was sure she'd be fine. Mason was to be home later that night. She got comfortable on the couch, with the television remote in hand she awaited Mason's return.

Nothing on television appealed to her, so she decided to read instead. It had been long before her visit to see Mason in November that she'd had time to read a novel. She looked over on the table beside her and there lay her favorite book. Picking it up, she smiled. Perhaps tonight, this is the book God wanted her to read.

One of Callie's favorite books in the Bible was Acts. In Acts, the writer tells about the Apostle Paul's conversion. The moment Paul stopped persecuting Christians and became a believer himself. No one believed Paul would do it. He had tormented, stoned, and even killed believers. Why would such a man turn to God?

Once he did. No one believed him. Who could ever imagine God forgiving this particular man? Yet he did. He changed. Completely. Miraculously.

When he found others who were Christians, they didn't believe that he had changed either. One man thought he was mad. He even told him so. Yet Paul told the man, "I am not mad, but speak the words of truth and reason. I have changed so I may open eyes, to turn others from darkness to light, and from the power of Satan to God, that they may receive forgiveness of sins and an inheritance among those who have a pure faith in Jesus."

Callie took her job seriously. She wanted others to see God in her and follow Him, too, but she was just a mere reflection. He'd been good to her through her marriage with Miles and even after his death. She never felt alone, but blanketed in His love and shelter.

Callie rested her eyes from reading and thought about what she'd read.

Callie's kitchen door shut, and she jolted awake. She didn't think Miriam was returning. She was waiting for Mason. That's right. He was coming home. She rubbed her tired eyes, sat up on the couch, to go to the door.

As she struggled to get up off the couch, someone suddenly stood beside her. Helping her. She looked up into the face of Blaine smiling back at her.

"Hello, Callie."

She dropped to the couch. Her expression must have scared Blaine, because tears filled her eyes. "Blaine!"

"It's me. I'm back."

Callie looked at Blaine and then at Mason who now stood in the room, smiling at her.

"Blaine? How? When?" Tears now filled Callie's eyes. "What are you doing here?"

"I'm your companion. Aren't I?"

Tears now escaped her eyes and moistened her cheeks. "Oh Blaine. Where have you been?"

Blaine sat down and hugged her. "Callie, I'm so sorry for leaving you. I'm here now. It doesn't matter where I was."

Callie laughed, "Well that's true." She looked up at Mason who now made his way to her.

"Surprise Nana!" He pulled out a tissue from his pocket and handed it to Callie. "You're gonna need one of these."

"Oh my." Callie wiped her cheeks with the tissue and cried some more. "Oh Blaine. I'm so happy you've returned." They leaned together and hugged. "Oh Blaine, I love you!"

"I know you do, Callie. I believe you really do."

Blaine leaned back and looked into the face of her dear friend. Not a stranger anymore. The light from Callie's eyes seemed so familiar and at that moment, she thought of the black woman at the mission. They both held a light that couldn't be extinguished. A light Blaine was drawn to. She never wanted to leave its glow. Like the tinsel on Callie's Christmas tree. Their light reflected so that others could see God and His love.

That night Blaine and Mason went on another walk. This time, Mason didn't stuff his hands into his pockets, but took her hand and held it up against his chest.

"Blaine. I have something to tell you."

Blaine stopped. "What?"

Mason faced her on the sidewalk as snow began to fall. Large, beautiful flakes. Some landed on his head, melted in his hair. His face was the most handsome face she'd ever seen. His expression gave her chills as well as hope and the promise of an exciting future. She prayed she could trust it, but somehow she knew she could. He was Callie's grandson. She also saw the same light. That amazing light that never stopped.

"Blaine. I love you!"

Blaine couldn't believe her ears. She'd rarely heard these words. They were new. Foreign. Yet now she believed them. She knew, without a doubt, she could trust Mason's words.

"When I stood out on this sidewalk just last week, I thought I'd never see you again. And I couldn't believe how much it hurt. How much I longed to hold you like I am now. And I stood out here and asked God to allow me another chance.

"The funny thing about the request was that I wanted it to be right here. Not in Chicago. Not anywhere else, but right here where we've taken so many walks together. I wanted to tell you here while watching Nana gaze at us through the front window."

They both laughed. "Is she there?" Blaine wanted to turn to see but she didn't want to take her eyes off Mason's face.

Mason looked beyond her and smiled, "Yup."

"Mason." His eyes returned to look at her. "I'm just beginning to know what real love really is. I want to wait to tell you that I love you when I really, really mean it. Is that okay?"

"Very okay."

He didn't look hurt or dejected. "But I can say this to be true. I've never thought of anyone like I think of you. You bring me hope and peace like I've ever imagined could happen to me. When I understand fully God's love, then I can fully understand your love. Does that make sense?"

Mason grinned like Blaine imagined how Miles' would have smiled. "Yes it does."

Blaine took a step closer to him. "But when I do, I will not say it lightly or without meaning. I will truly believe what I say."

"I wouldn't want it any other way."

"I don't want to live lies any longer. I need to understand fully what real love is from the One who created it. The One who loves like no other. And as I learn more about it, I will learn to love you with that kind of love. I'm sure of it."

"I can't wait." And without any hesitation, Mason kissed her lightly.

The lights on the porch blinked on and off.

About the Author

Elizabeth's first book, titled, **Under the Windowsill** is a coming-of-age story about a young woman named Kenna who runs away to Mackinac Island in search of a better life.

Elizabeth's second book, titled **Promise at Daybreak** has a Durand, Michigan setting and is about two elderly sisters who are forced together due to illness. They meet again to fulfill a pact they made at their mother's grave.

Elizabeth's third book, titled, **Just a Train Ride,** highlights a love story from the 1940s. An elderly woman recalls her story for a frustrated fellow passenger on a train from Chicago to Michigan.

For more information on where to find Wehman's books, check out her website at **www.elizabethwehman.com** or like her on Facebook at Elizabeth Wehman/Author for new and upcoming books.

Elizabeth lives in Owosso, Michigan with her husband. You may email her at elizabethwehman@yahoo.com.

Made in the USA
Middletown, DE
26 April 2019